The Geography of Voice
Canadian Literature of the South Asian Diaspora

D1666606

The Geography of Voice

Canadian Literature of the South Asian Diaspora

Diane McGifford

TSAR
Toronto
1992

The publishers acknowledge generous assistance
from the Ontario Arts Council, the Canada Council,
and the Ministry of Multiculturalism and Citizenship, Canada.

ISBN 0-920661-27-0

TSAR Publications
P.O. Box 6996, Station A
Toronto, M5W 1X7 Canada

Cover design: Holly Fisher
Cover art: *Purdah* by Amir Alibhai

Contents

Introduction

The Geography of Voice is the second in a series of South Asian
Canadian collections. The first, *Shakti's Words,* was published in 1990.
Its purposes were to offer students and general readers the selected
poetry of proven and promising South Asian Canadian women, and
at the same time to represent the richness, diversity, and individuality
of their voices. The third book, a collection of critical essays on South
Asian Canadian literature and of interviews with South Asian writers,
is in the planning stages. Although the second anthology is more ex-
tensive than the first–it includes both genders and three genres–its
purposes are similar to those of *Shakti's Words.* The second collection, too, is designed for the general reader and for the student, and
the emphasis is on formal and thematic multiplicity and diversity, established and evolving writers, and the individuality of South Asian
Canadian voices–this time those of men and women in poetry, prose
fiction, and drama.

Each voice in the anthology belongs to an individual Canadian
writer, but together, I think, they bear witness to the distinctive circumstances of South Asian Canadian experience and writing. This
distinctiveness is conspicuous when the work is set outside Canada,
often in the country of the writer's birth. Consider, for example,
Farida Karodia's *Daughters of the Twilight,* set in small-town South
Africa, or Rohinton Mistry's "The Ghost of Firozsha Baag," set in a
Bombay tenement. Both works, written in Canada by Canadians,
record and depend on pre-Canadian experience, particularly the for-
tunes of foreign birth. Here Canadian society goes unscathed, and
Canadians are free to savour the edifying cultural distinctiveness of
these works and to shake their liberal Canadian heads, aghast at the
barbarous racist policies of South Africa and amused by the quaint

Bombay Parsi community. Yet one of this anthology's principal intentions is to depict the distinctiveness of the "in Canada" South Asian immigrant experience, a distinctiveness that leaves most of us wincing and ashamed.

South Asians in Canada usually find that the cold, forbidding Canadian climate is outmatched by the icy, hostile social environment where they feel themselves doubly marginalized: first because they are immigrants and second because they belong to racial, often linguistic, and usually religious minorities. Mainstream Canadians may be openly antagonistic, judging South Asians as simply too different, simply the "wrong" kind of immigrant; or the racism and bigotry may be more subtle. Whatever the face of intolerance, the effects are comparable and nobody should be shocked that the alienation of the immigrant and the bitter stings of racism and religious bigotry, painful daily realities for South Asian Canadian writers, are important factors in shaping their lives, politics, and art. *The Geography of Voice* acknowledges the historical and social influences on writing and is unapologetic about publishing what some critics disdainfully label "political art." The collection treats "political art" respectively, a reflection of the belief that all art, including the work of the white, patriarchal canon is political, although this latter school will insist on designating its garb "universal," pretending that the emperor wears no clothes when, in this case, he nearly always does.

Membership in a marginalized group, of course, may give a writer a few advantages–more of this later–and social, religious, or racial issues, while never far away, are not the whole of South Asian Canadian writing. These writers are not always blatantly overtly political. Rienzi Crusz writes as many domestic passionate lyrics as he does explicitly political poems. So do Lakshmi Gill and Uma Parameswaran. Nazneen Sadiq's protagonist, Naila Siraj, in *Ice Bangles* seeks authenticity and empowerment through her engagement with community and with work. Because Sadiq concentrates on Naila's personal transformation from reticent immigrant to poised Canadian professional woman, racism and sexism though present remain peripheral problems. Still, in some ways Naila Siraj is atypical: she comes from an upper middle-class Pakistani family and has been educated in a Roman Catholic school. Naila speaks better English than most Canadians and wears her class like a protective charm. Nurdin Lalani in M G Vassanji's *No New Land* is not screened by education, class, or money. Instead, he is too taxed by the very human problem of his burgeoning middle-aged sexuality to think of the politics of racism and his victimization. But the reader isn't, and Vassanji cleverly leaves the political dimensions of Nurdin's situation to the reader, creating a moral book which is compassionate and free of didacticism, a book which forces the reader to identify the personal as the political.

In both *The Geography of Voice* and *Shakti's Words* the term "South Asian Canadian literature" refers to the writings of Canadians who trace their origins from one of the countries of the Indian sub-continent: writers who have come directly to Canada from one of these countries or indirectly by way of Britain or a former British colony, usually East or South Africa, or the Caribbean or the Pacific Islands. This anthology includes authors from countries of the Indian subcontinent and from each pattern of the diaspora. The term South Asian then refers only to origins–not, for example, to a single geographical location, a particular national group, or a specific religion. It's worth noting that many of the writers here have never seen the South Asian countries of their ancestors and in some cases several generations of a family have experienced transcontinental shifts, say from India, to England, to Canada.

Clearly the racial, religious, cultural, and linguistic diversity of these people, accented by immigration patterns and the various waves of the diaspora, makes for a heady mix. Culturally, religiously, educationally, and experimentally, South Asian Canadian writers are a remarkably varied assembly. They do not come tabula rasa nor with begging bowls in hand, ready to be re-fashioned as Anglo- or Franco-Canadians, but as vibrant, talented people, schooled in the literary forms of their indigenous and adopted languages, in the vernacular forms of English, and in the traditional forms of English literature. South Asian Canadians are proud of their ancient civilizations and traditions and determined to make their inheritance part of their Canadian writing. This is true in all genres, but consider, for instance, the work of South Asian Canadian dramatists. *Nautanki*, a form of North Indian village theatre, has inspired Rahul Varma as playwright and as artistic director of Teesri Duniya, a Montreal multicultural theatre group. Varma's multicultural vision encourages him to coauthor plays, and *Isolated Incident*, appearing in this anthology, was written with Stephen Orlov. Rana Bose's *On the Double* and the theatre troupe of which he is a founding member, Le Groupe Culturel

Montreal Serai, are indebted to the experimental street theatre of
Calcutta, popularized during the 1960s. These playwrights have imported the theatrical models and conventions of their mother cul-
tures, joining them with those of Canadian theatre to produce
intercultural drama. Both Rana Bose and Rahul Varma value their
cultural identities, and yet want to redefine multiculturalism, to de-
ghettoize and de-hyphenate it. Their aim is to have their work
evaluated alongside other Canadian plays, not patronized, labelled as
picturesque, folksy, a hybrid strain of ethnic drama. The first
beneficiary of their work should be Canadian theatre. First, new
forms, ideas, and perspectives mean renewed vigour and life, and
second, their work can help generate a pluralistic theatre, one which
more accurately reflects the Canadian consciousness.

South Asian people have been immigrating to Canada for nearly a
hundred years. The first immigrants were Sikhs who, about the turn
of the century, came to British Columbia to work in the lumber in-
dustry. What Uma Parameswaran calls "the gold-rush" period of immigration to Canada began in the 1960s with an influx of
well-educated professionals. Before this second wave, South Asian
Canadians, living mostly on the West Coast, were writing in Punjabi,
Urdu, or Gujarati, but the arrival of the scholars and professionals
meant the advent of creative writing in English. Now, thirty years of
South Asian Canadian literature in English, the prodigious literary
output of the 1980s, and the indisputable merit of this work–evident
in the number of literary prizes to the South Asian Canadian community, most recently Rohinton Mistry's Governor General's Award
for *Such a Long Journey* (1991)–make it clear that an anthology of
South Asian Canadian literature is long overdue. Unquestionably
South Asian Canadian literature is here to stay.

Yet, while anthologies can make a range of literature available in
schools and libraries, availability and accessability are not the same.
My implication is that South Asian Canadians are scholars and critics
as well as dramatists, poets, novelists, and short-story writers, and that
their scholarship and criticism are essential if we are to read the
literature with perspective and intelligence. *A Meeting of Streams:
South Asian Canadian Literature* (Toronto: TSAR, 1985) is an early
but substantial evaluative overview of this literature, based upon sur-
veys by Suwanda Sugunasiri, Arun Mukherjee, Surjeet Kalsey, and
others. Anthologies of Canadian Urdu and Punjabi writing are con-

tained in early issues of *The Toronto South Asian Review*. More recently, the Spring 1992 issue of *Canadian Literature* is devoted to essays on South Asian writing in Canada; and a forthcoming article "The South Asian Diaspora in Canada: An Overview" by Uma Parameswaran is an excellent introduction. Parameswaran foregoes theories, preferring to make concrete suggestions and gives names, titles, observations, and even some history, for example, a brief description of the *Komagata Maru* affair which she describes as "one of the worst racist episodes in Canadian history." *Other Solitudes: Canadian Multicultural Fictions* (Toronto: Oxford, 1990) edited by Linda Hutcheon and Marion Richmond contains interviews with Himani Bannerji, Rohinton Mistry, and Neil Bissoondath, interviews which wrestle with the tough questions of racism, multiculturalism, and literature, and let the writers speak forthrightly about their writing and the conditions in which they write.

Critics like Arun Mukherjee, who writes from a global and socialist perspective, or Himani Bannerji, who writes from the perspective of a feminist with membership in a racial minority, inform us of alternative literary styles and stances, casting light on the stodginess and elitism of the critics who have been blinded by privilege. Mukherjee's "The Vocabulary of the 'Universal': The Cultural Imperialism of the Universalist Criteria of Western Literary Criticism" (in *Towards An Aesthetic of Opposition: Essays on Literature, Criticism, and Cultural Imperialism*, [Toronto: Williams Wallace, 1988]) quarrels with the universalist approach to criticism, particularly its tendency to de-radicalize Third World literature, take away its teeth, and so indirectly promulgate "cultural imperialism." She enjoins critics of the universalist school to do their homework, to familiarize themselves with the specifics of an author's culture before passing judgment, and to understand that the new Commonwealth writers have developed their own indigenous vernacular forms which differ from those of Western literary tradition. Bannerji, too, in her insightful, stylistically unorthodox, anti-essay "The Sound Barrier: Translating Ourselves in Language and Experience" addresses specifics, the dislocation of sensibility that Asian *women* (and she does address women) encounter in Canada, particularly their experience of "otherization." She intimates that "crossing the sound barrier" requires new forms and content and that these must be rooted in a writer's apparently "untranslatable" circumstances. Her essay is itself the very model of what she advocates.

These critics have done the ground work for South Asian Canadian criticism and suggested paths it should and shouldn't take. The work continues. There is a flourishing interest in the writing of the diaspora –the Spring 1992 issue of the academic journal *Canadian Literature,* as mentioned above, is devoted to South Asian Canadian writing, and now most major Canadian magazines regularly review South Asian Canadian books. Add these to the sheer volume and quality of South Asian Canadian literature, the presence of a strong national press and its literary journal (TSAR), and the decision by the *Toronto South Asian Review* to publish a collection of critical essays and interviews. The dark days for South Asian Canadian writing are over. It has caught on and its campaign for recognition as real Canadian literature, to be taught as *Canadian* literature in schools and universities, is well underway.

South Asian Canadian drama, like literary criticism, has passed through its nascent stages and is now part of the theatrical life in several Canadian cities, particularly Vancouver and Montreal. Montreal Serai and Teesri Duniya have, for several years, written and staged their own plays. Their theatre is popular, unabashedly political, determined to expose injustices and hold these up to public scrutiny. The two plays reproduced here, Rana Bose's *On the Double* and *Isolated Incident* by Rahul Varma and Stephen Orlov, take as their subjects, respectively, the double standard which oppresses women and the "isolated incident" argument sometimes used in the courts to protect perpetrators in racially motivated crimes.

Each play typifies the theatre of its group and shows a different aspect of social/political exploitation. By returning theatre to its grassroots and reclaiming the energy of street theatre, these groups and plays speak with the voices of the disenfranchised and show that those most separated from power are often most adept at dissecting its workings and revealing its corruption. With the Spring 1992 acquittals in the Rodney King affair in Los Angeles and the subsequent race riots there and in Toronto and other cities, analyses of racism, sexism, and violence and public education on these issues are vital. We would all agree that the public is better educated by dramas than by race riots. These dramatists, proven artists and educators, are in the business of teaching and delighting their audiences.

Immigrant writers understand the intricacies of power, its methods of manipulation, colonization, silencing, and exclusion. The upheavals of re-locating and re-shaping their lives, the advantages of untutored vision and less jaded responses, the shock of racism and bigotry, mean personally won knowledge, mean having something to say. The women poets in this anthology have not hesitated to speak their minds. Women, immigrants, members of racial and religious minorities, often academics and so employed in a systemically discriminatory sphere–clearly the women are survivors and fighters, facts which have shaped their creative work. Suniti Namjoshi's *Feminist Fables* and *The Blue Donkey Fables* quite obviously proceed from her feminist-lesbian consciousness and her scholarly, international perspective, though her wit and peppery iconoclasm are her own. The title of Himani Bannerji's *doing time* makes a succinct statement about being female and Asian in Canada. Gill and Kalsey are, as well, unflinching in their attacks on racism and sexism, and Parameswaran, who is a deft lyricist with a gift for political-lyrical poetry, is working on a book of poems celebrating women and entitled *Of Women I Sing*. Of course, these poets are not one-note-Joannas; their thematic range comprises the personal, the cultural, the classical, the literary. As scholars and as teachers, they are well versed in literary traditions and theories of criticism. They know a lot about poetry and writing, and write about everything–write as creative women whose experiments with structure and form, whose clever tongues and acute ears, mark their dedication to craft and to poetry.

The men tend to have made their names as prose writers, with notable exceptions. Rienzi Crusz is a gifted and prolific poet with six books of poetry between 1975 and 1992, the most recent of which is *The Rain Doesn't Know Me Any More* (TSAR). (One of his poems, published here, gives the title to this anthology.) With his passionate, nimble voice and his technical dexterity, Crusz can do just about anything, certainly animate traditional forms with his individual talent and even subvert some of the tired ones. To read his poetry is to enter a Cruszian world where the heat and richness of his native Sri Lanka vie with the cold and austerity of his adopted Canada, the Sun-Man with the snowmen, all set against the immigrant's unfolding saga of living and loving in a new, strange world. Like Parameswaran in her fine poetic sequence *Trishanku*, Crusz takes us to the very heart of the immigrant's story, from bewildered dislocation in poems like "Sun-Man in Suburbia" to bewildered reconciliation in poems like "The

Rain Doesn't Know Me Any More." Nor should we ignore his moving elegies, his love poems, his domestic humour, his religious or spiritual work, his self-directed irony. Crusz's poems are thick with imagery, dense with the exotic names, things, and myths of his mother land, beautifully crafted, wonderfully allusive; it's quite impossible to do his work justice in an anthology.

Cyril Dabydeen, a novelist, short-story writer, editor, and poet, is, like his female contemporaries, outraged by racism. Certainly his early poems address the racism inherent in a wide range of Western institutions, for example, Canadian immigration policies in "Lady Icarus," and call for alternate readings of colonial history in the Americas, as in "Ancestry." Dabydeen, of course, has his lighter moments; see "Interludes," or better still read *Islands Lovelier Than a Vision*. In his more recent poems in *Coastland: New and Selected Poems*, Dabydeen moves to that typically Canadian encounter: the showdown with the wilderness that turns out to live as much in the spirit as in the landscape. Still, if his theme is familiar to Canadian readers, Dabydeen's imagery is atypical, drawn from the land of his birth and ancestors, and so takes him full circle back home and brings his history to his Canadian present.

The outsider, man on the margins, is a major figure in Arnold Itwaru's poetry, a point made in the title of "visit" and in the ironic title "arrival." Itwaru, whose poetic hallmark is his rhythmic, uncompromising language, has found the perfect tongue to articulate his stark visions and his erotic celebrations. Since his voice crosses national borders, his poetry is, in one sense, as Canadian as can be, with the proviso that his imagery frequently comes from his native Guyana. The protagonist in his novel, *Shanti*, which begins in Canada but takes place in Guyana–thanks to retrospective narration–is a woman living in the edges, and though her edges are assuredly Guyanese, Canadian women have no trouble recognizing themselves in her story.

Among the other South Asian Canadian poets, Asoka Weerasinghe, born in Sri Lanka, is alert to the ravages of colonialism and racism, inside and outside Canada, and writes of them. Yet at times he is domestic, loving, even romantic. Ajmer Rode's early meditative lyrics are experimentations in form and language, preparations for his more mature work which tends to longer lines and complex social issues, interspersed with fine lyrical passages. Other poets, like Krisantha Sri Bhaggiyadatta and Suwanda Sugunasiri, combine the realist's vision with the satirist's wit; one hopes that their relative silence of the last few years will soon end.

Generally South Asian Canadian women have written more poetry and the men more prose. I beg the obvious question and emphasize that this is merely a trend, that both genders have written well in each genre, and that in prose fiction, as in poetry, the diversity is indubitable and impressive: extending to voice, theme, style, setting, and historical period; encompassing the sophisticated, the amusing, the ironic, the political, and the plainly naive. There are a variety of authorial perspectives; expatriate views of the motherland filtered through years of Canadian experience; immigrant stories of life in Canada; pieces by the children of immigrants, those not quite immigrants and not quite born Canadians. It's important to make the point that these works are Canadian because in nearly every case they were written in Canada by Canadians, had to be written here. More important is the question of when Canada will recognize these writers as genuine A-one, honest-to-goodness Canadian, rather than consider them exotic cultural embellishments or imitations, albeit colourful ones, of the real thing.

The prose pieces in this anthology have been selected first for literary merit and second because, as a collection, their themes, voices, and writers reflect the diversity just discussed. The careful reader, aware that all people in Canada are immigrants (aboriginals excluded), may just call these writers–many of whom have lived here for decades–Canadians, writers of Canadian literature. Of course, there will always be those who decry divergences from the mainstream and promote segregation into ethnic groups and bands of "hyphenated Canadians," but by working to broaden the definition of Canadian writing, Canadians can show they value cultural perspectives outside the dominant white patriarchal one. Certainly Rohinton Mistry's 1991 Governor-General's award for *Such a Long Journey* pushes the established boundaries of Canadian literature and is an important step towards a genuine enlightened literary pluralism.

Rohinton Mistry, Arnold Itwaru, and Farida Karodia are among those authors whose work (at least that reprinted in this anthology) was written in Canada and set in the mother country: Bombay, Guyana, and South Africa, respectively. Sam Selvon's "The Harvester," from *The Plains of Caroni*, set in the Caribbean, was written in England before he immigrated to Canada. Spatial and temporal distance appear to accord these writers a clarity of vision that was elusive before leaving home. Distance from the motherland is not the only element these books share. Selvon's concerns in "The Harvester"–the nobility of the people, their hard lives, and the threat of mechanization–are the subtext in Itwaru's *Shanti*. This novel and Karodia's *Daughters of the Twilight* examine the individual and social consequences of colonialism, racism, and sexism. Mistry's subject and tone in "The Ghost of Firozsha Baag" are a little lighter, though not unrelated, and despite his good humour and delight in people, Mistry doesn't shy away from the exploitation and bigotry haunting old Jacqueline, a Catholic ayah in a Parsi household.

Nazneen Sadiq (*Ice Bangles*), Neil Bissoondath ("Dancing"), and M G Vassanji (*No New Land*) hop continents from country of origin to country of adoption and record the complexities of becoming Canadian. There is, however, nothing formulaic about their approaches; each writer has an explicit signature and gives an individual, sometimes unexpected, twist to the prototypical quest for belonging. For example, Vassanji's protagonist jostles between his sexual desire, inflamed by an "easy" culture, and memories of his father's puritanical attitudes to sexuality. Nurdin brings his history with him, and reconciling himself to his new country, to the present, requires reconciling himself to his austere past. On the other hand, Sheila in Bissoondath's "Dancing" isn't given a chance to sort out her cultural confusion. Sheila, a new immigrant to Canada, learns that her fellow Trinidadians can be as racist as any white Canadian. Disillusioned and bewildered, all she can do is keep on dancing, join her people who ironically will stop her from belonging. Bissoondath regards racism as an international disease and his public and fictional expressions of this opinion have been roundly criticized, often by those who should know better.

Ved Devajee (Réshard Gool) in *The Nemesis Casket* and Bharati Mukherjee in "The Management of Grief" examine the bequests of colonialism, exploitation and cultural arrogance. Ved Devajee–a persona or pseudonym of Réshard Gool–writes about the colonial consciousness, a very Canadian subject, from an international perspective and with a cosmopolitan sophistication and polish. One must be careful in talking about *The Nemesis Casket*, since its structural and narrative mysteries tease critics and defy definitive readings. The excerpt here, from "Marshall," Part One of the trilogy forming

The Nemesis Casket, is only intended to be a leap into the literary and literal mysteries of the book. Bharati Mukherjee's poignant, flawlessly crafted work "The Management of Grief" ends what is almost a national silence to talk about the Air India Disaster, the Canadian tragedy that Canadians have tried to disown. In the story the Indian community manages grief because it is a community, one whose cultural and spiritual lives have developed rituals for coping with death and grief. The Canadians from Multiculturalism genuinely want to be of service, but their cultural insensitivity makes them nuisances, silly and condescending, not helpful. Mukherjee juxtaposes Shaila Bhave with Judith Templeton, although her principal focus is not the distance between the two women, but the "management of grief."

With Ven Begamudré, who came to Canada when he was six, South Asian Canadian writing completes one cycle and begins another, since Begamudré, the son of immigrants, is a second generation Canadian. In *A Planet of Eccentrics*, he mostly turns the tables and becomes the Canadian gone to India in search of inspiration. This is true of the story reprinted here, "The Evil Eye." Yet, Begamudré is equally at home in Europe or Regina, Saskatchewan; his cross-cultural writing and history may suggest a new kind of Canadian writer, a transcultural citizen of the global village. To conclude, however, I want to return to the previous generation, specifically to Uma Parameswaran's "How We Won the Olympic Gold". The "we" in her title makes another statement about South Asian Canadian writing. This "we" is her insistence that she and her writing are Canadian, that she–and here I take liberties with Margaret Atwood–has planted herself "in this country/ like a flag."

Whether citizens of the global village, tenacious flowering flags, or firmly planted ones, South Asian Canadians are here to stay, though in a changing country, politically, socially, and culturally. The Canadian flag in the 1990s no longer waves over a nation neatly divided into English and French Canadians–Christians, of course, with lip service paid to aboriginal people and to Jews. The constitutional crises of the 1980s and 1990s attest to internal dissention and desires to redefine Canada; a walk in any major urban centre and increasingly in rural areas reveals the racial, religious and ethnic diversity of the Canadian mosaic, and internationally Canada is part of a new Commonwealth, a reconstructed body of nations, and may soon be part of a continental free-trade agreement. Commensurate with these transformations, Canadian literature has shifted beyond the old oppressive archetypes, so constrictive in their concepts of excellence. Modern Canadian writers have deconstructed the literary canon, and in particular women and ethnic and racial minorities are building "rooms of their own," making space for just about anybody who loves language and form, has something to say, and knows how to say it. The writers in this anthology are part of this new indefinable canon, and they have the freshness and energy, the fervour and commitment of youth. Yet, their traditions and hard lives have given them the vision and compassion of age. When we read them, we sense new friends, though somehow familiar, splendidly dressed, and grown wise.

Diane McGifford

I. Poetry

Himani Bannerji

A Letter for Home

I still have a stake on this land
It is true that I have walked a long way
carrying an earthen jar
With the ashes of my ancestors, earth from my land,
some grains and oil, and my cast off umbilicus.
I have buried this urn here
under my hearth, and built a fire
that I feed daily, and watch the shapes
gather and give me the news
from the other world.
I do not bind my tresses in exile
a speck of ash lies on my full plate
and at night in bed I feel the house
vibrating with the life still left throbbing
in the earth where my umbilicus lies buried.
I dream often that the council of elders
have pronounced their verdict
and waking, remember at dawn
a dead man, a peasant,
who ran to the very edge
of his lost land, in the face of bullets,
falling, stretched his arms,
grabbed a handful of earth
and staked his claim.

Upon Hearing Beverly Glen Copeland

Last night she drummed me Africa

and brought darkness   stars
and the wet greenery of the night forest
into this prison of stone
civilization of Greece and Rome
the England of Hawkins and Victoria
fell from us
a heap of soiled clothes
discarded in the new night of history
wind blew from the savannahs
from the clear scent of the waterfalls
southern plantations opened their gates
and the vision of a black mother child in arms
framed by the circle of a dim light
and the furrowed face of a man
intent on fathoming the dark

burst into flames
broke chains
fists fires and fleeting forms
into the night
agitation
cries of victory

yet the centre   the still centre
the still torso of the drummer
rooted like a palm tree
into the earth
and the drum

the form of the world
calling   gathering
reminding

last night she drummed me Africa

"Paki Go Home"

1.
3 pm
sunless
winter sleeping in the womb of the afternoon
wondering how to say this
to reason or scream or cry or whisper
or write on the walls
reduced again
cut at the knees, hands chopped, eyes blinded
mouth stopped, voices lost.

fear anger contempt
thin filaments of ice and fire
wire the bodies
my own, of hers, of his,
the young and the old.

And a grenade explodes
in the sunless afternoon
and words run down
like frothy white spit
down her bent head
down the serene parting of her dark hair
as she stands too visible
from home to bus stop to home
raucous, hyena laughter,
"Paki, Go Home!"

2.
the moon covers her face
Pock-marked and anxious
in the withered fingers of the winter trees.
The light of her sadness runs like tears
down the concrete hills, tarmac rivers
and the gullies of the cities.
The wind still carries the secret chuckle
The rustle of canes
as black brown bodies flee into the night
blanched by the salt waters of the moon.
Strange dark fruits on tropical trees
swing in the breeze gently.

3.
Now, and then again
we must organize.
The woman wiping the slur spit
from her face, the child standing
at the edge of the playground silent, stopped.
the man twisted in despair,
disabled at the city gates.
Even the child in the womb
must find a voice
sound in unison
organize.
Like a song, like a roar
like a prophecy that changes the world.

To organize, to fight the slaver's dogs,
to find the hand, the foot, the tongue,
the body dismembered
organ by organ rejoined
organized.

Soul breathed in
until she, he
the young, the old is whole.
Until the hand acts moved by the mind
and the walls, the prisons, the chains of lead or gold
tear, crumble, wither into dust
and the dead bury the dead
until yesterdays never return.

To Sylvia Plath

Sylvia,

I was thinking about your death. It seems to me that you were done with fathers and sought a rest, returning to mother in that stove, that modern day hearth out of which life issues in the shape of food daily prepared, the brown warmth of the baked goods. The stove from its fixed centre draws the whole household. It is to this centre you returned seeking to be lulled, to be regathered into that bellyshape. After all we cannot return anymore to the safe darkness of the mother body, to be rocked by the waves, barely hanging by a thin cord. When we emerge it is to the world of the fathers, strife gathers strength, we struggle and only in sleep return to that warm dark home. But you were tired, the day of the fathers was long and bitter. So you sought your rest and found it in the sweet sickness of gas, in the death of the Jewish child, in the concentration camp of the hearth.

Krisantha Sri Bhaggiyadatta

Barbara Frum the sun sets early

Barbara Frum the sun sets early
on my side of the street
because of that high rise you own
that shaved mountain
of smooth stone and dark glasses
blows wind in my ears
howling freezing those thin flaps
fashioning currency of icicles on my eyes.
I cannot see. I cannot hear.
All before my true time.

As my vision sets
losing daylight hours
at night, I witness you
reading bedtime news
dispensing sedatives
to a tired nation
interrogating the destabilized
asking answers of the established
answers which you yourself forget
as you ask the next question
and expect us to forget

barbara, i wake up every morning
with you in my head

the night before resounding
in that drum, my body;
then i look out the window
and see that whistling monolith. . .

○ Winter '84

I tell the corner store owner
"pretty cold out there"
he says
"ain't what it used to be"
"oh," I say, "why is that"
innocently
tensing
wondering if coloured immigration
has affected the seasons . . .
"they've been fooling around
with the weather,"
he says
(his wife nods)
"ever since they sent a man
to the moon
it hasn't been right"

"oh," i say,
breathing out
intrigued
"yeah, i know what you mean"

in the valley of the towers

in the valley of the towers
of king & bay
the base of the toronto-dominion, royal bank
first canadian place, royal trust, bank of nova scotia:

secretaries, clerks (1,2,&3) lunching with junior junior
management, mail boys scurrying, senior management
striding
in close huddle, new immigrants & tourists breathing in
vast
scenery:

music by Latin Fever, a band with a Cuban Leader
and white
musicians in black suits playing "Manhattan skyline."
One woman
on the bandstand in low cleavaged formal wear red
corsage tapping
high heel shoes singing "songs from all over the
world: South America, US & Italy!" and "a song you
haven't
heard in a long time, 'You Light Up My Life.' " Low
applause.

midst the dull & gleam of high rise filing cabinets, one
tree
islands of earth encased by concrete squares, people
munching
fast food, between the 10-storey layers of parked cars: i
glimpse

the nondescript Strathcona Hotel where they lock migrant
workers
prior to deportation; where some kill themselves trying to
escape
or not wanting to go back. . .

Rienzi Crusz

Elegy

Father
you were a great mathematician,
loved God and the jambu fruit.

You deserve a poem
exact as the sun, with no beginning, no end,
just an intense line of light
curving to pure circle.

How can I, a child
trace even a tangent
to your perfect geometries,
the vast afternoons of your brain
in which you walked so easily
with Euclid and Pythagoras?

And how can I compose
that mathematical prayer
of your living, the way
you chased the ultimate equation,
the something that flowed
from heaven to earth
earth to heaven?

I'll compose
from the genius of my childhood,
use my crayons to draw the perfect tangent
straight to the tip of your tongue:
Ah, the fruit of the jambu!
How I shuddered and shook the tree,
and you and I
shared the sweet red pulp
of our mouth's yearnings.

Sun-Man in Suburbia

When the Sun-Man
moved into suburbia,
his neighbours
had already hammered out
their strips of civilization:
    green lawns
    smooth as thighs,
    sunning
    in the ooze of summer.

Here,
    there was no place
    for the violence of weeds,
    leap of grass,
    round yellow snouts
    of dandelion.

The tame lawn-scaped mate
    must bare his skin
    to the slow burn of sun,
    bend his back
    to the crawl of mower,
    and keep his scowl

only under the deep vein.

So the Sun-Man
    kept his vigils,
    fed the bonfires
    of suburbia
    with the yellow blood
    of dandelion,
    thin ribs of weed,
    crying blood-let faces
    of grass.

But when he held up
his green mirror of civilization
to the face of the sun,
he saw
    the flare of dragon's teeth,
    the sun-god darken
    with the vengeance of locusts.

This summer,
    when roots have pulsed
    to the beat of spring rain,
    he'll let his grass grow wild
    like the hair on his dog Bonzo;
    let weeds jut
    their bird-boned jaws
    and dandelions laugh
    through their yellow teeth;
    he'll gently spread his hair
    in the tall grass,
    wrap his brown skin
    with the green arrogance of summer,
    and sleep
    under a forgiving sun.

The Elephant Who Would Be a Poet

High noon. The piranha sun
cuts to the bone
Anula, the heaving elephant,
froths at the mouth.
The logging ends.

Without command
he eases his huge body to the ground,
rolls over,
makes new architecture
from his thick legs,
four columns vertical
to the sun.

The confused mahout
refuses the poem
in this new equilibrium,
this crazy theatre of the mind,

this new way
of looking at the real world. . .

Love poem

for Anne

For you, brown lover,
with buffalo curd and palmyrah honey
still sweet on your lips,

the raven winging in your hair,

I offer the immigrant land
with no contrary season,
only summer,
and summer and summer.

No white laming cold before the thaw,
no cutting nodule of spring,
no fallen leaves to confuse your feet,
only the consummate thing,

the full-blown rose, the sun
in batik exuberance.

Now also ask for the sweet warm rain,
the once monsoon harvest of fruit:
jambu, mango and mangosteen;
guava and rambuttan, the tender cadju

wrapped in green leaves, the jaggery bell
of the godambara-rotti man,
and I will tease the Asian condiment
from the summer almirahs of this land.

What you deserve will be
what you always had
in your warm rich blood:
the green land.

ℰ Dark Antonyms in Paradise

O my beloved country,
I return like the prodigal,
stay for sixty days
and sixty nights; return,

to warm my arthritic bones,
listen to your heart-beat,
your new song, what media

and the London *Economist* declared
was the new redemption, the prosperity
Hongkong and Singapore style.
How JR,* like the great Dutugemunu
builds another brazen palace
by the marshes of Kotte,
and now rests in his silken sarong
and ripened dreams.

Two million rupees
flow daily like milk and honey
to your desert bowls, your people's
sweat in Dubai and Oman,
the sweet sands of Arabia;
and a hundred thousand now eat cake,
where once they couldn't find
a fistful of rice.

And a man from Attanagala
ends his life
with a gulp of ECOTAX.
And so did his wife and two daughters
two months earlier. The coroner
regretted the lack of early
psychiatric treatment.

I've seen the bustle and buzz
of your Free Trade Zone,
the new adventures, American banks,
Japanese technology,
how hundreds of village girls
with money on their morning faces
move briskly to man the spindles, the levers
that make their new-found bread.

And a seventy-year-old man,
distressed over his prolonged illness
from snakebite,
throws himself body and soul
before the Galle Evening Express.

And how your Galle Road highway throbs
to the low hum of the Mercedes,
a thousand Toyota bodies moving
like a cluster of dragonflies in the sun;
and the trishaws, IZUKI buses
in which your brown bodies ride
with the disciplined patience of ants.

And a twelve-year-old student
embraces his sweet grave
with a generous potion of PARAQUAT
because his mother chided him
for quarrelling with his sister.

Five-star hotels now gleam
in the Sri Lanka sun, tourists
dip their bottoms
in the everlasting blue
of your circling sea, wrap
their pink skins in cotton and silks,
the loud embrace of batik;
and your craft boutiques burst
at their seams with elephant and ivory,
the filigree effusions
of your artistic people.

And another twelve-year-old
chooses an untimely grave
with ENDREX,
because his teacher caned him
for forgetting his drawing book.

O my beloved country,
your paradise story goes on
with dark antonyms to match.
But take a bow, an encore,
and an encore for the warm brilliance
of your new sun.
I pray
for slum corners of your kingdom,
your soul.

*J.R. Jayawardene, President of Sri Lanka

Elegy #2

Morning. Black hammering gab of crow.
Trying to tell me something?

Sudden magpie alone
promising sorrow to wear on my face;

That same night, I heard the jaktree owl hoot
from its darkened throat;

Cats took the parapet wall and hissed,
then caterwauled their psalms for the dying.

Father, you died with morning on your face,
fulfilled the prophecies of birds.

I, rocked in the hammock of the sun,
your gentle ways,

refused the dark harbingers,
saw nothing

in the sliced face of the moon,
the broken reservoirs of your heart,

only believed   the God
on your wizened face,

your love now silent
and hard as wood.

Song of the Immigrant

It's time
to break your elephant and wood apple dream.
Honey and curd in your mouth,
the kingfisher ablaze by the Mahaveli's edge—
time to cast off
your batik sarong and wooden thongs,
the exotic shackles round your throat.

You only read
the language of signs,
a long silence in the snow,
a dark music   silent
and hammered in your blood.

No more shall the elders say:
Hold your tongue and wait,
this night will pass.
The civilized nerves
will first grow taut, then break;
then sleep beside your alien breath,
then love you with a tentative smile,
even bleed for your leftover pain.

21

Now you may talk loudly of crows
as stars in a dark night,
conjure peacocks from harvest cornfields,
look straight into the sun, the whipping snow
and not blink at all.
Be happy now.
Only death
can redeem
the original dream.

Song for the Indian River Man

(Indian River, Keene, 10 May, 1986)

For Murray Black

Up river: darkness falls
thick as jute.
Our boat rides anchor.
The cul de sac wears its lily pads
like a necklace.
Now here, now there,
the brackish pane cracks and closes,
walleye and bass
electric in their roamings.

A dragonfly reconnoiters.
Mosquitoes sense new summer flesh.
We're armed:
"Off" thick on exposed skin;
a rod in each hand, a net for hauling,
we wear jackets like medieval armour.

No light now but the sky's opening,
a filament weak as a night bulb's.
Darkness abets. We slowly sink

(with bullfrog, lilypad,
the tall wildrice beyond the shoreline)
into the dark hammock
of the river.

Through the evening haze,
I watch the river man's rugged face,
his strong hands, the way
he threads his lure, whips his line
like a rainbow's arc.
Soon, a 4-lb small-mouth bass
will fall for his art,
break surface with blood
on its heaving gills.

I often wondered
about the blank spaces of friendship:
his long silences, drifting years,
rumours about his crucible of fire,
how once he tried to walk on water.
What endured? the melody in his old piano,
heady rhythms of guitar,
the wide open spaces of his heart?

Now here he was
fashioning a perfect ecology:
the missing piece in the river's face.
Where else would this man,
ever restless, ever wanting to be still,
find the perfect metaphor?
He was gone. Now only the river,
the dark beautiful night on the waters.

The Geography of Voice

My lady, so close to me
for so long,
your pale mouth spills decibels
high and low about my ears,
voices that divide like geography
from a cool cutting bitch's tone,
to mongrel dialect,
epiphanies and laughter.

In the cold cotton-white land
where your hibiscus heart
freezes to its roots,
you talk from the head, cold
and final as winter's argument.

Travelling south, out of town,
the sun flavouring you like gravy,
you turn ethnic, a voice
dragging sun-tones, a vocabulary
much like your Sri Lankan grandmother's.

Back to your cradled beginnings
where you heard the elephant
challenge the inconsistent moon,
pariah dogs barking
at nothing but hot air, children
crying "sadhu, sadhu" on their way
to the Temple,
you are belly laughter, epiphanic voice
drumming the limbs of the Kandyan dancer.

Bouquet to My Colonial Masters

Gauguin's woman under another sun
raped. How silence spilled
from an abattoir of tongues.

And you still show me
your polished bannisters,
your country estates,
green, columned and groomed.

How your freighters coughed black,
then guffawed and left   heavy
with coconut and tea,
cardamon, cinnamon and ivory,
the sandalwood artifacts
still leaking their exotic perfume
from the dark holds.

And through it all
I heard the Englishman's siesta snore,
the civilized cooing
of civilized men
gulping their velvet whiskies,
as brown waiters bent and bowed
to the evening noise of their masters.

So what was left to keep?
Shakespeare!
a tongue to speak with,
some words to remember.
Today,
we are all poets
for having suffered the chains,
for having learnt the language.

The Rain Doesn't Know Me Any More

I shape forgotten metaphor:
curved tusks, howdah and mahout;
splash the Bird of Paradise
against a cemetery of cars,
seek the root in cabook earth,
the dream   that meandered, got lost
in an orgasm of blood.

I who held the palm-tree's silhouette
against the going sun, a woman,
a child   long enough
to divide a continent,
have new revelations:
I have circled the sun.
The white marshmallow land
is now mine, conquered,
cussed upon, loved.

Look at this dreaming face,
these new muscles, tempered bones,
black eyes   blue
with a new landscape,
legs dancing the white slopes
like a dervish.
Against paddy-bird havocking in tall grass,
bluejay   raucous, cardinals
the color of blood.
For the home-coming catamaran,
747 screaming,
wounding the night like a spear.

The monsoon rain

doesn't know me any more.
I'm now snow-bank child, bundled,
with snot under my nose,
snowflake magic in both hands.
Once, rice and curry, passion juice,
now, hot dogs and fries,
Black Forest Ham on Rye.

So what's the essential story ?
Nothing   but a journey done,
a horizon that never stands still.

Poem

My son,
the blood I spilled for you
was real.
For twenty years I waited
at the City Gates
for darkness to fall, for stars
to guide my immigrant feet.
Only by dying
do we learn the true rhythms
of the heart, by crying,
how to laugh from the belly.

He Who Talks to the Raven

talks to God,
      black-feathered and beaked
with toenails growing inward,
      a mouth full of caw.
Superb surveyor of the skies,

postman to history
happening by the second,
    fowl-mouthed, he sings
the sweetest song, black eyed
    he outdoes the morning sun.

He who talks to the raven
    shares parables,
some windows of possibility:
    if the water's at the bottom
of the pitcher,
    throw   pebble after pebble
and the level will rise like bread
    to the top.
If the desert churns your thirst
    know that there's water
breeding in the cactus.

He who talks to the raven
    talks to the bird humming
with ESP in its brain.
    Who knows the distant agony
of the goat even as the anaconda
    unhinges its jaws;
the byways of the eagle's ether flight
    before it traps
the rabbit's frozen eyes.

He who talks to the raven
    long enough, learns
how the sweet wood apple
    disappears in the elephant's mouth,
how to say   caw caw caw
    when the gongs of hunger
ring like church bells.
    How when something lurches,
is ready to strike,
    can suddenly stride

into the face of the sun,
    keep the rose between his teeth
and say: caw caw caw.

This bird is diplomat
    and bore.
Will take your gifts
    and demand for more, insist
that you understand its importunate ways,
    love it, stroke its velvet wing.

When the raven talks,
    listen,
it's God
    in ultimate disguise.

Cyril Dabydeen

Interludes

For Craig Tapping

The woman in the library, in her twenties
reads zealously, searching with her eyes
the bones of the page, blood of gremlin close to her nose

Longing for tidbits of where she comes, from

that Maritime place; here now in this Haida country
the sea lingers in her blue-and-white collar–

Newfoundland or Nova Scotia, what does it matter?
A time of rum-running; meanwhile I imagine
cricket galore, reading the CLR James column

In the *London Times,* scoring divisions and subdivisions,
boundaries in my mind, entertaining Catholic whites
(De Venturul, De Gannes, De La Bastide)

I make further strokes, as I watch middle-class browns
and blacks, those running faster down the pitch;
a mighty spring next, throwing the ball like the tide

Such a time when local players or even a woman
in the nineteenth century could organize a tour to England

or Canada. Yes, take some blacks who could bowl faster!

Woman, your friendly looks, eyes, invite me to indulge
this pastime of reading, in this rage
of runs and homesickness

Exiles: A Sequence

#101

He stole into the sun
and garnered himself a place

It was so from the beginning;
with the seasons in his dreams—
he expresses the drama of himself

—describing events to everyone
living alone in the cold & ice.

His body grows old, as he loosens up,
mouth opening in the eternal longing
for more sun. He walks along,
Oedipus-like—

sweltering with leaves glazed,
the omen of windows rattling:
shingled all around

Such solid remnants—
offering hope because of where
he came from, whence he must return

#102

Pretending to be part of the self
he followed you to the source
the sun in his heart–

still the source of his dream,
overturning one more time,
he makes amends, listening

with cocked ear, mouth
opening like a tunnel . . .
everything in his grasp

He talked as if abundance
was everywhere. Obsidian again,
he remembered his own tragic fate–

how he once nurtured the desert,
chattering at the edge of the sea
when the sirens came

voices locked in his head,
memory of madness,
caves form as in a dream–
he withdrew into himself
singing, until peninsulas
crumbled at his feet

The Forest

I.
I've come from that ridiculous forest
where things grow waywardly,
jaguars snarling on tree-tops
as I am amazed–

looking distantly at you,
my heart pounding.

I'm stuck with being prehensile,
knotting lianas of thighs,
legs, toes, letting out
frustration, a thunder's belch,
the stomach's disgrace–
a language, other proverbs.

II.
Laughter of stones dropping
into water, a large river
making faces;
a grimace next, as I am unable
to reach perfection; and let
the waves ride side by side
while billows take over;
mangrove also bend, buttressed,
the one ship caught
on the edge of the horizon,
anchored there for a hundred years
or more; an emblem or leaden tongue,
dried out

III.
Inhaling the odour of other places,
beached whales, trees that sway,
leaves swooping down like maddened birds;
at the house we try to separate out
our souls from boards, shingles;
the palaver of wood in thick silence,
accents tripped over, syllable after syllable;
a dozen years later we move on.

Further trees in my midst; waves, houses.
A rainbow expressing colour of skin,
the longing for other virtues really;

the clouds mocking our intelligence;
now spent, eager as I am—
and immensely awry.

Foreign Legions

This is a surfeit, believe me—
I am circumscribed in the desire to traverse
Whole landmarks; the rage in me
As I am not scuttled or going beyond.
Now cockeyed because of hibiscus or bougainvillaea,
I contain myself with a tropical burning;
This too is belief; the spirit harks at luminosity,
The sun itself leaping forward in the constancy
Of rain, the slush of fewer days around,
The weather falsifying grass,
The squelch critical as syllogism.

Thrilled by the furore of other days,
Other longings, a strange madness takes over—
The sun in a myriad of rivers in the late afternoon,
And how splendid the lakes, alluvium of a special kind.

I gather all the selves mirrored in the display
Of leaves, and one moment is more fragmentary
Than all the other. Water scuttles,
Displaying ripples like oblivion.

I hold on to a stopped mouth, ear;
I am vanquished for a while as I sit down
At the edge of the forest and talk in tongues
Of silence, mirroring other longings—
Take me, I say, to the butterfly's wings,
The world itself welcoming me as I am
The imagination's leap and spirited blood.

Disaster comes soon after, and I am stuck
In one place; I am hailed from afar, standing tall,
Both feet splayed out. Moongazer too I am,
Whirling with shadows, without anxiety–
And let the dreams take over, let the tides
Vanquish all others while I wait
For the rebirth far ahead–
The moment's mammoth start.

Elephants Make Good Stepladders

It isn't the same as growing up
On a different side of the tropics–

After all they are worlds apart,
Even though I've been accustomed to hearing

About India's tigers–
Not elephants.
How I wished for more than youthful
Visits to Circuses in a colonial town;

To hear a real elephant's grunt,
To watch its trunk come alive–

To climb with stepladder ease
As I am in the heart of the jungle:

This more than TV Wonderland or Disneyworld,
The trunk lifts up, lowers–

Water pours out as if from the clouds;
With Shakuntala innocence

I experience the thrill of monsoon magic
Hands folded, I contemplate the subcontinent's

Pastime flood; bending forward,
Water at my knees–

I meet the elephant eye to eye.

Ramabai Espinet

Hosay Night

Like a key turning
In the rusty iron lock of memory,
Shadows filter past the thin
Skinless eye of moon now
Cutting through the knife-blue sky
And, like echoes off an old skin drum
Drawn across the lash of memory
The mind pitter-patters

Hosay Night in deep-edged
St James dark where
Drumsticks rain fire on Potoy's back
I was a small boy on Flag Night
A small girl on Ganges Street
Watching the tadjahs; near the mosque door
The sun and moon kissed
Straw fires lined the streets

Stirring a dim morning dream
Of colder times, ancient streets,
Fires for warming hands, and drums,
Tribesmen, plainsmen, my grandfather's
Pale eyes and swarthy hands. . .
A journey outside the lodge
Of memory, the cutting edge

Of bitter cane

Behind the moon and God's back
Pain knowing no end
We lived alone, like
Shadow murdering shadow
The stars alone for safety
Tassas beating in the dark
Rum, stickfight, chulhahs
Flights to nowhere

This land is home to me
Now homeless, a true refugee
Of the soul's last corner
Saddhu days and babu days
And Mai in ohrni days
Lost to me–like elephants
And silks, the dhows of Naipaul's
Yearning, not mine

In the Jungle

I am a stranger
Everywhere.

Dawn breaks up an iron plateau
Of night
Colder and denser than spit.
And the unpromised day
Becalmed
Collects the grimy tears
Of morning, marooned in moulting light.

Mouldy, mildewed, spent
So early in the morning.
My hands bear callouses
Of stranger washtubs

Than those which bent
My mother's aching back,
My lament for futility–
Miles of soiled labour
Acres of razor-cruel cane
Slashing dusty brown legs
Pus forced onto wooden hospital floors
(Soon to be hosed and disinfected)–
Dwindles into forlorn recognition
Of misplacement
Of displacement...

It is not for nothing
That we inherited a massive
Unknown and unknowable presence.
Our ignorance and labour
Fed your morning cups
Your cosy breakfasts
Your India ink.

And, it's like this:
There's me here
And everything else outside.
No friend, really,
Nor lover, except in the dismal
Despairing caches of silence
And longing
Something abstract, barely felt
Never held.

There is a wrongness in the air,
Murderous winds,
Rain beating upon corpses
Cadaverous rain
Echoing hardness
Knowing disdain.

Instruments of Love and War

Hearts beating at the sandy border
Dry white moondust
In the shadowless glare
Of moonland

This is the season for attack
For no faltering gaze
And sounds of no orchestra
For demolition

Make me a shield
A coat of mail
Forged for the heart
Of my brother

Tides in the desert
Red running, parting
The watering ways
Of dread

If my blood runs weak
In the rum-hot night:
A big gun encore flashing
Like the bloody 4th of July

Bombs are raining on Baghdad
As snow whitens this side
Of the mountain
Sepulchre

In The Village
A band of jazz musicians
Sing of avarice, of Tell me
Why, Why

Tell me why when
Ice sets in iron-blue eyes
The fer-de-lance of factories
Makes armour

In the shops
Bending sideways, a curve
Of lovely cheek, my mother
My aunt

Buying pots of flowers
Cyclamens, Hydrangeas, early
Easter lilies, sunshine
Fences of morning glories

As shells tear through tongues
Rising from desert dust
Curling in arches of smoke
Of flame

Only a killsack
In the theatre of war
Over miles of desert dead
Oil slicks and worse

Fleshless trees, with
Blood trunks and no
Yellow-bellied ribbons
For masking

Instruments of war
Love past caring
Verisimilitude of mothergrief
And no morning glories. . .

Lakshmi Gill

Letter to a Prospective Immigrant

And what about that tired myth: Canada the Cold?
Not a myth, I assure you. Don't come naked.
In ten years your proud figure
will bend like natives hunched under coats.

Here the body must deny nature
stay virginal or abort, no womb-issues.
Housewhores are mad, in league with perverse
witches, cripples and wild dogs.
Make no mistake: divided, you fall.

Of your soul, beware. They deal with devilcommerce
profit in the ruthless ascent of defenses,
seal themselves in brass towers. Oh, are they lonely
afterwards! Friends scattered all over the forest,
bushed like the poet said.

This is no cotton candy country
no penny arcade;   come prepared
slide off your merry-go-round
and jump over the gymhorse
like the little people with set faces
wristbandaged in skintights.

Joy? There is no joy. Just a long, dull ache

icehot (not even pain) of want.
They need an orgy, communion, sacrifice, expiation.
If you can bring blessings, come then
(don't expect blessings in return); hell does not give
but takes.

Marshland Wind

off the marshes against the wooden
kitchen door rattling it like teeth
growling garm that won't let me come
out, my hands pressed to the wall
my voice deadened by the howl
through the eaves surrounding this
falling house, caging an intruder

Honour Roll

Within the hole
of our life here
in Sackville, we
draw the veil down
around our heads
making mole-Mass
celebrations daily
grateful for Marc's
& Evelyne's & Karam's
existence, our flesh
and soul.

Night Watch

I will to lie awake

to the children's drama:
sounds of Marc's reading
in his room then soothing
breathing by eleven. . .
I suspend my dreams
for the vision of Evelyne
standing by my bed
in the dark awakened
by her nightmare. . .
I listen to the footfalls
in the hallway of Karam
running from horror. . .
and on nights when all is well
I sleep with one eye open.

Third Street

The family was all there:
papa, mommy, Sis Mur
and my dead sister Eve.
We were armed against
the native Moros
who with big knives
waited out side the gates.
Our house was dark.

Breathless at our station
my sisters crouched
beside the long front window
with the torn wire screen

and I double-humped
within the side window frame.

When night was darkest
they attacked
jumping over the wooden gate
over the stone wall
spilling over the garden
crashing through the loose
garage door, the servants'
quarters, up the dark flight
of stairs of the basement
and finally axed down
our wooden front door
with the faulty lock.

It's always the same
the enemy dark at the gate
finding the same route
into our house
through the loose hinges
and torn screens.

Letter to Gemma, Activist

Your postcard from Peking
said it all.
Poetry is a luxury
where action is necessary.
Words won't change
the morality of leaders
and words won't bring
food on the table
of the people.
To the liberation of mankind!
Lenin said,

and he meant that positively.
These negative imaginings
will not transform humanity,
not even, just me.
When we played with bows and arrows
as children,
you played on
while I stopped to analyze
the string, the wood,
the feather, the knot,
how it all tied together,
traced the flight in the air.
What is left for us when
we reach our third decade
and lay aside our toys?
     our joys?

Out of Canada

It assaults me at every turn:
my eyes are offended
by what they see–the bright
sunlight on the snow
icy shafts that pierce straight
to my head. . .

I cannot die here, on the streets
of Moncton, I tell myself over and over–
people wouldn't know where
to send my body.

I cannot die here in this country
where would I be buried? Not like poet
John who drank himself to death, lying there
in Sackville, all the way from Manchester.
Where else could they send him? I can still

see his bright eyes piercing me, how happy
he was for discovering ghazal–it didn't save him.
There are no shields against this land
for poets like us.
But I will not go under.
I will sit at the foothills of the Himalayas
and leave hard Canada for the hardy Canadians.

Arnold Itwaru

visit

down this footpath of puddles   marabuntas and tumbled greens
my voice is a breath of smoke
under the blazing sky
i do not remember so fiercely hot

once i roamed the morass that wanders still amidst the dams
deep with the tender breath of fresh-cut grass
and fresh-ploughed earth

that was another world where jamoons and semitoos
were forever ripe
where bunches of red pepper exerted strong lure
not the saddening green that chokingly rises
in the putrid land and encroaching jungle
around blackened faces and drained bodies
i hardly recognize

the sandkoker trees are shedding their leaves now
yellow fallen leaves upon their thorn-strewn ground of
fecund sour grass no grazing cow would eat

in some of the fields the sugarcane has been burnt
blackened in the soot of this labouring mud
these people   my people
are still at work

their cutlasses still flashing in desperate need
in the toiling fields of the merciless sun

so many chasms separate us   i with my dreams on the other side
of the horizon
where the winter is bitter
far from this shore and land of singing water
across the distant sands of my childhood play

in the stream beneath the consolation of blue skies
fish and ducks are swimming   as if nothing has changed
but the houses are in ruins
and the young who i do not know
and the old who remember certain versions of me
each day stare in emptiness at the passage of their years
each day fearing each other's growing treachery
and there is nothing i can say
i who once lived and worked here

i will go to the watch house by the sea and listen to the rising
tide
beyond the rot and ruin
the insidious decay in every footpath and dream here

i cannot bear anymore the stories of rape and murder
the brutal anguish of mutual hatreds turned inwards
people hacked and mangled to death in broad daylight
and the begging
tattered children and adults begging for food
in this fertile land of many waters
this land and earth of my birth

i will go to the watch house behind the wall of the sea and
listen
past the sorrow and the rage and the confusion in me
past the ragblown roadless wheezing in the dying of this day
flesh eating bone in the hollows of each evening

across the buckling bridges
today's women   empire's offal   strike their womb's stirring
cursed in labouring birth and labour until death

the towns are defaced and barred
decrepit prisons against the enfrenzied horror of the street
caged-in dreams of yesterday and yesterday
and of children and hope gone New York Toronto London way

blow softly on them Atlantic   it is the least you could do

blow softly as they cower from each day's drain and glare
and the ooze that distorts the pulsing eye

prepare them
prepare them
prepare me
in the gathering dusk
of this oceaned nocturne
far away

arrival

this is the place
mark its name
the streets you must learn to remember

there are special songs here
they do not sing of you
in them you do not exist
but to exist you must learn to love them
you must believe them when they say
there are no sacrificial lambs here

the houses are warm

there's bread there's wine

bless yourself
you have arrived

    listen
keys   rattle
locks   click
doors   slam
   silence

matin mornings

matin mornings in cowpasture days
confession behind wax-smelling altars
dead man
dead cross

the brethren sing sweet Jesus walking Galilee
they hear the slurp and slap of mud in the footpaths of sleep
their cries legioned in sugarcane fields
calypsoes   rum   Saturday-night brawls

confess, rumbles the pulpited ghost breathing
sin redemption eternal blemish

the brethren of little faith confess sun-cursed sins
in need and hard work and unending need

they know how sweet The Name sounds in believers' ears
they confess   unworthy servants   servants scratching empty
palms   they confess

the morning drinks them up and moves on

Body Rites

(chant seven)

the sounds of this night
are of another time

they rise and fall within our breathing
beyond the sonatas and tombs
the madrigals in alien voices
across the turbulence of streets
and roadways of our passage

they are already memory
something gained something lost
in the departures of our meeting
as we go from place to place
placing ourselves in our unfolding

Surjeet Kalsey

I Want My Chaos Back

(28 August 1983, Harbourfront Toronto)

today I am three thousand miles away
from throbbing bubbling figurines of
my flesh . . . how much I miss their presence . . .
how much . . . the very thought of not being
with them makes my heart droop.
The honest voices,
            the soft touches
the house filled with their noise
I am dying to hear, to feel.
This is a real loneliness.
This is a real barrenness

I want to walk with you all,
        I want my chaos back.
I miss the noise.
I miss the confusing sounds of my two
passions: children and creativity.
What have I created in the company of
you my love, I would never be able to
create without you. I miss you all
very much, Your presence, our noise,
I want my chaos back.
Touch me on this piece of paper,
sending you in it lots of love

A Woman with a Hole in Her Heart

A mole on her forehead
a bluish dark grey bruise
that Adam gave to Eve
on their marriage anniversary
and smeared her fate
with the blame of his fall.

Don't tell me
woman is a woman–a mistake of nature
a rib of adam, or a broom, a mop, or anything etc. etc.

Her self begins where your thinking ends
She blooms like the first crux of the Universe-
the glory of all created existence. . .
Until,
until someone crushes her under his foot
until she is isolated from the human
until some voice rustles in her ears:
reminding her
that she has a hole in her heart.

The hole left behind
when she pulled the nail driven
by her mother on the very first day
she saw the light, by saying:
they wanted their male heir
not YOU a female.

My mother had a hole in her heart too,
and her mother, and her mother's mother
and her mother's mother too. . .

Voices of the Dead

Fragile/ arrow/ this side up/
handle with care/ secret is secured/
safe in this black box/
the meaning of life is so brittle/
never thought/
humans and their flesh/ blown in the air/
shredded so cruelly/ never thought of it/

Not even a thin veil/ peel of an onion
was between life and death
it was/a vast devastating ocean/
from where throbbing starts/from where
stillness takes over/there was't
any sign/any line in between/the wind
and the surging/surfing of the high waves/
. . . and what was/that moment /when
an ocean/ was dried up/within me/ I don't
know/ when the earth/ was shattered
within me/ I can recall the moment/ when I
turned to a stone/ and many people after.

Countless faces, countless eyes
stopped at this shore/ cross-roads
of the ocean and the sky/ to find out
any clue of the 329 bodies/ shreds
metal scrap/ vanished in the
ocean within few moments. . .
WHY? WHAT FOR?

I forgot to breathe with many
slivers in my heart.

          some maniac force
still saying:

whichever sound will voice the reason
whichever ear will hear the reason
whichever pen will print the reason
whichever eye will read the reason
will be handled with care/ will be
se/ver/ed with care!

Black box can keep the secret only
not the truth: before the blow out
all the people on board were alive/
the black box cannot bring them
back in flesh and blood, it cannot
bring back their breath.

Suniti Namjoshi

Further Adventures of the One-Eyed Monkey

One sunny afternoon when the one-eyed monkey had
wandered into the forest behind the river, she came
across a woman meditating fiercely. The monkey
recognized the famous ascetic–she was the wife of
a brahmin who was even more famous–so she leapt
into the branches of a large peepal and sat very still,
not wanting to disturb her. Suddenly she heard a
tremendous crashing, and the god, Indra, fell through
the treetops and landed in the clearing. The woman
ignored him, but the god knocked her down and
proceeded to rape her. Then the god disappeared, and
the brahmin appeared. He understood at once that
his wife had been raped, so he petitioned the higher
gods to avenge the wrong he had thus suffered. Lord
Vishnu appeared and asked if there were witnesses.
"Only a one-eyed monkey," said the brahmin. The
monkey was asked to describe what had happened.
Now the monkey had a great deal of respect for the
woman sage, so she gave her testimony as accurately
as possible. When she had finished, Lord Vishnu
declared that the god, Indra, had committed a great
sin, in that he had sinned against a brahmin. It was
necessary for the god to purify himself by performing
a sacrifice. Indra was summoned and performed the
sacrifice that requires a stallion. And so it came

about that a horse was killed, a god purified, a
brahmin appeased, a woman ruined, and a monkey
left feeling thoroughly puzzled.

Philomel

She had her tongue ripped out, and then she sang
down through the centuries. So that it seems only
fitting that the art she practises should be art for
art's sake, and never spelt out, no, never reduced
to its mere message–that would appal.

(Tereus raped Philomela and cut out her tongue in
order to silence her. She was then transformed into
the "poetic" nightingale which sings so sweetly through
Western tradition.)

On that island. . .

On that island where all the men turned into pigs
–there was no exception, the hero dreamt–
I stood there watching the local antics
and I found myself enjoying them.
The brilliant sun was bouncing off each porcelain back
and they looked so pink, so pretty, so piglike
with their snouts and trotters in lacquered black
that I confess I was charmed, forgot my dislike
of men behaving like pigs, and of women
who catered to them. So I said to Circe,
"They delight and dazzle. But what next? What then?
Is it all a matter of sheer artistry?
Of prancing in a patterned tapestry?
Are they pleasure-giving pigs or ordinary men?"
"Oh well," she smiled. "They serve a function.
Piglets must please.
But tomorrow, if you like, we'll try another species."

It's not that the landscape...

Birds and Pine Tree, style of Kano Motonobu (1426-1559)
(Eugene Fuller Memorial Collection)

It's not that the landscape is colourless,
though, the fact is, it's barely dawn.
It's just the birds, their fragile happiness,
their unconscious tenderness, which they shed on
everything, till bird and tree and light are one.
Oh neither you nor I could enter there.
We'd tread on the grass, we'd switch on the sun
and baffle the landscape with our mere
humanity. We would cast long shadows,
discolour the world we had come upon.
But we can watch the birds: who comes, who goes,
how their shared delight pleases everyone,
and how, being ignorant birds and unaware,
they live at ease in their native air.

Eurydice

Death was rather sudden, but pleasant enough.
He came. I rose, gliding smoothly through
the green wood. The going was easy, not rough;
I had no hesitation about what to do.
Death made it simple: he led, I followed.
There was no question, he knew that I would.
And I didn't mind at all that he choose the road;
I was his forever, that was understood.
And so, when my lover came, brave and confident,

and won me from Death by means of his charm,
what could I do, but prove obedient?
He led. I followed till some slight alarm
made him look back, and then I fled, since he
was not Death's master, but a slave, like me.

Transit Gloria

"Let's face it," the zoologist remarked, "the donkey is not a heroic beast."

"That isn't true," protested the Blue Donkey.

"You mean it isn't palatable. But what does it matter? Heroism isn't everything."

"No, I mean it isn't true. There have been dozens of distinguished donkeys."

"Name one."

"Shanti."

"Who?"

"Shanti, my grandmother."

"Never heard of her."

"That just shows you don't know what you're talking about."

"All right," returned the zoologist. "Let's talk about Shanti. In how many battles did she engage and how much territory did she conquer?"

"What?" asked the Blue Donkey.

"Let's try again. Was she big and brawny and extremely powerful?"

"No," replied the Blue Donkey. "No, she was an ordinary size, but appearances don't matter."

"Very well," continued the zoologist. "Could she bray loudly? Did she win arguments?"

"Her voice was gentle, soft and low," murmured the Blue Donkey, beginning to feel she was losing ground.

"Well, was she a sex symbol?"

"A what?"

"Never mind." The zoologist shrugged. "Look, she wasn't a general, she wasn't a politician, she wasn't a star. What exactly was her claim to fame?"

"She was intelligent," said the Blue Donkey.

"What?"

"In-tel-li-gent."

"There you are." The zoologist looked extremely pleased. "Would you agree that donkeys on the whole do not argue, do not fight and do not dazzle?"

"Well, no, they don't." The Blue Donkey paused. "It isn't sensible."

"Precisely." The zoologist was beaming now. "I have studied donkeys, and that is how donkeys think. Now, at last, do you take my point?"

"Yes," muttered the Blue Donkey gloomily. "In order to win I have to be stupid."

Uma Parameswaran

Tara's Mother-in-law:

What kind of place you've brought me to, Son?
Where the windows are always closed
And the front door it is always locked?
And no rangoli designs on porch steps
To say please come in?
How you can expect Lakshmi to come, son?
You think she'll care to enter
Where the same air goes round and round?
She "the lotus-seated consort
    of him who reposes
    on the primeval ocean of milk?"
You think they'll bless this food
    three days old
    you store in cans and ice-cupboard?

Son, son, it gives me great joy
to see you so well settled,
children and wife and all
Though my hairs do stand on end
When your wife holds hands with men
And you with other men's wives.
But I am glad, son, I really am
That you are settled good good
And thought to bring me all the way
to see this lovely house and car and all.

But I cannot breathe this stale air
With yesterday's cooking smells
going round and round.
Son, cooking is an every day thing
Not a Sunday work alone
And son, cooking should smell good
The leaping aromas
    of turmeric and green coriander,
    and mustard seeds popped in hot oil
that flavour food, not stink up the air.

Open the windows, son.

I am too used to the sounds
    of living things;
Of birds in the morning
Of rain and wind at night,
Not the drone of furnace fan
    and hiss of hot blasts
    and whoosh whoosh of washing machine.

Open the windows, son,
And let me go back
    to sun and air
    and sweat and even flies and all
But not this, not this.

Dilip:

Amma, I like school.
It is such fun.
We play most of the time
And sing songs in French.
Amma, fingerpainting is such fun

So many bright bright colours
And we can use all we want.
Amma, if a crayon breaks
You can just throw it away
And take a new one!
Ma, you think you could change my name
To Jim or David or something?
Amma I love recess time.
Did you see the tyres?
The tyres tied together?
And you can climb up
and sit inside and swing?
Such fun!
When the snow comes, Ma,
I'll get less brown won't I?
It would be nice to be white,
    more like everyone else
    you know?
I can do everything on the jungle-gym
That Petey can. I'll show you Saturday.
No school on Saturdays.
Just think, Amma, no school
Ever on Saturdays!
Except that it isn't so good
When you like school, you know?

Usha:

A river meandering motherly through the plain
my children wading in my placid waters.
I felt your steel feet planted astride my limbs,
felt my water rise in the catchment of your cofferdam
as you reared your wall to enfold me.

    Did you think, my love, you could hold me

in the matted coils of your hair
and funnel me out as and when you please?

With a sudden shower that truant boy opened
the floodgates of desire, swept my unleashed waters
on your unready bosom, and then ran away,
trilling his flute, into the winter fog.

Did I think, my love, I could
straighten the buckled-in pillars
of your spans to receive
my awakened tides?

Arise, my love, for out of the battered foam of my waters,
out of the pulverized stone of your loins
he has forged his song:

Rejoice, for though I am gone, the imprint of my hand
is on this crumbled wall and on these hungry waters
bound each to each through me.

Rejoice, that the fields you fed may draw
new strength from your embraces.

Demeter I Miss You

Demeter I miss you more than I dare avow
Here where love for mother is suspect.

I sought you along the Aegean
in the very fields where Persephone
Danced the year long; I only found
The virgin enshrined in grottos

Over Aphrodites baring their bosom
To the gaze of men.

I hoped to find you weeping by the Assiniboine
here where Pluto holds her in throe
eight long moons;
Caryatids I see stretched on the sand
that burgeon into lycra-padded fronts
when it is time to gyrate
to dizzy drumbeats
ere supporting pillars of erstwhile stone.

Demeter I miss you more than I dare avow
in this breastless land forlorn.

Long ago I have seen you
on the banks of the holy river;
Ganga dripping down your dark hair
Unveiling you like dawn stripping the east
Of his mourning cloak;
The transparent cloth clings
To your broad hips, contours
Your child birth mottled belly
And brings into sharp relief
Your breasts, cashew fruits
With giant seeds
Waiting to suckle

A Wedding Song

Spring came softly this year.

It was a long winter for the Assiniboine–
    with blizzards whistling across the prairies
    and snow steadily covering banks and water
    that had frozen with a sudden summer frost.

Under the snow and the long freeze

The river had felt earth's mother touch,
Felt the roots of the tree waiting, waiting,
And the sun's laser rays warming
Her deep waters into thawing, slowly thawing.

When Spring's deft fingers broke the ice,
The river was ready, and her waters rose—
    not with the flood of yesteryears—
But gently, gently, as the lotus rises
At Lakshmi's feet.

We who had seen winter come suddenly,
    had turned up our thermostats
    brought out our wintercoats
    and driven in gas-heated cars
    along the frozen river, our Assiniboine,
Had only distantly thought of the lonely swirling
Of her warm waters locked under ice unending.

But the tree waited, patiently waited,
For the river to rise
And feed his roots
That he may bloom.

Ajmer Rode

Try a Red Hot Coal

Try a red hot coal on your palm
your hand may not burn
the Sun that rose faithfully
for a billion years
may not rise tomorrow
the table in front of you
stuck by Gravitation
may fly to the ceiling
any moment.

absurd?
maybe

but my imagination has refused
to circle around the Sun
forever.

Under a Sewer Bridge

freedom
freedom what
freedom what? of pen?
freedom what? of pen? of tongue?
freedom what? of pen? of tongue? never
freedom what? of pen? of tongue? never. if ever
so what? says Ramu, born grown and disposed of
       u
       n
       d
       e
       r
     a sewer bridge

Mustard Flowers

If you see an old man sitting alone
at the bus stand and wonder who he is
I can tell you.
He is my father.
He is not waiting for a bus or a friend,
nor is he taking a brief rest before
resuming his walk.
He doesn't intend to shop in the
nearby stores either.
He is just sitting there on the bench.

Occasionally he smiles and talks.
No one listens.
Nobody is interested
And he doesn't seem to care
if someone listens or not.

A stream of cars, buses, and people
flows by on the road.
A river of images, metaphors and
similes flows through his head.
When everything stops
at the traffic lights it is midnight
back in his village. Morning starts
when lights turn green.
When someone honks his neighbour's
dog barks.

When a yellow car passes by
a thousand mustard flowers
bloom in his head.

A tall man passes with his shadow
vanishing behind him. My father
thinks of Pauli who left his village
for Malaya and
never came back. A smile appears
on his lips and disappears.

When nothing interesting seems to
happen he talks to
his other self:
Where were you born and where
have you come?
Who brought you here?
Shall you ever go back?
It is all destiny, yes a play of
destiny, you see.

He muses
and nods his head:
And where will you die my dear?

The thought of death is most
interesting and lingers on.
He stops talking, and thinks of the
Fraser Street chapel where he
attends funerals sometimes.
He thinks about the black
and red decorations and
imagines himself resting peacefully,
a line of people
passing by looking at him
for the last time.
His eyes are lit. Perhaps
this is the image he
enjoys most
before it is demolished
with the rude arrival of a bus.

A pain spreads over
his forehead,
passengers get down and
walk away briskly like ants.
the bus leaves.
He looks
at the traffic again to see
if a yellow car is passing by.

Once She Dreamed

Once she dreamed she was Mileva,
the long haired Serbian girl
Who married Einstein. She quietly
watched when Einstein twisted

the absolutely
flat space with his hands.
She watched
when Einstein broke the absolute
flow of time into pieces and
spun them around at the different
speeds.
She was there when Einstein
reconstructed the shattered universe.
As he became greater and greater
he grew modest and tender.
When finally the World came to
touch his hands
Mileva smiled and left.
She still liked to live in her own
absolute space
and move at her own pace.

Once she dreamed she was
Francis Gilot,
the young woman who married
Pablo Picasso.
She saw Picasso and the tip of
his brush
tearing apart the calm surrounding
the objects on his canvas.
She saw faces turning into cubes
and cones.
When Picasso was engulfed
in cubes of fame
Gilot left.
She said she wouldn't become a cube.

Then she dreamed of Jeanny
the lady who married Karl Marx.
Jeanny read stories to their
hungry children
as Marx fed the hungry of the

world in his imagination.
As his beard curled more and more,
Jeanny saw Marx grow into a
prophet trying to define a future
for mankind, trying to
unseat the lords.
When infuriated Gods came
upon him
Jeanny stood at the door wondering
what to do.

Last night she dreamed nothing.
Her eyes refused to close.
A sad vacuum expanded in her
and burst.
The man she married
quietly disappeared.
She says he was confused, depressed
and needed care.

Spanish Banks

The grey sands
invite me to follow the
receding sea water
to recognize a clam shell
that could be the house
where my ancestors began.

I walk slowly and with
respect.

Suwanda Sugunasiri

Women on Tape

side one

Ia. Chair in the Corner

1.
On the second shift
in the London kitchen as I
walk in. . .

"Sorry I couldn't
meet you at Gatwick. . . But
y'know
really
I love it
believe me
every minute of it
back from work.
Even Polish
the silver and brass
move the furniture
around
and
back again.

"Energy I'd say
energy

that's what.
Guess I've been brought up that way!"

2.
"Has it been
honestly, a week, since
we left London driving through
Paris and Monte Carlo and Rome. . .?
The night out
in Venice the dinner
at Rio Grande the wandering minstrels
the wine
the lulling train ride.

"You're my brother.
Like one at least.
He's a good man, this
my man
your buddy.

"But . . .
but how long
how long I mean
tell me
can I be
as but a chair
in the corner?"

3.
"Great to be back
in my wonderful
kitchen
'I'm sick
of cooking'? Oh,
words on a wallplate! Just
a joke. Reminds
me to love
cooking."

4.
"This my man
a good man. . ."

Ib. Wives of London

She came
to bid us goodbye
out of the house
down the stairs
("elevators bore me")
thrilled at each step
to the road
the bank the supermarket
the smile
exuberant decorating
the face.

Yesterday she
served us a scrumptious meal.
"Cooked
all day," her husband said with
a mocking pompous grin
"Not
all day," she protests.

"Yesterday he
lunched with the Israeli ambassador tommorrow
off to Hawaii. The UN
pays him but not
me.
Would be interesting
to play cards
with him; beat me
all the time
way back when.

"I unstitch and stitch

my jackets and skirts
to fit myself in;
add lace brocade colour;
look in the mirror
lipstck rouge
pummelling the face.

"Just look at that
water, how beautiful, meandering
down the street
into the drain.
Have you this scene in Toronto?

"I
can take the Metro from one end
to the other.
He
does the driving
carefully
well-calculated.
"Tonight Jakarta
stopover with his folks en route, who knows!
Perhaps a swim a sip
of the local arrack under the fan."

"Come again,"
she says, waving
she smiles
the wet tear over the lined face
grown of long years,
the wife
in London Paris Geneva Tokyo.

side two

IIa. Guardians and Angels

Skiing
I watch on tv

sun I enjoy
by the window.
The little ones' crying
running falling smiling
make my day.
The ocean
of German around me too much
to fathom,
he swims
navigates with so much ease
the four walls my guardian
angels
he
the breadwinner
my saviour.

IIb. Song of Femininity

In an Egyptian mummy coffin
DuMaurier Players
deep in eternal slumber beside
a wine cellar rotting
inside out
the smell enough
to kill the dead
scotch vodka gin strewn in splinters
of glass the outer shell
plastered with Playboy Penthouse
centrefolds dissipating
at the touch.

The lotus
in the pond
walking by
in peacock plumes the maxis midis
crushing
under the draped sari beckoning
the nymph the mother the lover
in me strutting

to a foxtrot strumming
a song of femininity.
The woman I am
released from bondage!

Asoka Weerasinghe

Trilogy

(curfew in Ceylon, April 1971)

1. THE BIRTH OF INSURGENTS

When I went home
April showered me with bombs
and bullets.

The hunched hills whispered
rumours of treason
spreading like sheaves
of daggers over paddy-fields;
while idling knowledge copulated
to bear murderers
in woods where once blossomed
orchids and hibiscus.

I was at home
when April showered
guns and bullets.
Eight borrowed helicopters
droned like ailing mosquitoes,
while offspring of the guilty
book-peddled in Paris and Oxford.

2. THE INSURGENTS

Blood falling

Blood trickling
         drenching the earth,

Blood dripping

Blood clotting
         the dread in forests,
where you are flowers
where flowers do not bloom.

I could only send you
         the Arctic wind,
to heal your cries
         of bullet wounds,
and let you share my tomb
         with your dead.

3. THE PLIGHT OF INSURGENTS

The water-weeds wept
bruised for him who was silenced
by one bullet hole in his skull.
Under my feet brown-water swept
at noontide, braiding streaks of blood,
and nine soldiers guarding the barb-wired
bridge could only mock grave-smiles.

Metamorphosis

Even the Gods are jealous of this paradise.
Where once only the colonial masters
enjoyed buttered-scones and iced Ceylon tea,
at Colombo's Grand Oriental Hotel at three.

Even the Gods were jealous of this paradise.
Where once only the British civil servants
could afford to eat Granny Smiths apples and grapes,
and cover home-windows with Kashmir-silk drapes.

Even the Gods were jealous of this paradise.
Where once a few rich had mynahs in their lofts
and black-tied foreigners fox-trotted at night,
as I watched through hotel windows envying the sight.

The Gods are still jealous of this paradise.
Even though the names of the patrons have changed
from Cargill, Miller, MacDonald and Sims,
to Sliva, Banda, Selvadas and Cassim.

Even the Gods are still jealous of this paradise.

Four Poems for Anikka Maya

1.
We sit in a boat
in tandem nearly
    every evening
taking the live cocoon
    within you
for a ride.
We kiss a whole day's
tea from our lips,
    kiss Palmolive soap
among our slippery laughter
    cautious
not to drown whomever
    we are supposed to be taking
for a ride.
    My both hands soapy
I touch you from behind
    and bathe you and him or her
and embrace you
    around the fattening stomach
through the soaking water.

2.
In the green-surgical morning
"I am glad you made it."
When you arrived yearning
for a breath of fresh air
avoiding my anxious gaze,
I had parked myself
on a stainless sterilized stool
beside a uterine blood pool.
I felt proud of you and amazed
being so clever to find
your way out from the umbilical maze

in a foetal crouch and pursed eyes.
While carried by your armpits
the quartz light half flooded
your turquoise face and lit
the limbs dangling from your hip
that stretched straining your lips
to claim your share of our space.
One half of my brain prayed
and wished as expected of me,
and the other half faintly recited
Dylan Thomas poems for your mother
as well as my numbed memory
could remember in a dazed hurry.
Beside me your mother's
breathing body a dissected corpse,
still humming Christmas carols,
waited eagerly to try
and harmonize with the chord
of your first primal cry.

3.
Poems in my Carmelite head
under a green skull cap,
I breathe irrational vows
through masked nostrils
waiting for the life
that would penetrate the air
within blue moments
chalked in blood
strung by the navel
gasping for oxygen.

You had courage to let a scalpel
stab an incision
and let the healing hands
string your stomach with
Teflon sutures
like Paraguayan harp criss-crossing

the plum-skinned flesh
plucking the music
of the early morning hymns.

4.
Sharing lullaby concerts
listening to music lying in my lap,
and mesmerized trapped
by a red-flowered wall quilt
I kiss the soles of your sleek
soft porcelain feet to the built
up rhythms of the calypso music.
When growing old, I hope
you will cope
with the pancaked kisses,
and not have to limp
counting the misses
in fear of crushing each one of them.

II. Fiction

Ven Begamudré

The Evil Eye

Sinu lies at the base of a shrine to Goddess Saraswati. His arms are crossed behind his head. He clutches a reed with his toes, paints indigo white clouds up from the river into an ultramarine sky. Searching for prey, a brahmin kite wheels into view, threatens to spoil his composition. With two flicks of his foot, he paints a curved v, reddish-brown, pierces the wings with sunflower rays, and fixes the kite to the sun. He rolls onto his stomach, digs his elbows into the damp earth, and props his chin on his hands. Distant unseen goatherds call to their flocks, gather them for the journey home.

Townspeople often smile when Sinu passes, but none can guess how he feels. Happy is not the word. He feels bubbly. Not like the bubbles he once blew from soapy water. Those were many-hued like the squares, now long dried, of his watercolour paintbox. He feels like the bubbles in bisleri soda–invisible until someone shakes a bottle the way his parents have shaken him by announcing they have found him a bride. Fields of ripening sugar cane stretch from the river to Nanjangud Town. By the time they are ready to harvest, he will return with a girl named Janaki, a South Indian born and raised in the North.

He looks at the goddess in her shrine, a niche of whitewashed mud opening onto the river. A crescent moon rises from her brow, and her head tilts towards one shoulder. With two of her hands, she clutches a veena. One is poised near the instrument's neck; the fingers of the other hand pluck the strings. She asks, *What shall I play for you next?* He replies, *Whatever you wish.* In the third hand she holds a book. Her fourth hand reaches for the head of a swan rising from the lotus at her feet. Now she asks, *Who will read my poetry or listen to my music while you are gone?* He fingers a petal of the lotus where chipped red paint reveals grey stone. *Janaki will help me restore you,* he promises. *We shall listen on moonlit nights to your songs.*

He rises and bids the goddess farewell, then crosses the lower canal by a foot bridge and fans his way though sugar cane to the Nanjangud Road. He always takes the long way home, for he wants no one to know where he hides after school. By the time he reaches the eastern edge of the town, coconut palms cast their shadows towards him. Even as he nears his father's house, Sinu's footsteps slow.

His mother Sharada never tires of telling him his father Iruve had always wanted a son. When Sinu's eldest sister was born, Iruve was too young to worry about having fathered a girl. With the second, third, and fourth girl, he began to feel cheated. He found fault with even his growing prosperity, for he wanted to watch his own son, not some overseer, supervise the harvest. After the birth of the fifth girl, he began fearing for his soul. "Who will bring me a daughter-in-law from the city?" he cried.

"What is one daughter-in-law from a city against five sons-in-law from our district?" Sharada asked.

He spat on the floor, next to her foot, but her toes barely twitched. "My soul shall not go to heaven if my pyre is lit by a son-in-law," he scoffed. "Even you should know that." He left her nursing the baby and trudged through his fields. No one knew where Iruve hid.

The sixth time Sharada gave birth, he remained hidden in his fields until past sunset. He returned to find the latest child asleep in the crook of her arm.

She folded back the towel wrapped around the child and weakly said, "A boy finally. Let us name him Srinivas." She crooned over the baby, "Sinu? Welcome, Sinu."

That very night, squinting by the glow of a kerosene lamp, Iruve painted over "Kempe Gowda House" and painted "Srinivas House." The new name dried unevenly on the whitewashed stone, but Iruve thought it grand. Not everyone owned a house as posh as that belonging to the Kempe Gowda clan; not everyone could name his house after a son. Next, Iruve applied black paste around Sinu's eyes. It would deceive the evil eye into thinking he was deformed, unworthy of attention.

Iruve delighted in his every discovery about his baby son. "See, he

sees his toes," Iruve said; or, "Listen, I tell you he is speaking words."
On Sinu's first birthday, Iruve took him to a portrait studio in Mysore
City. There they posed in front of a painting of yew trees among the
ruins of a Christian church. He had the photo tinted and displayed it,
his first coloured photo, in the main room.

This evening, Sinu finds his every move watched. "Eat more slowly," Iruve says. "Do you want your future in-laws to think we are ill-
bred?" Sinu forces himself to eat so slowly, he is still eating when the
others are finished. "Hurry, you lame bullock," Iruve says. "Do you
want your future in-laws to think you expect the world to revolve
around you."

Sinu looks to Sharada, but she looks away. After Iruve leaves, she
pulls Sinu to her, cradles his head in her lap. "Never mind, son," she
says. "Your father is afraid only that the evil eye will notice if he
praises you. It is so full of mischief, there is none so vigilant as the evil
eye. Think, though. If he did not love you, would he have secured a
bride from Delhi itself?" Sinu looks up to see tears in Sharada's eyes.
"My son, my son," she croons. "You will soon be a man." She hugs
him so close her fleshy arms feel like the jaws of a velvet vice. He
clutches her wrists, but still he feels as though he will drown in her
flesh, smother beneath her breasts. One sags onto his brow, the other
onto this throat. He has always felt trapped like this, in a house that
feels like the womb: his father with a tongue as searing as flame; his
mother with breasts like sodden earth.

He wonders whether his sisters would envy him if they knew he
dreams his own death. Sometimes he dreams Iruve throws him into a
fire made of dung cakes. Other times, he dreams Sharada buries him
alive in a field. Soon his days in brahmacharaya, in studentship, will
end. He will enter the second stage of his life, that of the householder.
Only then can he pursue the three ends of man: pleasure, material
gain, and virtue.

Best of all will be pleasure.

With all the sights of Delhi awaiting them, the family has little time
to linger over those in Bombay. Sinu spends two days dashing in
Iruve's tow to landmarks like Colaba Causeway and Sassoon Dock,
Taraporewella Aquarium and the Hanging Gardens on Malabar Hill.
Sharada spends her days immobile on Chowpatty Beach. There she
snacks on kulfi ice cream while she chuckles at the antics of contor-
tionists and sandcastle sculptors. At night, breezes blow off Bombay

Harbour. Perhaps it is these breezes; perhaps it is the hectic pace Iruve sets; whatever the cause, Sinu reaches Delhi in the first flush of a fever. Everyone mistakes the light in his eyes for excitement. On the morning of the one day he and Janaki will spend alone before their marriage, he wakes to find not dew but a faint white dust on the compound of her uncle's house. People here call it frost.

Janaki speaks Hindi and English; Sinu speaks Kannada and little else. Despite their difficulty in understanding one another, he does not tire of their outing. At home he has only to look up from his plate, and Sharada calls for sambar and rice. He has only to raise his tumbler and his youngest sister mixes water with curds. She is still unmarried, for no one wants a girl with protruding teeth. Yet Janaki allows him to open doors for her, allows him to pay for autorickshaws with coins that jingle in his pocket.

There is so much to see in Connaught Place alone, they spend the entire morning in the white colonnades, the arts and crafts shops, the airline offices with their coloured photos from Fiji and New Zealand. After lunch in a hotel restaurant, they linger silently until Janaki speaks of Jaipur, where her eldest brother lives: of the Old Town's pink sandstone buildings, which sparkle like jewels in the desert setting; Jantra Mantra, the observatory with its gigantic sun dial; the jewellers' market, Johari Bazaar. She frowns when he says in Kannada, "I will buy every jewel there for you," but he does not repeat himself in English.

He leads her back to the Rajasthan Emporium and bids her wait outside with her back to the window. There he examines rows of Rajput miniatures. They lie on velvet below glass. He has spent most of the money Iruve gave him but, before Sinu left the house, Sharada pressed a twenty-rupee note into his hand. She whispered, "You show the girl what we are worth." The note buys a single ivory square no large than a square of paint in his watercolour box. The miniature depicts a warrior prince in amber robes and a cinnabar turban. While leaving, Sinu notices a painting of a Rajput lady, gold and viridian green on a surface lacquered black; painted in the style called nirmala, or perfect. She cradles a lotus in the palm of one hand. After whispered entreaties, the clerk agrees to exchange a second miniature for the wristwatch Sharada bought Sinu in preparation for this journey. The second miniature is of a princess.

He rejoins Janaki on the pavement. The brown-paper packet he holds should make him feel worthy, but he feels ashamed as though he has betrayed someone with his extravagance. He thrusts the packet at her, then hurries away with his hands buried in the pockets of her father's warmest cardigan. He hugs himself, but not tightly enough to suppress a shiver. How cold it is here during Chaligula, the season northerners call Shishira, the one Britishers call simply the cold season. No wonder hawkers rub mustard oil on their bodies to keep warm. No wonder some even stand with braziers suspended under their garments. He turns when Janaki touches his elbow.

Her questioning eyes confound him when he tries to explain. He nearly says, "A sample only of what I can offer." Instead he forces himself to say, "A promise we shall visit Jaipur after we are wed." When she blushes, so does he, and they stand face to face inches apart. He knows she feels anxious about the first night they must spend together. One does not speak of such things. If only his parents would not insist the second ceremony, the tying of the kankanam that will herald their complete union, await their return to Nanjangud.

"Let us be off," he says. When she reminds him they still have the afternoon, reminds him of the old fort Purana Qila and of Humayun's Tomb, he shakes his head. "We must walk," he says. He confesses he has squandered all his money, even parted with his wristwatch, all for her. He waits for her to scold him, but she does not.

They cover a furlong before she touches his elbow again. "Thank you," she says.

They walk in silence after that, sometimes drifting apart, sometimes drifting so closely their sleeves brush. By the time they reach her father's house, sweat drenches Sinu's hair; yet his throat feels like the moulted skin of a lizard, brittle and cold. After he claims, "We were robbed," Janaki hurries from the room. He prays she will keep the miniatures a secret.

It will be their first of many.

On the evening of the fourth day of the wedding, Sinu arrives at the house of Janaki's father. Music blares from loudspeakers to tell the district a marriage is still underway. As befits the groom, Sinu wears his finest clothes, gifts from her uncle; yet no sooner does Sinu enter the compound than her brothers strip him to his new dhoti. They lead him to the inner courtyard and seat him near the fire blazing on a dais. His skin glistens with mustard oil and turmeric; he begins to perspire. When he wipes his face with his hands, he secretly wipes away tears.

He has eaten nothing since his sunrise meal of crisped rice and curds. He wants to sleep. This grand adventure, this journey all the way north to secure a bride has become a gauntlet of rites.

He and Janaki have observed malai-matral three times. She sat astride her uncle's shoulders; Sinu sat astride her eldest brother's. Both Sinu and Janaki wore two garlands of marigold and jasmine entwined. They tried not to laugh, for the garlands tickled their necks and ears. After her uncle and her brother stopped face to face, grinning and grimacing, Sinu took one of his garlands and placed it around her neck. By this he showed he willingly shared half his spiritual force with her. She, in turn, did the same.

They have also observed nalangu for three evenings. They sat facing one another on mats. First he stretched out his legs, and she rubbed turmeric paste on them. The yellow paste stung and closed his pores; yet he bit the inside of his mouth to keep from smiling when she touched the soles of his feet. She allowed herself a smile when he, in turn, did the same for her. Then she took up two handfuls of crisp yellow rice, raised them above his head, and scattered the rice in the air. He, in turn, did the same. Iruve laughed with Sharada, for only now could anyone see the bride and groom at play. Once married, Sinu and Janaki would play behind closed doors as husband and wife. They sat side by side while the women of her family passed a plate over their heads. On it was a mixture of turmeric and slaked lime to cast off the evil from the evil eye. Then, while the women sang accompanied by men playing pipes, Janaki's mother distributed sandalwood paste, flowers and fruits: papaya, guava, tender coconut.

Sinu repeats the Sanskrit phrases sung by the priests to induce a proper frame of mind:

"As man by himself is an imperfect being. Husband and wife are halves of a spiritual whole, the husband the left, the wife the right."

"Man and wife wed in the presence of Agni, the god of fire, and because the gods attend the marriage, no human may sever its tie."

"Marriage is a sacrament, not a contract. Though the husband may die, he will wait for his wife in the heaven world, and both will return once more to wed."

At last the priests judge him ready. Her mother leads Janaki into the courtyard. The end of Janaki's gold-embroidered sari covers her head. She stops at the dais, allows her mother to uncover her eyes, and Sinu and Janaki gaze at one another. Designs drawn with sandalwood paste cover her hands, her feet, her face. She, too, has eaten little since sunrise. She sits thankfully next to him on the dais, and they pretend to ignore one another while the ceremony continues. The women of her family create a pass-not by waving a camphor flame around the dais. The pass-not will confound invisible beings contemplating malice.

Guests come and go. They eat and drink in the house of Janaki's father, but Sinu and Janaki must wait. By midnight, he feels so keen of sense that every act he witnesses appears significant: the smile on one of her unmarried classmates, the raised eyebrow of her distant male cousin. Smoke from the fire burns Sinu's eyes, incense clouds his throat; yet most of all, worst of all, he feels chilled.

The priests make their final blessings, and the ceremony ends. Janaki's close relations and friends bring jewellery and clothes. In return they receive fruit or pan supari: betel leaves stuffed with slaked lime and areca nut. Distant relations and ordinary friends give small amounts of money. It will buy her a ring. They receive pinches of yellow rice and, laughing, shower it on Sinu and Janaki.

Sinu wraps a shawl about his shoulders. When he rises to make his ablutions, he staggers. People around him laugh, and he rubs his legs as though they have lost their feeling. A few minutes more, and he can eat. A few hours more, and he can sleep through sunrise. When he passes his parents, already seated for yet another feast, Sharada looks up with pride in her moist eyes. Then she looks at Iruve as though pleading with him to admit he is also proud of his son.

Iruve's lips purse. He eyes the plantain leaf on which his meal will soon be served. At last he says, "You look so handsome, son. So much like a man."

Sinu feels cheated, for such words would have meant more had his father spoken them freely. Sinu nods his thanks and leaves his parents to their meal. Even as he finishes washing, his mother screams. Janaki's father, Sinu's father-in-law now, bursts into the room.

"Your father is no more!" he shouts. He gestures as though throwing away his heart like a worthless possession. He pulls Sinu, staggering, into the main room.

Sharada sobs while she cradles Iruve's head in her lap, smothers him with her breasts. Sinu's legs grow numb. He finds himself on the floor.

Making no apology, guests flee the house. Music no longer blares in the compound.

Through daybreak and morning, Sinu and Janaki remain with Iruve's corpse while Sharada wails in a tiny room beyond the kitchen. Like Sinu, Janaki sits cross-legged next to the body, but she remains motionless while he rocks with his hands clasped over his ears. At last he stretches out on a mat. Sharada's screams keep him awake.

At noon, the city corporation van arrives to carry the corpse to the crematorium. Sinu climbs onto the back alone, but even here he cannot find solitude. People stare at him through the high glass sides of the black van. He feels so chilled that, later, when an attendant rolls the corpse through the open steel doors of the crematorium, Sinu takes a step towards the flames.

The attendant raises his palm inches from Sinu's chest. "Not you, sir," he insists.

When Sinu returns to the house, his father-in-law says, "You are welcome to remain here until the immersion. We have no heating coil for your bath, but you may not go out now in any event. I see the chill air does not agree with you."

For ten days, Sinu, Sharada, and Janaki never once leave the house. At night the two women sleep, but each sunrise finds him looking more haggard. At home he takes a head bath only once a week; now he must take one every day, and that with cool water. While the days wear on, he wanders about the house. There is no place to hide. Often he staggers as though the flesh has been scooped from his limbs. He no longer feels bubbly. He feels like a single bubble: sometimes so hollow, he expects his chest to collapse onto his spine; other times stretched so tightly, he thinks he may burst. If only Janaki could keep him warm at night, but that cannot yet be. They exchange many looks, but they exchange few words beyond, "Rest yourself," or, "Take some food."

On the eleventh day after the cremation, Sinu, Janaki, and Sharada hire a taxicab to drive them to the outskirts of Delhi. Sharada fills the front with her bulk, squeezes the driver against his door. Sinu holds an unglazed pot containing ashes. Once, when the taxicab jolts and the lid scrapes aside, ash falls on his thigh. He brushes away the ash, then licks a fingertip and tries to erase the yellow-grey smear. Janaki stops him by placing her hand on his and his cheeks burn. At a small temple on the bank of the Jamuna River, the taxicab stops. They are downstream from the city, towards Agra. There, Janaki has told him,

North Indian couples observe a rite called honeymoon. They view Taj Mahal by moonlight.

Sharada hires an old priest. After she pays him he walks, clad only in his breechclout, into the river. Just then, a young woman fans her way through reeds, clambers up the bank some distance away. Sinu's eyes linger on the wet sari clinging to her breasts.

"I cannot do this," he tells Janaki, "Appa's ashes belong in the Kabini River." Before she can say anything, he moans, "Oh, God, I am so cold." He stumbles down the stone steps into the river. For a moment, the hollowness leaves him. He feels his heart beat in his chest if only because a hand seems to clutch it under the water. He wants to immerse the ashes and be done with them, but the priest makes him wash himself and stand with his hands clasped during an endless Sanskrit prayer. When the priest finally nods, Sinu takes the clay pot from the bottom step. Clasping the lid, he lowers the pot, turns it upside down, and pushes it through the surface. Bubbles rise; the clay pot sinks. He emerges trembling to find Sharada gazing balefully at him.

"You should have scattered the ashes," she says. "Not drowned them like that, son."

During the long rail journey from Delhi to Bombay from Bombay to Miraj Junction, from Miraj to Bangalore and then Mysore City, from Mysore to Nanjangud Town, Sinu pretends all is well. He knows he should feel warmer coming home, back to where the sun traps even brahminy kites with its rays, but the chill spreads from his hands and feet through his limbs to his heart. Srinivas House no longer feels like a womb; it feels like a Muslim or even a Christian tomb. When his lungs begin gurgling with fluid, he finds little comfort in Janaki's embrace. He knows she piles shawls on him, chafes his wrists to speed the flow of blood, and feeds him scalding tea with a spoon, but it all seems wasted effort, wasted like the years his parents spent in schooling him–all those years when he longed for praise.

One night he wakes to find Janaki cradling his head in her lap. He raises a hand to touch her face. He has done nothing wrong. He has so much still to do. He wants to say, "Promise me you will restore the statue. The shrine of Goddess Saraswati will be our secret place."

"What is it?" Janaki asks. When she bends closer, his hand slides into the hollow of her throat, down onto her blouse. She unbuttons it, moulds his hand onto her breast.

He mutters, "Promise me–"

The world turns white, wet and softly white, and a boy floats on the surface of a river, floats between water and air. Waves rock him, breezes nudge him, yet he lingers to twirl like a lotus freed from its roots. He sinks with his reflection in the quicksilvered surface waves. Warm mud blankets him; reeds embrace him. Many-hued bubbles glide from his mouth when he smiles. They break the surface, rise through an ultramarine sky, pass indigo white clouds, and pluck free a kite drying on the still damp sun.

Neil Bissoondath

Dancing

I was nothing more than a maid back home in Trinidad, just a ordinary fifty-dollar-a month maid. I didn't have no uniform but I did get
off early Saturdays. I didn't work Sundays, except when they had a
party. Then I'd go and wash up the dishes and the boss'd give me a
few dollars extra.

My house, if you could call it a house, wasn't nothing more than a
two-room shack, well, in truth, a one-room shack with a big cupboard
I did use as a bedroom. With one medium-size person in there you
couldn't find room to squeeze in a cockaroach. The place wasn't no
big thing to look at, you understand. A rusty galvanized roof that leak
every time it rain, wood walls I decorate with some calendars and my
palm-leaf from the Palm Sunday service. In one corner I did have a
old table with a couple a chairs. In the opposite corner, under the window, my kitchen, with a small gas stove and a big bowl for washing
dishes. I didn't have pipes in my house, so every morning I had to fetch
water from a standpipe around the corner, one bucket for the kitchen
bowl, one for the little bathroom behind the house. And, except for
the latrine next to the bathroom, that was it, the whole calabash. No
big thing. But the place was always clean though, and had enough
space for me.

It was in a back trace, behind a big, two-storey house belonging to
a Indian doctor-fella. The land was his and he always telling me in a
half-jokey kind of way that he going to tear down my house and put
up a orchid garden. But he didn't mean it, in truth. He wasn't a too-
too bad fella. He did throw a poojah from time to time and as soon as

the prayers stop and the conch shell stop blowing, Kali the yardboy always bring me a plate of food from the doc.

The first of every month the doc and the yardboy did walk around with spray pumps on their back, spraying-spraying. The drains was white with poison afterward, but I never had no trouble with mosquito or fly or even silverfish. So the doc wasn't a bad neighbour, although I ain't fooling myself, I well know he was just helping himself and I was getting the droppings. People like that in Trinidad, you know, don't let the poojah food fool you. You could be deading in his front yard in the middle of the night and doc not coming out the house. I count three people dead outside his house and their family calling-calling and the doc never even so much as show his face. We wasn't friends, the doc and me. I tell him "Mornin" and he tell me "Mornin" and that was that.

I worked for a Indian family for seven, eight years. Nice people. Not like the doc. Good people. And that's another thing. Down here Black people have Indian maid and Indian people have Black maid. White people does mix them up, it don't matter to them. Black people say, Black people don't know how to work. Indian people say, Indian people always thiefing-thiefing. Me, I did always work for Indian people. They have a way of treating you that make you feel you was part of the family. Like every Christmas, Mum–I did call the missus that, just like her children–Mum give me a cake she make with her own two hand. It did always have white icening all over it, and a lot of red cherry. They was the kind of people who never mind if I wanted to ketch some tv after I finished my work. I'd drag up a kitchen chair behind them in the living room, drinking coffee to try to keep the eyes open. And sometimes when I get too tired the boss did drive me home. Understand my meaning clear, though. They was good people, but strick. They'd fire you in two-twos if you not careful with your work.

Nice people, as I say, but the money . . . Fifty dollars a month can't hardly buy shoe polish for a centipede. I talked to the pastor about it and he tell me ask for a raise. All they gimme is ten dollars more, so I went back to the pastor. You know what he say? "Why don't you be-come a secketary, Sister James? Go to secketarial school down in Port of Spain."

Well, I start to laugh. I say, "Pastor, you good for the soul but you ain't so hot when it come to the stomach." Well, I never! Me, who hardly know how to read and write, you could see me as one of them prim an proper secketaries in a nice air-condition office? Please take this lettah, Miss James. Bring me that file, Miss James. Just like on tv! I learn fast-fast servant job was only work for somebody like me.

That was life in Trinidad.

Then I get a letter from my sister Annie up in Toronto. She didn't write too often but when she set her mind to it she could almost turn out a whole book. She talk on and on bout Caribana, and she send some pictures she cut out from the newspaper. It look so strange to see Trinidadians in Carnival costumes dancing and jumping in them big, wide streets. Then she go on bout all the money she was making and how easy her life was. I don't mind saying that make me cry, but the tears dry up fast-fast. She write how Canadians racialist as hell. She say they hate black people for so and she tell me bout an ad on tv showing a black girl eating a banana pudding. Why they give banana to the Black? Annie say is because they think she look like a monkey. I couldn't bring myself to understand how people so bad. Annie say they jump out of the stomach like that. I telling you, man, is a terrible thing how people born racialist.

Anyways, Annie ask me to come up to Canada and live with she. She wanted to sponsor me and say she could help me find a job in two-twos. First I think, No way. Then, later that night in bed, I take a good look at myself. I had thirty years, my little shack and sixty dollars a month. Annie was making five times that Canadian, ten times that Trinidadian. I did always believe, since I was a little girl, that I'd get pregnant one day and catch a man, like most of the women around me. But the Lord never mean for me to make baby. I don't mind saying I try good and hard but it just wasn't in the cards. I thought, No man, no child, a shack, a servant job, sixty dollars a month. What my life was going to be like when I reach sixty? I think hard all night and all next day, and for a whole week.

After the Sunday service, I told the pastor bout Annie's letter. Quick-quick he say, "Go, Sister James, it is God's doing. He has answered your prayers."

I didn't bother to tell him that I didn't pray to God for help. I figure he already have His hands full with people like the doc.

Then it jump into my head to go ask the doc what to do. He was always flying off to New York and Toronto. So I thought he could give me more practical advices.

I went to see him that morning self. He was in the garden just behind the high iron gate watering the anthuriums. Kali the yardboy was shovelling leftover manure back into a half empty cocoa bag. I remember the manure did have a strong-strong smell because they did just finish spreading it on the flower beds.

The doc was talking to himself. He say, "A very table masterpiece of gardening." Or something like that. That was the doc. A couple of times when I was walking home I hear him talking to his friends and it was big and fancy-words, if you please. But when he talk to me or Kali or we kind of people, he did start talking like us quick-quick. Maybe he think we going to like him more. Or maybe he think we doesn't understand good English. I always want to tell him that we not children, we grow up too. But why bother?

I knock on the gate.

The doc look up and say, "Mornin, Miss Sheila."

"Mornin, doctor."

"Went to church this mornin, Miss Sheila?"

"Yes, doctor."

"Nice anthuriums, not so?"

"Very nice anthuriums, doctor. Is not everybody could grow them flowers like you."

He shakes his shoulders as if to say, That ain't no news. Then he say, "Is hard work but they pretty for spite, you don't think so?"

I remember the day a dog dig up one of the anthuriums and the doc take a hoe to the poor animal and break his head in two. There was blood all over the place and the dog drop down stone dead. The owner start to kick up a fuss and the doc call the police to cart the man off to jail. But that was just life in Trinidad and I didn't say nothing. But ever since then those pink heart-shape flowers remind me of that dog, as if the plants pick up some of the blood and the shape of the heart. It was after that that the doc put up the brick fence with broken bottles all along the tip and a heavy iron gate.

I say, "Doctor, I want to ask you for some advices."

He say, "I not working now, Miss Sheila, come back tomorrow during office hours."

"I not sick, doctor, is about another business." But still he turn away from me, all the time spraying-spraying with the hose.

Kali stop shovelling and say something to the doc.

The doc say, "What is this I hearing? Miss Sheila? You thinking bout leaving Trinidad?"

Kali start to laugh. I see the doc wanted to laugh too. He turn off the hose and drop it on the ground. He walk over to the gate. He say, "Is true, Miss Sheila?"

"Yes, doctor." And I get a strange feeling, as if somebody ketch me thiefing something.

"Canada?"

"Yes, doctor."

"Toronto?"

"Yes, doctor."

"So what you want to know, Miss Sheila?"

"I can't make up my mind, doctor. I don't know if to go or if to stay."

"And you want my advice?"

"I grateful for any help you could give me, doctor."

He start rubbing the dirt from his hands and he stand there, think-ing-thinking. Then he lean against the gate and say, "Miss Sheila, I going to tell you something I don't say very often because people don't like to hear the truth. They does get vex. But you know, Miss Sheila, people on this island too damn uppity for their own good. They lazy and they good-for-nothing. They don't like to work. And they so damn uppity they think they go to Canada or the States and life easy. Well, it not easy. It very,very hard and you have to work your ass off to get anywhere. Miss Sheila, what you could do? Eh? Tell me. I admire you for wanting to improve your life but what you think you going to do in Canada? You let some damn stupid uppity people put a damn stupid idea in your head and you ready to run off and lose everything you have. Your house, your job, everything. And why? Because of uppiti-ness. Don't think you going to be able to buy house up in Canada, you know. So, I advise you not to go, Miss Sheila. The grass never greener on the other side." He stop talking and take a cigarette from his shirt pocket and light it.

I didn't know what to say. I was confuse. I say, "Thanks, doctor. Good day, doctor," and start walking to my house. Before I even take two steps, I hear Kali say, "Them nigs think the world is for them and them alone."

And he and the doc start to laugh.

There I was, hands hurting like hell from suitcase and boxes and bags and I couldn't find the door handle. My head was still full of cotton wool from the plane and my stomach was bawling its head off for food. I just wanted to turn right round and say, "Take me back. The doc was right. I ain't going to be able to live in a place where doors ain't have no handle." But then a man in a uniform motion me to keep walking, as if he want me to bounce straight into the door. Well, if it have one thing I fraid is policeman, so I start to walk and, Lord, like the Red Sea parting for Moses, the door open by itself.

This make me feel good. I feel as if I get back at the customs man who did ask me all kind of nasty questions like, "You have any rum? Whisky? Plants? Food?" as if I look like one of them smugglers that does ply between Trinidad and Venezuela. I thought, I bet the doors don't open like that for him!

As I walk through the door I start feeling dizzy-dizzy. Everything look cloudy-cloudy, as if the building was just going to fade away or melt. I was so frighten I start to think I dreaming, like it wasn't me walking there at all but somebody else. It was almost like looking at a film in a cinema.

Then I hear a voice talking to me inside my head. It say, Sheila James, maid, of Mikey Trace, Trinidad, here you is, a big woman, walking in Toronto airport and you frighten. Why?

I force myself to look around. I see faces, faces round me faces. Some looking at me, some looking past me, and some even looking through me. I start feeling like a flowers vase on a table.

Then all of a sudden the cloudiness disappear and I see all the faces plain-plain. They was mostly white. My chest tighten up and I couldn't hardly breathe. I was surrounded by tourists. And not one of them was wearing a straw hat.

I hear another voice calling me, "Sheila! Sheila!" I look around but didn't see nobody, only all these strange faces. I start feeling small-small, like a douen. Suddenly it jump into my head to run headlong through the crowd but it was as if somebody did nail my foot to the floor: I couldn't move. Again like in a dream. A bad dream.

And then, bam!, like magic, I see all these black faces running towards me, pushing the tourists out of the way, almost fighting with one another to get to me first. I recognize Annie. She shout, "Sheila!" Then I see my brother Sylvester, and others I didn't know. Annie grab on to me and hug me tight-tight. Sylvester take my bags and give them to somebody else, then he start hugging me too. Somebody pat me on the back. I felt safe again. It was almost like being back in Trinidad.

Sylvester and the others drop Annie and me off at her flat in Vaughan Road. Annie was a little vex with Syl because he didn't want to stay and talk but I tell her I was tired and she let him go off to his party.

Annie boil up some water for tea and we sit down in the tiny living room to talk. I notice how old Annie was looking. Her face was heavy, it full-out in two years. And the skin under her eyes was dark-dark as if all her tiredness settle there. Like dust. Maybe it was the light. It always dark in Annie's apartment, even in the day. The windows small-small, and she does keep on only one light at a time. To save on the hydro bill, she say.

She ask me about friends and the neighbours and the pastor. It didn't have much family left in Trinidad to talk about. She ask about the doc. I tell she about his advices. She choops loud-loud and say, "Indian people bad for so, eh, child."

She ask about Georgie, our father's outside-child. I say "Georgie run into some trouble with the police, girl. He get drunk one evening and beat up a fella and almost kill him."

She say, "That boy bad since he small. So, what they do with him?"

"Nothing. The police charge him and they was going to take him to court. But you know how things does work in Trinidad. Georgie give a police friend some money. Every time they call him up for trial, the sergeant tell the judge, We can't find the file on this case, Me Lud, and finally the judge get fed up and throw the charge out. You know, he even bawl out the poor sergeant."

Annie laugh and shake her head. She say, "Good old Georgie. What he doing now?"

"The usual. Nothing at all. He looking after his papers for coming up here. Next year, probably."

Annie yawn and asked me if I hungry.

I say no, I did already eat on the plane: my stomach was tight-tight.

"You don't want some cake? I make it just for you."

I say no again, and she remember I did never eat much, even as a baby.

"Anyways," she say quietly, "I really glad you here now, girl. At last. Is about time."

What to say? I shake my head and close my eyes. I try to smile. "I really don't know, Annie girl. I still ain't too sure I doing the right thing. Everything so strange."

Annie listen to me and her face become serious-serious, like the pastor during sermon. But then she smile and say, "It have a lot of things for you to learn, and it ain't going to be easy, but you doing the best thing by coming here, believe me."

But it was too soon. With every minute passing, I was believing the doc was righter.

Annie take my hand in hers. I notice how much bigger hers was, and how much rings she was wearing. Just like our mother, a big woman with hands that make you feel like a little child again when she touch you.

She say, "Listen, Sheila" and I hear our mother talking. Sad-sad. From far away. And I think, Is because all of us leave her, she dead long time but now everybody gone, nobody in Trinidad, and who going to clean her grave and light her candles on All Saints? I close my eyes again, so Annie wouldn't see the tears.

She squeeze my hand and say, "Sheila? You alright? You want some more tea?"

She let go my hand, pick up my cup, and went into the kitchen. She say, "But, eh, eh, the tea cold already. Nothing does stay hot for long in this place." She run the water and put the kettle on the stove. When she come back in the living room I did already dry my eyes. She hand me a piece of cake on a saucer, sponge cake, I think, and sit down next to me.

She take a bite from her piece. "You know, chile," she say chewing wide-wide, "Toronto is a strange place. It have people here from all over the world–Italian, Greek, Chinee, Japanee, and some people you and me never even hear bout before. You does see a lot of old Italian women, and some not so old, running round in black dress looking like beetle. And Indians walking round with turban on their head. All of them doing as if they still in Rome or Calcutta." She stop and take another bite of the cake. "Well, girl, us West Indians just like them. Everybody here to make money, them and us." She watch me straight in the eye. "Tell me, you ketch what I saying?"

I say, "Yes, Annie," but in truth I was thinking bout the grave and the grass and the candles left over from last year and how lonely our mother was feeling.

"Is true most of them here to stay," she continue, "but don't forget they doesn't have a tropical island to go back to." And she laugh, but in a false way, as if is a thing she say many times before. She look at my cake still lying on the saucer, and then at me, but she didn't say nothing. "Anyways," she say, finishing off her piece, "you see how I still talking after two years. After two years, girl, you understanding what I saying?"

"So I mustn't forget how to talk. Then what? You want me to go dance shango and sing calypso in the street?"

"I don't think you ketch what I saying," Annie say. She put the saucer down on the floor, lean forwards and rub her eyes hard-hard. "What I mean is . . . you mustn't think, you can become Canajun. You have to become West Indian."

"What you mean, become West Indian?"

"I mean remain West Indian."

I think, Our mother born, live, dead, and bury in Trinidad. And again I see her grave. I choops, but soft-soft.

Annie say, "But eh, eh, why you choopsing for, girl?"

"How I going to change, eh?" I almost shout. "I's a Trinidadian. I born there and my passport say I from there. So how the hell I going to forget?" I was good and vex.

She shake her head slow-slow and say, "You still ain't ketch on. Look, Canajuns like to go to the islands for two weeks every year to enjoy the sun and the beach and the calypso. But is a different thing if we try to bring the calypso here. Then they doesn't want to hear it. So they always down on we for one reason or another. Us West Indians have to stick together, Sheila. Is the onliest way." Again her face remind me of the pastor in the middle of a hot sermon. You does feel his eyes heavy on you even though he looking at fifty-sixty people.

My head start to hurt. I say, "But it sound like if all-you fraid for so, like if all-you hiding from the other people here."

I think that make she want to give up. I could be stubborn when I want. Her voice sound tired-tired when she say, "Girl, you have so much to learn. Remember the ad I tell you bout in my letter, the one with the little girl eating the banana pudding?"

"Yes. On the plane I tell a fella what you say and he start laughing. He say is the most ridiculous thing he ever hear."

Annie lean back and groan loud-loud. "Oh Gawd, how it still have fools like that fella walking?"

"The fella was coloured, like us."

"Even worser. One of we own people. And the word is black, not coloured."

It almost look to me like if Annie was enjoying what she was saying. And I meet a lot of people like that in my time, people who like to moan and groan and make others feel sorry for them. But I didn't say nothing.

All the time shaking her head, Annie say, "Anyways, look eh, girl, you going to learn in time. But lemme tell you one thing, and listen to me good. You must stick with your own, don't think that any honky ever going to accept you as one of them. If you want friends, they going to have to be West Indian. Syl tell me so when I first come up to Toronto and is true. I doesn't even try to talk to white people now. I ain't have the time or use for racialists."

I was really tired out by that point so I just say, "Okay, Annie, whatever you say. You and Syl must know what you talking bout."

"Yeah, but you going to see for yourself," she say, yawning wide-wide. "But anyways, enough for tonight." She get up then suddenly she clap her hands and smile. "Oh Gawd, girl, I so happy you here. At last." She laugh. And I laugh, in a way. She pluck off her wig and say, "Come, let we go to bed, you must be tired out."

Before stretching out on the sofa, I finish off my cake. To make Annie happy.

Next morning Annie take me downtown in the subway. It wasn't a nice day. The snow was grey and the sky was grey. The wind cut right through the coat Annie give me and freeze out the last little bit of Trinidad heat I had left in me.

I don't mind saying I was frighten like hell the first time in the sub-way. Annie, really playing it up like tourist guide, say, "They does call it the chube in England but here we does say subway." I was amaze at the speed, and I kept looking at the wall flying past on both sides and wondering how I ever going to learn to use this thing. I kept comparing it to the twenty-cent taxi ride to Port of Spain, with the driver blowing horn and passing cars zoom-zoom. The wind use to be so strong you couldn't even spit out the window. But the subway though! The speed! But I couldn't tell Annie that. When she ask me what I think of it, I just shake my head and pretend it was no big thing. To tell the truth woulda make me look like a real chupidy. Annie wasn't too happy bout that. A little vex, she say, "You have to learn to use it, you can't take taxi here."

I doesn't remember a lot from my first time in Yonge Street. Just buildings, cars, white faces, grey snow. Everything was confuse. It was too much. The morning before I was still in my little shack in Mikey Trace, having a last tea with the neighbours–not the doc, or course, but he send Kali over with twenty Canadian dollars as a present–and this morning I was walking bold-bold in Toronto.

Too much.

We walk around a lot that day. We look at stores, we look at shops. She show me massage parlours and strip bars with pictures of naked women outside. In one corner I see something that give me a shock. White men bending their back over fork and pickaxe, digging a hole in the street. They was sweating and dirty and tired. Is hard to admit now, but I feel shame for them and I think, But they crazy or what? In Trinidad you never see white people doing that kinda work and it never jump into my head before that white people did do that kinda work. Is only when I see that Annie didn't pay no attention to them that I see my shame. I turn away from them fast-fast.

By the end of the day my foot was hurting real terrible and my right shoe was pinching me like a crab. Finally we get on the subway again and I was glad to be able to rest my bones, even with all kinda iron-face people around me. We stop at a new station and Syl was waiting for us in his car.

It was a fast drive. Syl did always have a heavy foot on the gas pedal. I remember trees without leaf, big buildings, a long bridge, the longest I ever see, longer than the Caroni bridge or any other bridge in Trinidad. By the way, that was one of the first things I notice, how big and long everything was. And when somebody tell me that you could put Trinidad into Lake Untarryo over eight times, my head start to spin. It have something very frightening in that.

Finally we get to Syl place, a high, grey, washout apartment building. The paint was peeling and the balconies was rusty for so. I say "Is the ghetto?" I was showing off. I wanted to use one of the words I pick up from a Trinidad neighbour with a sister in New York. But Syl and Annie just laugh and shake their heads.

Annie point to a low building across the street. "They does call that the Untarryo Science Centre."

"What they does keep in there?" I ask.

Annie say, "I hear they does keep all kinda scientific things, but I really don't know for sure."

"You never go see for yourself?" I ask.

Syl cut in with "And waste good money to see nonsense?" He laugh short-short and tell Annie to stop showing me chupidness.

We went in the building and Syl call the elevator. That was my first time in a elevator but I used to seeing the prim an proper secketaries going into one on tv, pushing a button, nothing moving and they come out somewhere else. Is a funny thing, but you ever notice that elevators doesn't move on tv? Is as if the rest of the building does do the moving up and down.

I look at Syl and I say, "Eh, eh, boy Syl, it look like you grow a little. You ain't find so, Annie? He not looking taller." Annie didn't reply but Syl blush and close his eyes, just like when he was a little boy. He did always like to hear people say he grow a little because he don't like being shorter than his sisters. He like to say he grow up short because we did jump over his head when he small, but I doesn't believe that. "And I see you still like your fancy clothes." He was wearing a red shirt which hold him tight-tight at the waist and green pants as tight as a skin on a coocoomber. I notice his shoes did have four-inch heels and I realize that was why he was looking taller, but I didn't mention it. Syl have a short temper when it come to his shortness and his fanciness. I didn't talk about his beard neither. Annie tell me he was growing it for three months and it still look as if he didn't shave yesterday.

We get off at the eight storey and walk down a long-long corridor. Same door after same door after same door. Annie say, "I could never live in a highrise. It remind me of a funeral home, with coffin pile on coffin." We turn a corner and I hear the music, a calypso from two or three carnivals back.

Syl didn't have a big apartment, only one bedroom. All the furniture was push to one side, so the floor was free for dancing. The stereo was on the couch, with a pile of records on the floor next to it. There was a table in one corner with glasses and ice and drinks on it.

Somebody shout from the kitchen, drowning out the calypso, "Syl, is you, man? Where the hell you keeping the rum?"

Syl say, "You finish the first bottle already?"

The voice say "Long time, man. You know I doesn't wait around."

Syl say, "Leave it for now, man, come meet my sister Sheila."

Annie, vex, say, "Fitzie hand go break if he don't have a drink in it always."

A big black man wearing a pink shirt-jac come out from the

kitchen. Syl say, "This is Fitzie. He with the tourist office up here."

A pile of people follow Fitzie from the kitchen and more came out of the bedroom. Syl wasn't finish introducing me when the buzzer buzz and more people arrive. The record finish and somebody put on another one. People start to dance. A man smelling of rum grab on to my waist and start to move. It was a old song, stale. I didn't feel like dancing. I push the man away and went to get some Coke. The Coke didn't taste right, it was different from the one in Trinidad, sweeter and with more bubbles. It make me burp. Fitzie pat me on the back.

The front door open, a crowd of people rush in dancing and singing with the record before they even get inside properly. I couldn't believe so much people was going to fit in such a small room. Somebody turn up the music even louder. Syl give up trying to tell me people's names. It didn't matter. The music was pushing my brain around inside my head, I couldn't think straight, couldn't hardly even stand up straight. Fitzie say to me, "Is just like being back home in Trinidad, not so?"

I ask Annie where the bathroom was and I went in there and start to cry even before I close the door.

I don't know how long I stay in the bathroom. I kept looking in the mirror and asking myself what the hell I was doing in this country. I was missing my little shack. I wanted to jump on a plane back home right away, before the doc could break down the shack and put up his orchid garden. It was probably too late, the doc wasn't a man to wait around, but all I wanted was that shack and my little bedroom. I kept seeing the pastor saying goodbye, and the neighbours toting away the bed and dishes, the palm-leaf on the floor, the calendars in the rubbish.

Somebody pound on the door and I hear Annie saying, "Sheila, you awright? Sheila, girl, talk to me."

I hear Fitzie say, "Maybe she sick. You know, the change of water does affect a lot of people."

I wipe my eyes and unlock the door. A man push in, looking desperate, and Annie pull me out fast-fast. She say, "What happen? You feeling sick?"

I shake my head and say, "No, is awright. Is only that it have too much people in here. But don't worry, I awright now."

"You want to go home?"

Fitzie say, "I'll drive you."

"No, really, I awright now."

We went back into the living room. It was dark. People was dancing.

West Indians always ready for a party to start but never ready for it to end. It didn't take long before the air in the apartment was use up. Everybody was breathing everybody else stale air, the place stinking like a rubbish dump. Curry, rum, whisky, smoke, ganja and cigarette both. And the record player still blasting out old Sparrow calypso.

I start to sweat like cheese on a hot day. Somehow people find enough room to form a line and they manage to move together, just like Carnival day in Frederick Street, stamping and shuffling, stamping and shuffling, and shouting their head off. Syl, in the middle of the line, grab on to my arm and pull me in. I feel as if I didn't have no strength left. I just moving with the line, Syl pulling me back and pushing me forwards.

Finally the song end and the line break up, everybody heaving for air, some people just falling to the floor with tiredness. I couldn't breathe. It was like trying to pull in warm soup through my nose. I push through the crowd to a open window. A group of people was standing in front of it, drinking and smoking.

Fitzie was talking. "These people can't even prononks names right. They does say Young Street when everybody who know what is what know is plain an obvious is really Yon-zhe. Like in French. But that is what does happen when you ain't got a culcheer to call your own, you does lose your language, you does forget how to talk."

A young man with hair frizzy and puff-out like a half-use scouring pad say, "At least we have calypso and steelband."

"And limbo."

"And reggae."

"And callaloo."

Fitzie spot me listening. "Eh, eh, Sheila man," he say, "but you making yourself scarce tonight. All-you know Sheila, Syl sister?"

Everybody say hello.

Fitzie ask me how it going and I say it very hot in here.

The young man with the scouring pad hair laugh and say, "Just like Trinidad."

Everybody laugh.

Fitzie say, "Yeah, man, just like home."

The young man say, "Is the warmth I does miss, and I not talking only about the sun but people too. Man, I remember Trinidad people always leave their doors open day and night, and you could walk in at any time without calling first. Canajuns not like that. Doors shut up tight, eyes cold and hands in pocket. They's not a welcoming people."

I was going to tell them bout the doc, with the big house and the fence and broken bottles. I wanted to say even me did always keep my shack shut up because if you have nothing worth thiefing, people will still thief it, just for spite. But I didn't want to talk, I just wanted to breathe. Besides, Syl done tell me he don't like people talking at his fetes. He only like to see people dancing and eating and drinking. Seeing people sitting around and talking does make him vex. He say is not a Trinidadian thing to do.

I manage to get to the windowsill and I look out at the city. The lights! I never see so much lights before, yellow and white and red, line after line of lights, stretching far-far away in the distance, as if they have no end. That was what Port of Spain did look like from the Lady Young lookout at night, only it was smaller and it come to an end at the sea, where you could see the ships sitting in the docks. But after looking at this, I don't think I could admire Port of Spain again. This does make you dizzy, it does fill your eye till you can't take any more.

Fitzie the Tourist Board man say, "You looking at the lights?"

"Yes."

"They nice. But can't compare with the Lady Young though."

I didn't say nothing. I felt ashamed, but I couldn't say why.

He ask me to dance. Reggae music was playing. I not too partial to reggae. It does sound like the same thing over and over again if they playing "Rasta Man" or "White Christmas". So I say no, next song. He grab my arm rough-rough and pull me. I say, "Okay, okay, I give up." Then he hold me tight-tight against him, so that I smell his cologne and his sweat and his rum and his cigarettes and he start moving, pushing his thigh up between my legs. I try to pull away but he was holding on too tight, doing all the moving for the two of us.

About halfway through the song somebody start shouting for Syl. The front door was open and a white man was standing just outside in the corridor. My heart start to beat hard-hard. The voice call for Syl again. Fitzie stop moving and loosen his grip on me. Everybody else stop dancing. They was just standing there, some still holding on, staring through the door. All the talking stop. The music was pounding through the room. A cold draft of air from the window hit my back and make Fitzie hands feel hot-hot on me.

I take a long, hard look at the white man. His face was a greyish whitish colour, like a wax candle, and all crease up. He was pudgy like a baby. He was standing hands on hips trying to look relaxed but only looking not-too-comfortable. I think his hair was brown.

Fitzie say, "I bet I know what that son-of-a-bitch want."

Annie come up to me, put her arm around my shoulder.

The man take a step closer to the door, as if he want to come in. I feel Fitzie tense up, but it seem to me the man was only trying to get a better look inside.

Fitzie say, "Like he looking in a zoo, or what?"

Then Syl appear at the door, shorter than the man but wider, tougher looking. Syl say loud-loud, "What you want here?"

I couldn't hear what the man was saying but I see his lips moving.

Syl lean on the door frame, shaking his head. Then he choops loud-loud.

The man take a step backward, waving his hands around in the air.

The song come to an end, the turntable click off. I could hear myself breathing.

Syl choops again and say, "You call the cops and I go take you and them to the Untarryo Human Right Commission. Is trouble you want, is trouble you go get."

The man put his hands in his pants pockets and open his mouth but before he could talk somebody else push himself between Syl and the man. It was a short, fat Indian fella by the name of Ram. He did arrive at the party drunk. A white girl was with him, drunk too. Annie tell me she wasn't his wife, she was his girlfriend. His wife was home pregnant and vomiting half the time.

Ram say, "What going on here, Syl boy?"

Syl say, "This son-of-a-bitch say the music too loud. He complaining. He say he going to call the police."

Ram say, "The music too loud?"

The man say, "I just want it turned down. I don't want to have to call the police."

Ram laugh loud-loud, put his arm around Syl shoulder and say, "Syl, boy, the music too loud. It disturbing the neighbours. So what we going to do about this?"

"Ram, boy, it have only one thing to do, yes."

"Yes, boy Syl, only one thing."

Ram put his hand to his nose, blow twice, rub the cold between his fingers and then wipe his fingers clean on the white man's sweater.

The white man pull back and push Ram away. Then he turn grey-grey and rush off, leaving Syl and Ram in the door.

I start to feel sick.

Ram and Syl, laughing hard-hard, hug on to each other.

The young man with the scouring pad hair run to the door and shout down the corridor, "Blasted racialist honky!"

Fitzie run up to Syl and Ram shouting, "Well done, man, well done. All-you really show that son-of-a-bitch."

The young man say, "Nice going, man, you really know how to handle them."

Annie say, "Good, good."

Suddenly everybody was laughing. A few people start to clap.

Syl take a rum bottle and drink long and hard. He fill his mouth till a little bit run down his chin. Ram shout, "Leave some for me, man," grab the bottle and take a mouthful too.

Syl spot me and call me over. I was finding it hard to smile but I try anyways. He put his hand on my shoulder and Annie put her arm around my waist. Syl eyes was red like blood and he couldn't talk right. After some mumbling and stumbling, he manage to say, "Sheila, girl, you see what just happen there? Remember it, remember it good. Is the first time you run into something like that but it ain't going to be the last. You see how I handle him? You think you could do that? Eh? You think you could do that?"

I didn't know what to say. I was feeling I didn't want to treat nobody like that and I didn't know if I could. Finally I just say, "Yes, Syl," without knowing myself what I mean.

Ram say, "Screw all of them."

I say, "Maybe we should go back home?"

Annie say, "But it early still, girl."

I say, "No, I mean Trinidad." Our mother's grave, and the grass and the candles was in my head again.

Syl dig his fingers into my shoulder. "Never let me hear you saying that again. Don't think it! We have every right to be here. They owe us. And we going to collect, you hear me?"

I say, "Syl, I ain't come here to fight." I start crying.

Annie say rough-rough, "Don't do that," and it wasn't my Annie, it wasn't Annie like our mother, it was a different Annie.

Then Syl grab me and shout, "Somebody put on the music. Turn it up loud-loud. For everybody to hear! This whole damn building! Come, girl, dance. Dance like you never dance before."

And I dance.

I dance an dance an dance.

I dance like I never dance before.

Ved Devajee (Réshard Gool)

The Nemesis Casket

Here in the Caribbean we are refugees again; we carry personal rations of soap. Shortages. In Guyana it was rice and table salt. Now in Haiti, it's electricity and water. The drought is into its second month but overlooking Port-au-Prince, in Petionville, the more expensive hotels refill Olympic swimming pools three mornings a week.

Our bedroom furniture resurrects the turn of the century. The house belonged to a German aristocrat–a cousin of Vestinghuis–who went bankrupt. After sunset–which is brief here–I loll in the old brass bedstead, cross-examining the elaborate scroll of the ceiling, brooding upon Marshall. Like a cigarette or a drink you have mislaid and can't recall where. Marshall has become an obsession, almost an illness. I can't decide where to assign meanings.

Last night, downstairs, Dianne had a Duke Ellington seventy-eight on the ancient, wind-up gramophone. Whenever she tramped across the bare floorboards, Satin Doll missed a beat. At one point the music totally ceased. I tried the lights but they had gone, too: once again, I wondered whether Canada would duplicate the fate of Haiti: whether we would survive the current, ruthless plunder of our remaining, non-renewable resources.

This morning Dianne asked pointblank what was wrong. Why at the Embassy party had Marshall and I been so distant towards each other? The question was unexpected.

We were in her studio. I had my back towards her upright easel. In the tall mirror she was using for a self-portrait, I caught a side glimpse of myself staring past the shutters at the early light flat as sheet metal over the harbour; tide marks on the jetties; seagulls occasionally

121

riding high, opal sky.

We had been laughing.

She had stopped mixing paint on her palette, looked up, and said:
"Toasted cheese is very nice,
It is so nice
I had it twice!
–how's that for a poem? I've got talent, haven't I? A real gift, huh?"

I nodded indulgently. It was hard to discipline memory; to think this morning was like trying to gallop through molasses.

"Listen," Dianne continued, "there was an American at the Embassy party last night. From Delaware, I think. Every time he farted he said to himself, very softly: well done!"

She laughed so heartily tears sprouted and hung like earrings from the pupils of her large, oval eyes. The dawn sky was on her eyes and in the droplets–a delicate silver-blue: also hints of green (her dressing-gown) and of rust (her hair). In the wall mirror, the self-portrait was strangely still and dry-eyed; the hair looked richer, more autumnal–closer to the life.

For a moment I forgot Marshall, laughed, and almost immediately, she asked:

"What's with you guys? You and Marshall?"

I returned an absentminded gaze towards the waterfront. The sea burned now–a vast ditch of hot glue; above it was a truce–an armistice –where earlier the air had been defiant with roosters. Occasionally, in the distance, near the Iron Market, you heard complaints of other animals–goats, mostly–tethered to the backs of hand-carts that hadn't been moved into shade.

"It's complicated," I said. In the backyard of the house next door, a large woman in a magenta morning-gown was plaiting a young girl's pigtails. The trunk of the immense mango tree–under which the woman sat–had been whitewashed against termites. When the child fidgeted it received vicious smacks across the buttocks.

Dianne said:

"Sometimes you're like a rooming-house window with a vacancy sign. You're not here. Not anywhere!"

It took me a moment to grasp what she was saying. I felt as if I was being bombarded from several directions–the woman next door who was waving at me, Marshall, now Dianne. I was about to explain what the woman meant, then I realized it was not her radiant greeting or child abuse or other remnants of Caribbean slavery which needed explanation, but Marshall . . . that look in his eyes last night: caution, fear of fresh betrayal, craving for special love.

"Hold on a sec," I said, and left the room. On the stairs I remembered how the day before yesterday–or was it before that?–I had broken my watchstrap: how the boundless timepiece had felt–fatter than money. Among my notes I couldn't track down what I had wanted to show Dianne. Other casket transcripts became absorbing side-tracks.

Later, over lunch, at Le Rond Point, Dianne was generous.

"You don't need to apologise," she said. "I do it myself. All the time. That's what's happening when you ask sometimes what I'm thinking–"

"No," I interrupted, "it's not like following a train of thought. It's–well, certain things are too raw here . . . too tragic!"

"You mean, like that woman this morning? Her loud shoes. She's the Minister of Agriculture's mistress, you know."

"His placée," I clarified. "Not quite kept woman. Or concubine. Placage is very French."

"She'd been beating the child, hadn't she?"

I released an exclamation of authentic surprise.

Dianne laughed, and when she hesitated, I laughed too.

I knew she knew what I had laughed at, but she had to make sure.

"What are you laughing at?"

I simulated an expression of unimpeachable innocence.

"Nothing," I said. "I just felt delirious."

"What was it?"

"I'm not telling."

"You cheap bastard," she said, "you spoilsport!"

"There's no way," I protested with mock gravity, "I want to be told I'm a one-track, thought-polluted academic!"

We both laughed: conceding I'd been right. At the same time I couldn't help wondering what had prompted her not to declare how professional she was–or more typically: how artists were trained to see.

As if she'd been reading my mind, she returned to the woman. "You said tragic, but she wasn't, was she?"

I nodded: again thinking of Marshall.

"Not," she went on, "like the woman in the Mahogany Market last week?"

I expelled another gasp of surprise.

No longer coy or conceited, she shrugged. "You were drunk. You told me. I remembered."

I hadn't wanted to disinter the incident–the plump whore in her wedding dress (church-white, starched) eyes jammed with desolation.

Dianne leaned sideways to lay one arm across my shoulders.

I raised a hand to her arm for comfort and we apologized to one another with our eyes.

In the street while we were waiting for a cab or a tap-tap going in our direction, she examined a corner of the sky, and said (almost as an afterthought):

"–but Marshall's not raw, is he?"

I was too stunned to respond. Not only had she run one scenario to earth, but now–less wittingly–she had started another.

I hesitated, then I asked if she remembered the University of Haiti convocation: the gilt-edged invitations, the pedantic speeches, the camera-men pretending their video machines were loaded. . .

"Wait!" she interrupted, and reminded me of the presentations.

"Four hours in the heat!" she protested, visibly re-living conscientious disbelief.

"Two girls fainted," I affirmed. One by one, gowned students again trooped across the makeshift stage to be awarded–what? Not diplomas. No: nothing credible. Four hours . . . a hundred or so students baking in imported, worsted gowns . . . a noon-hot, airless room . . . then, within expensive, hand-embossed folders–nothing. Just a few sheets of white paper on which–for yet another half hour–they took down summer school class schedules!

Dianne laughed harshly. The situation, in her view, was grotesque; for me, it was a revelation. It placed Marshall in a perspective less riddled by awe and guilt and exasperation. In the tap-tap I tried to explain myself, but somehow couldn't. It was as if my mind was a theatre on fire, and too many ideas feverishly crowded the only exit.

At home I went to work at once; within a few hours, Marshall's dossier looked more coherent. Or so I thought.

Dianne was at her studio table, revising her book on Haitian iconography. Sometimes I admired her flexibility: the ease and speed with which she could move between different ideas and contexts.

"Did you know," she asked when she caught sight of me in the doorway, "that Luther liked women with long hair, that Burke preferred delicate fragile women, that the Papuans revere women with big noses, whereas the Mangaians are partial to well-shaped genitals?"

She bent forward to inspect a notebook entry.

"It says here," she announced with passionate incredulity, "that women in the Middle Ages rubbed themselves in cow dung mixed with wine!"

I laughed.

"Praxiteles," I said, "thought the navel should be exactly between the breasts and the genitals."

"The dirty old rational Greek!"

I eyed her mischievously.

"By contrast," I began, "the sort of woman I–"

The mood in her eyes stopped me. She rose, and–in one movement –kissed me on one cheek and gently plucked the dossier out of my hands.

It was almost as if there had been no banter between us. The moment she had set eyes on the dossier she had read my purposes and reacted accordingly.

So as not to be in the way, I left. Outside the house I found a publique, and went to the Oloffson where I knocked back a few glasses of Barbancourt and listened to a man playing an intricate Rara melody on the vaccine.

The man was so impressive that an hour later I phoned Dianne. She said she had a few pages left, and would join me soon.

By the time she arrived–women spend an inordinate amount of time prinking–my vaccine-player had left; so we took a *camionette* to Le Lambi. In between dances we sat on the balcony which stood on wooden piers above Mer Frappee, nursing drinks and fencing with each other's estimates of Marshall. At first she was considerate and circumspect, but soon her reservations surfaced. When one is hurt, one can be unfair. On this occasion I attacked her for wasting so much time dolling herself up. It was not until the next morning–when I re-examined the text–that I was able to take my medicine more manfully.

I knew she was right, but had to confirm suspicions.

I confronted her in the back garden. She had washed her hair, and was sitting–head upside down against her chest–so that (from bronze roots downward) a marvellous cascade of sorrel fire tumbled onto her lap.

"Fuck off!" she said in a sepulchral voice, from behind the fortress of hair. "I won't discuss Marshall. Not now, not ever."

There was a comb in her right hand. I picked up the hand and kissed the back of the wrist carefully, penitently.

After a thoughtful pause, still behind the hair, she said: "You think I'm wrong?"

I hadn't released the hand, and answered with another kiss upon the back of her wrist.

"Say that again," she urged, and in a single movement, tossed back her hair . . . her head. After the anonymity, her face–freckled naturally and by sunlight–looked vulnerable, the huge Spaniel eyes halfway between apologies and mischief.

This time I turned the hand, spread like petals the fingers, and kissed the heart of the palm.

"No," I said, after a moment. "I think you're right. But tell me again what's wrong. In detail."

All morning we discussed the text. Who, she wanted to know, was *The Child?* Was the tavern waiter the guy she'd met in Mexico? How were casket materials selected: on what grounds? She knew who Grace was, but would the general reader?

These were manageable questions. Clashes began over the casket.

Dianne wanted long introductions, or at least, annotations. By lunchtime, after she had backtracked several times, I relented too. As a joke, she suggested that I dedicate all explanation to her, Dianne, general reader *par excellence,* which is what a week later, quite humourlessly, I decided to do.

For Dianne
general reader
sans pareil

The Casket

Arnold Itwaru

Shanti

Shanti had never known this pall of silence, this growing stone, this uncertainty in her. Her hands were fearful of the surfaces and objects here–the new dishes, the new sink, the new stove, the new refrigerator, the cold porcelain kitchen counter, the cold arborite kitchen table, the cold solarium floor, the mop, the plastic bucket, the woodless walls.

It was difficult for her to be enthused about this house, their very own as Latch, her husband, would remind her. It was for her an unaccustomed structure. It was called a house. She supposed it was a house, but it was unlike any house in which she had ever lived. Made of concrete instead of wood, attached like an extension to the rooms on the other side of the wall called another house, where strangers lived–she found this disconcerting. It was a place where, regardless that she did things unviolated by public view, she felt violated by the rejecting silence of strangers with whom she shared the same wall. She felt both walled in and walled out in this roof over carpeted floors, carpeted corridors, carpeted stairs, a building over a windowless hole in the ground called a basement. It was an address, a domicile, not home.

In here she walled herself in, needing to hide again, to be freed from the outside, to be invisible. For the first time she had begun to shut the door when she was in during the day. She had begun to lock herself in, to try to shut out an amorphous, lurking menace out there.

Keeping the door closed like this was something she had learned only since she came here. In the villages of her life doors were closed

127

when no one was at home, when someone died, and at night. Wooden, open to the sun, the wind, the neighbours, friends, relatives–even the mosquitoes and sandflies when they were in season–life inside embraced life outside. But here, this side of her long flight from all she had known and loved and hated, here doors were always closed, always wall to wall of unfamiliarities, opaque glances, unknowing privacies on the other side of curtained windows, here where, unseen, she looked, locked in, away from the alien grass on the narrow green of her alien yard, her alien fence, the alien sidewalk, all engulfed in an alien silence.

There was another silence once, nights of dew on footpaths and windows heavy with jasmine and stars, nights when she could hear the village women singing before the occasion of certain Hindu weddings, the village women's plaintive unrehearsed labouring wail and chant within the thwacking clap and boom of ancient drums in the ancient darkness, that broken unmusical music which told of the loss of a paradisal idyll called India, a place Shanti had never known.

India was a name whose image was her enigmatic legacy. No one whom she had known had ever been to that magical place though they declared themselves Indian, followed customs said to be Indian, some even spoke snatches of Hindi punctured by broken English.

The singers did not know India. The people did not know India. Shanti did not know India. But this was of little consequence. Their ancestors were born in India. Civilisations and dim centuries had intervened since then, but they were nonetheless Indian. They held on to this, for in it there was at least some dignity.

But for Shanti, named after and within the OM, indivisible syllable of the self in tranquillity, the speech of peace, Shanti, peace, daughter of peace–there was shame. Shame wore her in the tattered dresses of her childhood–the two dresses, always the ones which were too torn and ragged to be worn to school, and thus became her "house dress," one of which was worn while the other was drying on the line. These dresses made of her a painful and indecent display. The men would stare in open lust at her exposed thighs, her back, her buttocks, her belly, wherever the torn fabric of her tatters exposed her innocent and personal flesh. Not only was she ashamed of this: she was also ashamed of herself.

In her shame she was afraid to leave the thatched cabbage-board mud floor two-room decaying shack that was her home, where the continuing illness of her father, an old consumptive bow-legged emaciated caricature of a man, was another source of pain for her. He moaned in agony nearly all night every night of her life. His limbs trembled when he walked, and sometimes he would stumble and fall, unable to make it to the latrine behind the starapple tree backyard. Shanti's mother would have to clean him and help him up, and it would hurt to see how humiliated he felt at these times.

This man, her mother would remind her, this man had worked all his life before he came to this. He was one of the best canecutters in the sugar estate. Yet, like the others, there was never enough to improve his condition. It was impossible for him to build a better life. He had given his youth, his manhood, his health to the sugar plantation, and now, in his illness, there was no money to pay the doctors or to purchase medicine. There was barely enough to eat, and had it not been for the meagre sale of vegetables and fruit at the roadside market which her mother was able to make, having rented a patch of land in the bush which she farmed, there would be no money for even this, and certainly none for clothing.

Shanti's mother's voice was a repressed wail, a choked lament, and upon exceptional occasions when, unbelievably, there was something to laugh about, she sounded as if she were sobbing, smitten by brief hysteria.

Shanti did not dream of India. She wished she were invisible. It seemed the only way. It was easier to be alone, not looked at, not seen, hidden, Shanti did not dream of India.

In the eternal yesterday the village women's singing voices seemed to know and to not know this in their harmony and discord. Chaotic, contradictory, they merged nonetheless in shame and pain and hope in their long night of troubled joy.

"Shanti," her mother would say, "lemme tell you dis, me daughta. Yuh mus guh to school. You mus learn, me daughta. Learn. Dis nah life fi yuh. Dis nah life, me tell yuh."

Shanti learned very quickly. She was driven by a fierce thirst for learning. With her school uniform neat and clean and well ironed, with no shameful rips or holes in it, she found school a precious world. She excelled. She was admired. Her teachers were certain she would go far and they paid special attention to her. She was going to get out of the shadow, the shame, the misery. She did not know how. But she was. Perhaps if she continued to pass all of her exams she might even be a school teacher. Teachers did not seem to suffer. They were not the poor.

But Shanti's pain was to be compounded. One afternoon when she returned home from school she found, to her alarm, Mr Booker, the yellow-haired blue-eyed heavy-browed big-nosed red-faced white overseer, standing on the earthen floor of the open gallery of her home. Her father sat, huddled in silence, staring unseeingly at a crack in the mud-daubed ground. He looked crushed. His legs trembled as though they had been severed. He coughed occasionally, unknowingly trying to smother it in the respected whiteman's presence. Her mother stood by the fireside, weeping silently.

"Hello, Shanti," Mr Booker said, smiling below his huge nose, sweat trickling down his red face.

"Ma, *what happened?*"

Thunder rumbled in ominous menace in the collapsing distance.

Was the sugar estate threatening again to take away their land? They had lived here for over forty years, but from time to time the plantation manager would send them a letter, stating that the land, their land, was the plantation's according to the plantation's survey, and should it be needed, they would be evicted.

Overseers did not visit with the local people. Overseers rode mules, horses, motor bikes. They drove jeeps. They were aggressive, proud, indifferent, these minor functionaries of the sugar empire. They ensured that the labourers worked without visible unrest. To aid them, some of the "locals" were employed as their agents, men who knew each worker by name, whose supervision was thus considerably effective. The plantation named these men "drivers," in the unconscious remembrance of the empire days of slavery and glory, when especially selected enslaved human beings were treated slightly better than their fellows to lord the slavemaster's will over their own kind. But no one said anything about this. These drivers were paid to protect the interests of the plantation, often against their very neighbours. And, filled with the importance of their status, they lived proudly and distinctly apart from the folk of lesser importance in the ranking and ordering of the empire. On remarkably exceptional occasions an overseer would deign to visit, with some degree of imputed adventure, one of these drivers at home.

But Shanti's father was never a driver. Her parents had long been removed from the plantation's payroll. They were deemed too old to withstand the physical strain and dangers of work in the sugarcane fields. They would not be able to keep up both the pace and output of the younger workers, and the plantation could not risk employing liabilities to cultivation, harvesting, production. In its economic wisdom it struck off Shanti's parents from the payroll. They were of no further use to the plantation. They had to find subsistence elsewhere. It did not matter that there was no other source of regular wages for them.

What did Mr Booker want? Why was he here? Why was Ma weeping? What happened to Pa?

The thunder rumbled.

Overseers were feared. They were disliked. And nearly everyone was afraid of the overseer, Mr Booker. He was an impatient, fierce, arrogant man, a proud representative of Great Britain, that magnificent power, the British Empire which Shanti's schooling spoke of in glowing terms.

Mr Booker once licked three canecutters who confronted him about not having been paid for half a punt of sugar cane which they had cut and loaded. Mr Booker told them to go fuck their mothers and to keep their illiterate selves away from him. Outraged, the men struck out at him, but he was quick, in excellent health, well trained in the "Art" of self-defence, and when he was finished with them, one man had a fractured rib, the other was bleeding from a broken nose, and the third lay buckled up, vomiting on the red brick plantation road.

"Hello, Shanti," Mr Booker said again. He stank of sweat and rum. He tried to smile but his lips curled in a gross quiver.

And Shanti heard it then: the ominous roar which preceded the blackening sky, the hot burning air. The strong sick sweet smell of acre upon acre of burning cane leaves, the fields of leaping flame, had always horrified her. Over the seasons several of the thatch-roofed houses in the village had been burnt to the ground, their dried cane-leaf roofs ignited in the chaotic velocity of thunderous tongues of fire. Once a woman's skirt was thus set ablaze and she was burnt to death. And this rage of fire rampaged in the horror of Shanti's dreams in which she ran, kicking, screaming, engulfed, burning. These cane fires always took her in their overwhelming suddenness.

"No money, me daughta, no *mo* money," she heard her mother's lament and wail in the fire's rage in her father's feeble silence in the gargantuan overseer's menacing presence.

Mr Booker stretched out his thick, muscular arm. The sun had turned red.

Shanti did not know what to do. The thought of running came to her like an inner betrayal. She could not move. She could not lift her feet off the ground which was her home.

"No mo money," her mother sobbed, her eyes fixed in the distant presence of the raging fire.

Shanti stiffened at the touch of Mr Booker's hand on her hair. She tried to push him off but her tearful resistance was of no use. His powerful hands drove up her skirt, her panties, her tender personal flesh, pinned her on the ground in colonising force and violation as the fire devoured her screams and horror. The earthen floor, the smoky eaves, her mother's wail, her father's urgent spasmodic coughing, drowned in blood in the battery and assault of Mr Booker's conquering empire lust. The skeletal figure of her father rose once and collapsed, and the smell of shit, stronger than the overseer's foul breath, filled the rage of the plantation night of her pain and darkness as she wept, vomited, wept, a wretched bundle of human nothingness on the earthen floor of the open gallery of that shack.

O me daughta, her mother wailed across the tides of horror. Me only daughta, me only chile, me flesh, me blood. She tried to touch her child, but Shanti recoiled from her and squirmed away in a weeping foetal retreat and helplessness.

My daughter, her mother told her, your father is dying and I am too weak to earn anything anymore. We do not have any money left. All this work, this lifetime of work, and nothing to show for it, my child. No more health, no more for food, nothing in this godforsaken world. Nothing, I tell you, nothing, nothing.

Farida Karodia

Daughters of the Twilight

The weeks dragged by. Things were quiet and I was bored. Weekdays weren't too bad, but I was beginning to get fed up with school too. Weekends were even worse, because there was nothing to do. I had read every book in the house, including the dozen or so fly-encrusted romances that were strung up in the front window and had been there ever since I could remember.

One Saturday morning, for want of something to do, I volunteered to pick up the post at the post office.

I returned with the pile of letters. I had already checked and there was nothing for me. I wasn't expecting a letter, yet I always went through the same exercise, sorting through the letters in the hope that there would be one for me. But it was always the same. Nothing. Yasmin's letters were addressed to Ma. Anything for me was usually enclosed in her letter.

Ma riffled though the letters and picked up a large manilla envelope. She frowned and carefully scrutinised the government's identification stamp as though it would provide some clue to the contents.

There was a long silence while she read the letter through carefully. I noticed the sudden rush of blood from her face and knew instinctively that something was wrong. I waited for her to say something. Papa noticed too.

"What have you got there?" he asked.

"It's a letter from the Group Areas Board."

There was a moment of silence. Ma looked up.

"What do they want?"

"They've assessed our property," she said distractedly, scanning the typewritten page again.

"What? When?" Papa asked, startled.

"1,200 rands. . . According to this, the house and shop are worth 1,200 rands."

"Are they mad? When did they assess it?" Papa demanded.

"They don't say. But I think it was the time that Afrikaner came by to inspect the property about four or five months ago."

"Why don't I know about it?" he asked.

"You were the one who spoke to him. Remember, you thought he was here to assess for property taxes?" she reminded him.

Papa had forgotten all about the incident. He nodded as it came back to him, his eyes narrowing. He had asked the man what he wanted but had got no answer from him. At that time they had thought nothing of the episode, but now it took on new significance.

I listened as my parents rehashed the incident, reading all sorts of relevance into how the man had walked, looked around and refused to answer questions.

"They're going to take over our home and our shop." Ma was aghast. She glanced from Nana to Papa in stunned silence.

"Not while I have a breath left in my body!" Papa declared. Then he laughed. "This is just another bureaucratic bungle. It's a mistake. We won't worry about it."

"What if it isn't?" Ma asked.

He sat down heavily, considering her question.

"What are we going to do?" she repeated thinking that he hadn't heard her.

"I don't know! But I won't let them take what we've worked for all these years! This is our house. We've built this business from scratch. There was nothing here when we arrived. We'll put up a fight. You just wait and see." Papa's eyes darkened. Along his temple a vein stood out like a knotted rope. His clenched hand jerked open and involuntarily twitched as it rested on the top of the old rolltop desk.

"Fight with what?" Nana demanded. "They'll come with bulldozers and flatten all of this whether you're in it or not. I've seen how the Group Areas Board operates. They declare an area white, then they come in and take over. They're not interested in owning these buildings. It's you they want out of this area. They don't care about your life or what you've put into this place. They don't care about anything except getting you out."

"I don't think they'll break this down. It's a solid structure. I think someone wants it–probably old Faurie or van Wyk," Papa said.

"We should have seen it coming, especially after what they did in the other small towns," Ma said. "Still, I think Abdul is right, we should put up a fight. We can't just go like lambs to the slaughter."

Tormented, Papa leaned forward in his chair, drawing a hand over the bald patch on his head. "What else do they say?"

Ma exchanged troubled glances with Nana, "Nothing more, except of course that the property is worth 1,200 rands. . ."

Papa came upright so quickly that the old spring in the swivel chair twanged. "It's worth a lot more than 1,200 rands. Look what we've done to the place. Look at all the improvements!"

"We'll discuss this when you've cooled off," Ma said.

"Why steal our property. They can just ask us to give it to them for nothing," he said with a touch of sarcasm.

"In the end they'll do just that," Nana remarked.

Her words incensed Papa even more.

"Mum, please," Ma muttered.

"This place is worth a lot more than 1,200 rands," he continued. "I can tell you. We built all of this from nothing. We sank all our money into the business and this property." There was an angry pause. "Go on, what else do they say?" he demanded.

"They've given us six months to find another place on our own, or . . . the alternative they present here is to move to McBain, which is a little less than halfway to Queenstown."

"I know where it is," he snapped. "It's in the bush. A pile of bricks in the veld beside the road."

"We've passed by it hundreds of times," Nana said, "never giving it a second glance. There's nothing there. Abdul's right. It's just a pile of bricks."

"Dear Lord," Ma signed wearily. "My home. . . Both my children were born here. I love this place." She drew her hand cross her face.

"We're not moving. This is our home and we're staying right here," Papa told them.

Something really frightful had happened to the family. I stood to one side watching my parents and I wondered how such a terrible dread could ever be dispelled. The fear and anxiety of a future filled with uncertainty was unbearable.

Ma nodded. "We'll see a lawyer. Abdul's right. We'll fight them. Why should we give up our home? Our livelihood is tied up here."

They were at the lawyer's office first thing when it opened on Monday morning.

He told them that there was nothing they could do. It was a law, an act of parliament, that each racial group be confined to its own area. He said that we had no alternative but to abide by any decision the Group Areas Board made.

They came home angry and disappointed.

"That man is a mangpara," Papa said as they stepped in the door.

Nana and I knew instantly that things had not gone right.

The adults talked of nothing else but this new threat.

"They leave one with nothing," Nana sighed, "not even your dignity."

"What's happening?" I asked.

Ma shook her head wearily. They were too preoccupied to explain it all to me.

"What's going to happen?" I persisted.

"Everything will be taken care of," Papa answered.

My parents and grandmother latched on to the phrase, taking refuge behind it whenever they became impatient with my questions. I wished that Yasmin was here. I missed her. I had no one to talk to now.

. . . .

The Men from the Group Areas Board came on the day that Papa and Daniel had gone to East London. From the front door Ma and I watched them pulling up in the police van, accompanied by the sergeant of police, two constables and their dogs.

"What is it?" Ma asked. At first we thought that they had brought bad news about Papa. But when Ma saw the guns and the dogs, the blood drained from her face.

"What do they want, Ma?" I asked.

My mother shook her head. She didn't know either.

"These men are from the Group Areas Board," Sergeant Klein told us, gesturing towards the dark-suited men. "They . . . we are to enforce your eviction."

Ma's face was stark with fear. Then she looked at Sergeant Klein.

It was all a mistake, she decided, expecting that the sergeant would rectify the ghastly error.

I thought so too. After all, he knew us, knew that we were harmless. Ma laughed mirthlessly, but there was no response from the circle of cold and dispassionate faces.

Nana, who had heard the commotion, came to investigate. "What's going on here? Has something happened to Abdul?"

Ma shook her head.

"What's going on, Meena?"

"I don't know, Nana."

Nana's questioning glance flew to the dark-suited strangers and then to the constables, finally coming to rest on Sergeant Klein, who was our only salvation. But he was studying the tips of his boots.

"We're locking up this property," one of the men said.

Nana was aghast. "Now?" she asked.

The man nodded.

"You can't do that. You're supposed to give us notice. We know the law. Besides, her husband isn't here. He's in East London," Nana started to explain.

I shook my head.

"You received your eviction notice some time ago," Sergeant Klein replied.

I exchanged troubled glances with my grandmother.

"No we didn't," Nana put in.

"We have a copy of that letter."

"But we didn't receive it," I cried.

"The letter was registered and we have documented proof that you got it."

I looked at Ma and it all became quite clear. Papa. It was the only explanation. He probably received the notice and destroyed it. Nana was right. He had been behaving very strangely.

"You've had enough time. Now move out of the way," one of the other men said.

Throughout this exchange Sergeant Klein stood to one side, staring at the wall behind us.

"You've left us no choice," the first man said. "The matter is now in the hands of the police."

The drumming of voices and the clattering in my head made it almost impossible to hear what was being said. This is Sterkstroom, I thought. This can't possibly be happening here. This is not a big city. People here are not evicted.

"We're not ready. We need time."

"Go phone your Papa," Ma instructed. Her bun had come undone; her large anguished eyes were turned on Sergeant Klein, pleading. Then her hands dropped to her sides in a gesture of helplessness. This was the image of my mother I took with me as I hurried away to phone Papa.

When I returned, two of the younger constables had pushed their way into the house.

"Get out! Get out!" Nana pressed her hand to her chest. "Leave us alone!" Then slowly, her back supported against the wall, she slid to the floor. She was breathing heavily, her face ashen. Ma and I helped her to the door, where one of the younger men roughly pushed us outside.

"Pas op!" the sergeant cried, startled as Nana staggered. She would have fallen had Mrs. Ollie not put her arm out to steady her.

In the passageway one of the young constables was dragging the blue stuffed chair from the bedroom.

"What are you doing?" Ma asked, horrified as he tossed it on to the sidewalk.

Nana covered her face with one hand, the other hanging limply at her side. Ma put her arms about Nana, supporting her while I righted the chair.

"Heinie, hienie, Khoskhaz!" Gladys shouted from the kitchen.

Ma helped Nana into the chair.

"Did you speak to your Papa?"

I nodded.

"Well, what did he say?"

"He said not to do anything. He's on his way."

"Fine thing after the mess he's made." Ma muttered. "Keep an eye on your Nana while I go and see what's happening to Gladys."

Nana's face was expressionless, one side pulling downwards. I sensed that something was wrong, but I didn't know then that she had suffered a slight stroke. I squeezed her hand reassuringly, dabbing at the spittle which dribbled from the corner of her mouth. The police would soon be gone and then we'd be able to move back in again.

"No! No! Please!" Ma's cry startled me out of these reflections.

I rushed to the kitchen. My mother was clinging to the arm of one of the constables, who was struggling to free himself. Ma held on as though her life depended on keeping him at bay.

Lying on the floor were pieces of broken porcelain.

"They belonged to my grandmother. Please leave them alone. Leave me alone! I'll do the packing. Why are you doing this to us Sergeant Klein? Why? This is our home!" she cried.

"I'm sorry Mrs Mohammed, I'm only doing my job," he muttered, and walked away.

But Mrs Ollie stopped him. "What are you doing to these people?" she demanded. "I know them. You know them too. They're not criminals. Why are you treating them like this? In God's name, man, what are you doing?"

"Look," Ma cried, spreading her arms. "My tea service, look at it," she said, choking on a sob. Suddenly there was a loud crash from the bedroom. We all rushed to the front. On the floor were the fragments of Ma's precious porcelain basin and jug.

"Oh God, no!" Ma picked up the larger pieces, holding the shard with its delicate pattern of blue forget-me-nots against her cheek. The other constable placed his hand on her shoulder, apparently intending to guide her out of the room, but she jerked free.

"I'll get her out," Mrs Ollie said anxiously.

Sergeant Klein nodded.

Ma leaned against the dresser, clutching the piece of porcelain, tears streaming down her cheeks. Mrs Ollie led her outside. "This belonged to my grandmother," Ma whispered bleakly.

"Kom nou, Delia. Kom," Mrs. Ollie whispered, glaring at the police.

Out on the sidewalk Ma stared vacantly at our scattered effects.

Many of the townspeople had gathered. Some of them helped others stood around, uneasy witnesses shuffling from one foot to the other.

"Are you all right, Mum?" Ma asked.

Nana nodded with great difficulty.

"I don't know what's wrong with her," I said.

"It's the shock."

"Come over to my place for a moment," Mrs. Ollie urged Ma and Nana.

Nana's head teetered. Ma frowned, her troubled glance studying Nana. I wrung my hands. I had seen that look in Nana's eyes, an expression of unspeakable terror.

"Take care of your grandmother," Mrs Ollie instructed. "I want to take your Ma inside for a moment. I want to get her a cup of tea. It'll help you to pull yourself together so you can think about what you're going to do."

"I don't like the way my mother looks. I should get her to a doctor," Ma said.

"Dr Uys is out of town. I'll get her a cup of tea."

Some of the bystanders helped to pick up our scattered clothing, which I hurriedly threw into cardboard boxes.

Mrs Ollie showed Ma indoors to a chair by the window.

When the tea was ready she stuck her head out of the front door. "Kom Meena, vat vir you ouma n'lekker koppie roibos tee."

I dropped what I was doing and went to fetch the cup of tea for Nana.

"Dankie," Nana said, accepting gratefully. Her mouth was not too bad now. She wasn't dribbling any more and I noticed that she was able to move her arm a little.

I held the cup to Nana's lips. Mrs Ollie had served the tea not in the enamel mugs they used every day but in her best china.

I returned the cup. Mrs Ollie and Ma were sipping their tea in silence, Ma with her head bowed, supporting the cup and saucer in her lap.

"Under the circumstances you might find this hard to believe," Mrs Ollie said in Afrikaans, "but we're not all like that." She gestured to the police. "I've been your friend for a long time. I know what you're going through. Hardship and pain are the same whether you're white, brown, black or green."

"You've been a good friend to me all these years Sinnah." Ma smiled sadly. "Sinnah Olivier . . . I'd almost forgotten your last name. All these years you've been Ollie because the children couldn't say Olivier."

I was about to leave when Ma said, "Keep an eye on Nana please, Meena."

Sounds from outside carried indoors and soon her eyes welled up again. They were emptying the store in the same manner as they had emptied the house.

"You can store your stuff in my shed. The cows will be all right outside," she said, accompanying Ma to the stoep.

"Thank you," Ma said. "Thank you so much. I'll leave the big items here . . . for a short while anyway."

"What are you going to do, Delia?"

"I suppose we'll have to move to McBain. There's nowhere else for us to go."

"That's ridiculous. The place is nothing but ruins."

Ma shrugged.

Mrs Ollie sighed. She studied Ma. She didn't have to say anything. It was all there in her eyes.

Ma turned to go. "Thanks for the tea . . . and everything," she said, offering her hand, but the Afrikaner woman ignored her outstretched hand and embraced her, right there in the middle of the street with half the town looking on.

"Good luck," she said.

"There's a phone call from East London," someone called from the doorway.

"It must be Abdul. I'd better go."

I rushed after her. Ma paused in the doorway to the store. The police were too busy carrying out their nefarious deeds to notice us. Ma took the phone and covered her ear to shut out the commotion. She watched them with a disaffected air, as though she had cut herself off from all that was happening here. In stunned silence she listened to the voice on the other end. One hand flailed behind her as she groped for a chair.

"What is it, Ma?" I asked.

"It's Aishabhen. Your Papa's had a heart attack," she said, motioning for me to come closer.

I took the phone from her.

"The doctor says he'll be all right. The attack came on just after you called this morning. I think it was the shock of what was happening there," Aishabhen said.

"Tell her I'll take the train. I'll be there tomorrow morning," Ma said. Then, as an afterthought, she took the phone. "Let me talk to him."

"That won't be necessary," Aishabhen told her. "You have enough to deal with right now. He'll be fine."

"Are you sure, Aisha?"

"Yes, I'm sure. He won't be in hospital for long. He's looking fine, Delia. Don't worry. He should be discharged tomorrow. He can stay with us for another week or so while he recovers."

"I really appreciate this."

"Are you all right?" she asked.

"Yes. My mother wasn't too well, but I think she's feeling a little better now. We'll be leaving for McBain in the morning."

"Let me know if you need anything. Would you like Farouk to come and help you?"

"No, we'll be fine, thank you. You've been a great help," Ma said. Drawing a hand wearily through her hair, she put the phone down.

With the weight of Papa's illness off her mind she was able to think a little more clearly about what we would do once we got to McBain.

"Will he be all right?" I asked, eyes bright with anxiety.

"Aishabhen says he was lucky it was a mild attack. She doesn't think it's anything to worry about. We'll call the hospital later," Ma said. For a moment she watched the police carrying the merchandise out of the shop, then she signed, shuddered and turned away. She walked away from the shop towards the house, changed direction and left the property through the side gate.

Most of our belongings and the stock from the shop were stored in Mrs Ollie's garage. The items which we needed immediately were packed into the old Buick, repossessed from Mr Erasmus.

Finally, Ma made arrangements for the transportation of the rest of our belongings to McBain by ox-wagon.

Mr Petersen, principal of SAPS, took us in for the night and Ma was able to take Nana to the doctor. Dr Uys's cursory examination revealed that Nana had had a mild stroke.

Gladys said that she would join us later when things were more settled. "What about Daniel's stuff?" she asked.

"We'll leave it with you. I don't think he wants to come to McBain," Ma said.

Early the next morning, before leaving the town, we stopped by the house. The doors were all padlocked.

Gladys stood on the front sidewalk until the car turned the corner at the end of the street.

We were leaving behind us not only our home but also a big chunk of our lives. Tears slid down Ma's cheeks as she watched Gladys's forlorn figure in the rear-view mirror.

I turned around for a last look. Both she and Daniel had been such an integral part of our lives, one of the many threads woven into the fabric of our existence.

"There's no use dwelling on the past. We have to go on," Ma said, brushing the dampness from her cheeks.

"God, some day they'll pay for this," I muttered.

"Not them. We're the ones who pay," Nana said.

"What will happen to Daniel when he gets back from East London?" I asked.

"I don't know. I suppose he'll come to McBain . . . I don't know, Meena. I don't know anything, anymore."

Rohinton Mistry

The Ghost of Firozsha Baag

I always believed in ghosts. When I was little I saw them in my father's small field in Goa. That was very long ago, before I came to Bombay to work as ayah.

Father also saw them, mostly by the well, drawing water. He would come in and tell us, the *bhoot* is thirsty again. But it never scared us. Most people in our village had seen ghosts. Everyone believed in them.

Not like in Firozsha Baag. First time I saw a ghost here and people found out, how much fun they made of me. Calling me crazy, saying it is time for old ayah to go back to Goa, back to her *muluk*, she is seeing things.

Two years ago on Christmas Eve I first saw the *bhoot*. No, it was really Christmas Day. At ten o'clock on Christmas Eve I went to Cooperage Stadium for midnight mass. Every year all of us Catholic ayahs from Firozsha Baag go for mass. But this time I came home alone, the others went somewhere with their boyfriends. Must have been two o'clock in the morning. Lift in B Block was out of order, so I started up slowly. Thinking how easy to climb three floors when I was younger, even with a full bazaar-bag.

After reaching first floor I stopped to rest. My breath was coming fast-fast. Fast-fast, like it does nowadays when I grind curry *masala* on the stone. Jaakaylee, my *bai* calls out, Jaakaylee, is *masala* ready? Thinks a sixty-three-old ayah can make *masala* as quick as she used to when she was fifteen. Yes, fifteen. The day after my fourteenth birthday I came by bus from Goa to Bombay. All day and night I rode the bus. I still remember when my father took me to bus station in Pan-jim. Now it is called Panaji. Joseph Uncle, who was mechanic in Mazagaon, met me at Bombay Central Station. So crowded it was, people running all around, shouting, screaming, and coolies with big-big trunks on their heads. Never will I forget that first day in Bombay. I just stood in one place, not knowing what to do, till Joseph Uncle saw me. Now it has been forty-nine years in this house as ayah, believe or don't believe. Forty-nine years in Firozsha Baag's B Block and they still don't say my name right. Is it so difficult to say Jacqueline? But they always say Jaakaylee. Or worse, Jaakayl.

All the fault is of old *bai* who died ten years ago. She was in charge till her son brought a wife, the new *bai* of the house. Old *bai* took English words and made them Parsi words. Easy chair was *igeechur,* French beans was *ferach beech,* and Jacqueline became Jaakaylee. Later I found out that all old Parsis did this, it was like they made their own private language.

So then new *bai* called me Jaakaylee also, and children do the same. I don't care about it now. If someone asks my name I say Jaakaylee. And I talk Parsi-Gujarati all the time instead of Konkani, even with other ayahs. Sometimes also little bits of English.

But I was saying. My breath was fast-fast when I reached first floor and stopped for rest. And then I noticed someone, looked like in a white gown. Like a man, but I could not see the face just body shape. *Kaun hai?* I asked in Hindi. Believe or don't believe, he vanished. Completely! I shook my head and started for second floor. Carefully, holding the railing, because the steps are so old, all slanting and crooked.

Then same thing happened. At the top of second floor he was wait-ing. And when I said, *kya hai?* believe or don't believe, he vanished again! Now I knew it must be a *bhoot.* I knew he would be on third floor also, and I was right. But I was not scared or anything.

I reached the third floor entrance and found my bedding which I had put outside before leaving. After midnight mass I always sleep outside, by the stairs, because *bai* and *seth* must not be woken up at two A.M., and they never give me a key. No ayah gets key to a flat. It is something I have learned, like I learned forty-nine years ago that life as ayah means living close to floor. All work I do, I do on floors, like grinding *masala,* cutting vegetables, cleaning rice. Food also is eaten sitting on floor, after serving them at dining-table. And my bedding is rolled out at night in kitchen-passage, on floor. No cot for me. Nowadays, my weight is much more than it used to be, and is getting very difficult to get up from floor. But I am managing.

So Christmas morning at two o'clock I opened my bedding and spread out my *saterunjee* by the stairs. Then stopped. The *bhoot* had vanished, and I was not scared or anything. But my father used to say some ghosts play mischief. The ghost of our field never did, he only took water from our well, but if this ghost of the stairs played mischief he might roll me downstairs, who was to say. So I thought about it and rang the doorbell.

After many, many rings *bai* opened, looking very mean. Mostly she looks okay, and when she dresses in nice sari for a wedding or something, and puts on all bangles and necklace, she looks really pretty, I must say. But now she looked so mean. Like she was going to bite somebody. Same kind of look she has every morning when she has just woken up, but this was much worse and meaner because it was so early in the morning. She was very angry, said I was going crazy, there was no ghost or anything, I was just telling lies not to sleep outside.

Then *seth* also woke up. He started laughing, saying he did not want any ghost to roll me downstairs because who would make *chai* in the morning. He was not angry, his mood was good. They went back to their room, and I knew why he was feeling happy when crrr-crr crrr-crr sound of their bed started coming in the dark.

When he was little I sang Konkani songs for him. *Mogacha Mary* and *Hanv Saiba*. Big man now, he's forgotten them and so have I. Forgetting my name, my language, my songs. But complaining I'm not, don't make mistake. I'm telling you, to have a job I was very lucky because in Goa there was nothing to do. From Panjim to Bombay on the bus I cried, leaving behind my brothers and sisters and parents, and all my village friends. But I knew leaving was best thing. My father had eleven children and very small field. Coming to Bombay was only thing to do. Even schooling I got first year, at night. Then *bai* said I must stop because who would serve dinner when *seth* came home from work, and who would carry away dirty dishes? But that was not the real reason. She thought I stole her eggs. There were six eggs yesterday evening, she would say, only five this morning, what happened to one? She used to think I took it with me to school to give to someone.

I was saying, it was very lucky for me to become ayah in Parsi house, and never will I forget that. Especially because I'm Goan Catholic and very dark skin colour. Parsis prefer Manglorean Catholics, they have light skin colour. For themselves also Parsis like light skin, and when Parsi baby is born that is the first and most important thing. If it is fair they say, O how nice light skin just like parents. But if it is dark skin they say, *arré* what is this *ayah no chhokro,* ayah's child.

All this doing was more in olden days, mostly among very rich *bais* and *seths*. They thought they were like British only, ruling India side by side. But don't make mistake, not just rich Parsis. Even all Marathi people in low class Tar Gully make fun of me when I went to buy grocery from *bunya*. Blackie, blackie, they would call out. Nowadays it does not happen because very dark skin colour is common in Bombay, so many people from south are coming here, Tamils and Keralites, with their funny *illay illay poe poe* language. Now people more used to different colours.

But still not to ghosts. Everybody in B Block found out about the *bhoot* of the stairs. They made so much fun of me all the time, children and grown-up people also.

And believe or don't believe, that was a ghost of mischief. Because just before Easter he came back. Not on the stairs this time but right in my bed. I'm telling you, he was sitting on my chest and bouncing up and down, and I couldn't push him off, so weak I was feeling (I'm a proper Catholic, I was fasting), couldn't even scream or anything (not because I was scared–he was choking me). Then someone woke up to go to WC and put on a light in the passage where I sleep. Only then did the rascal *bhoot* jump off and vanish.

This time I did not tell anyone. Already they were making so much fun of me. Children in Firozsha Baag would shout, ayah *bhoot!* ayah *bhoot!* every time they saw me. And a new Hindi film had come out, *Bhoot Bungla,* about a haunted house, so they would say, like the man on the radio, in a loud voice: SEE TODAY, at APSARA CINEMA, R K Anand's NEW fillum *Bhoooot Bungla,* starring JAAKAYLEE of BLOCK B! Just like that! O they made a lot of fun of me, but I did not care, I knew what I had seen.

Jaakaylee, bai calls out, is it ready yet? She wants to check curry masala. Too thick, she always says, grind it again, make it smoother. And she is right. I leave it thick purposely. Before, when I did it fine, she used to send me back anyway. O it pains in my old shoulders, grinding this masala, but they will never buy the automatic machine. Very rich people, my bai-seth. He is a chartered accountant. He has a nice motor-car, just like A Block priest, and like the one Dr Mody used to drive, which has not moved from the compound since the day he died. Bai says they should buy it from Mrs Mody, she wants it to go shopping. But a masala machine they will not buy. Jaakaylee must keep on doing till her arms fall out from shoulders.

How much teasing everyone was doing to me about the *bhoot*. It became great game among boys, pretending to be ghosts. One who started it all was Mr Mody's son, from third floor of C Block. One day they call Pesi *paadmaroo* because he makes dirty wind all the time. Good thing he is in boarding-school now. That family came to Firozsha Baag only few years ago, he was doctor for animals, a really nice man. But what a terrible boy. Must have been so shameful for Dr Mody. Such a kind man, what a shock everybody got when he died. But I'm telling you, that boy did a bad thing one night.

Vera and Dolly, the two fashionable sisters from C Block's first floor, went to nightshow at Eros Cinema, and Pesi knew. After nightshow was over, tock-tock they came in their high-heel shoes. It was when mini-skirts had just come out, and that is what they were wearing. Very *esskey-messkey*, so short I don't know how their *maibaap* allowed it. They said their daughters were going to foreign for studies, so maybe this kind of dressing was practice for over there. Anyway, they started up, the stairs were very dark. Then Pesi, wearing a white bedsheet and waiting under the staircase, jumped out shouting *bowe ré*. Vera and Dolly screamed so loudly, I'm telling you, and they started running.

Then Pesi did a really shameful thing. God knows where he got the idea from. Inside his sheet he had a torch, and he took it out and shined up into the girls' mini-skirts. Yes! He ran after them with his big torch shining in their skirts. And when Vera and Dolly reached the top they tripped and fell. That shameless boy just stood there with his light shining between their legs, seeing undies and everything, I'm telling you.

He ran away when all neighbours started opening their doors to see what is the matter, because everyone heard them screaming. All the men had good time with Vera and Dolly, pretending to be like concerned grown-up people, saying, it is all right, dears, don't worry, dears, just some bad boy, not a real ghost. And all the time petting-squeezing them as if to comfort them! Sheeh, these men!

149

Next day Pesi was telling his friends about it, how he shone the torch up their skirts and how they fell, and everything he saw. That boy, sheeh, terrible.

Afterwards, parents in Firozsha Baag made a very strict rule that no one plays the fool about ghosts because it can cause serious accident if sometime some old person is made scared and falls downstairs and breaks a bone or something or has heart attack. So there was no more ghost games and no more making fun of me. But I'm telling you, the *bhoot* kept coming every Friday night.

Curry is boiling nicely, smells very tasty. Bai tells me don't forget about curry, don't burn the dinner. How many times have I burned the dinner in forty-nine years, I should ask her. Believe or don't believe, not one time.

Yes, the *bhoot* came but he did not bounce any more upon my chest. Sometimes he just sat next to the bedding, other times he lay down beside me with his head on my chest, and if I tried to push him away he would hold me tighter. Or would try to put his hand up my gown or down from the neck. But I sleep with buttons up my collar, so it was difficult for the rascal. O what a ghost of mischief he was! Reminded me of Cajetan back in Panjim always trying to do same thing with girls at the cinema or beach. His parents' house was not far from Church of St Cajetan for whom he was named, but this boy was no saint, I'm telling you.

Calunqute and Anjuna beaches in those days were very quiet and beautiful. It was before foreigners all started coming, and no hippie-bippie business with *charas* and *ganja,* and no big-big hotels or nothing. Cajetan said to me once, let us go and see the fishermen. And we went, and started to wade a little, up to ankles, and Cajetan said let us go more. He rolled up his pants over the knees and I pulled up my skirt, and we went in deeper. Then a big wave made everything wet. We ran out and sat on the beach for my skirt to dry.

Us two were only ones there, fishermen were still out in boats. Sitting on the sand he made all funny eyes at me, like Hindi film hero, and put his hand on my thigh. I told him to stop or I would tell my father who would give him solid pasting and throw him in the well where the *bhoot* would take care of him. But he didn't stop. Not till the fishermen came. Sheeh, what a boy that was.

Back to kitchen. To make good curry needs lots of stirring while boiling.

I'm telling you, that Cajetan! Once, it was feast of St Francis Xavier, and the body was to be in a glass case at Church of Bom Jesus. Once every ten years is this very big event for Catholics. They were not going to do it any more because, believe or don't believe many years back some poor crazy woman took a bite from toe of St Francis Xavier. But then they changed their minds. Poor St Francis, it is not his luck to have a whole body–one day, Pope asked for a bone from the right arm, for people in Rome to see, and never sent it back; that is where it is till today.

But I was saying about Cajetan. All boys and girls from my village were going to Bom Jesus by bus. In church it was so crowded, and a long long line to walk by St Francis Xavier's glass case. Cajetan was standing behind my friend Lily, he had finished his fun with me, now it was Lily's turn. And I'm telling you, he kept bumping her and letting his hand touch her body like it was by accident in the crowd. Sheeh, even in church that boy could not behave.

And the ghost reminded me of Cajetan, whom I have not seen since I came to Bombay–what did I say, forty-nine years ago. Once a week the ghost came, and always on Friday. On Fridays I eat fish, so I started thinking, maybe he likes smell of fish. Then I just ate vegetarian, and yet he came. For almost a whole year the ghost slept with me, every Friday night, and Christmas was not far away.

And still no one knew about it, how he came to my bed, lay down with me, tried to touch me. There was one thing I was feeling so terrible about–even to Father D'Silva at Byculla Church I had not told anything for the whole year. Every time in confession I would keep completely quiet about it. But now Christmas was coming and I was feeling very bad, so first Sunday in December I told Father D'Silva everything and then I was feeling much better. Father D'Silva said I was blameless because it was not my wish to have the *bhoot* sleeping with me. But he gave three Hail Marys, and said eating fish again was okay if I wanted.

So on Friday of that week I had fish curry-rice and went to bed. And believe or don't believe, the *bhoot* did not come. After midnight, first I thought maybe he is late, maybe he has somewhere else to go. Then the clock in *bai*'s room went three times and I was really worried. Was he going to come in early morning while I was making tea? That would be terrible.

But he did not come. Why, I wondered. If he came to the bedding of a fat and ugly ayah all this time, now what was the matter? I could not understand. But then I said to myself, what are you thinking Jaakaylee, where is your head, do you really want the ghost to come sleep with you and touch you so shamefully?

After drinking my tea that morning I knew what had happened. The ghost did not come because of my confession. He was ashamed now. Because Father D'Silva knew about what he had been doing to me in the darkness every Friday night.

Next Friday night also there was no ghost. Now I was completely sure my confession had got rid of him and his shameless habits. But in a few days it would be Christmas Eve and time for midnight mass. I thought, maybe if he is ashamed to come into my bed, he could wait for me on the stairs like last year.

Time to cook rice now, time for seth to come home. Best quality Bamati rice we use, always, makes such a lovely fragrance while cooking, so tasty.

For midnight mass I left my bedding outside, and when I returned it was two A.M. But for worrying there was no reason. No ghost on any floor this time. I opened the bedding by the stairs, thinking about Cajetan, how scared he was when I said I would tell my father about his touching me. Did not ask me to go anywhere after that, no beaches, no cinema. Now same thing with the ghost. How scared men are of fathers.

The next morning *bai* opened the door, saying, good thing ghost took a holiday this year, if you had woken us again I would have killed you. I laughed a little and said Merry Christmas, *bai,* and she said same to me.

When *seth* woke up he also made a little joke. If they only knew that in one week they would say I had been right. Yes, on New Year's day they would start believing, when there was really no ghost. Never has been since the day I told Father D'Silva in confession. But I was not going to tell them they were mistaken, after such fun they made of me. Let them feel sorry now for saying Jaakaylee was crazy.

Bai and *seth* were going to New Year's Eve dance, somewhere in Bandra, for first time since children were born. She used to say they were too small to leave alone with ayah, but that year he kept saying please, now children were bigger. So she agreed. She kept telling me what to do and gave telephone number to call in case of emergency. Such fuss she made, I'm telling you, when they left for Bandra I was so nervous.

I said special prayer that nothing goes wrong, that children would eat dinner properly, not spill anything, go to bed without crying or trouble. If *bai* found out she would say, what did I tell you, children cannot be left with ayah. And then she would give poor *seth* hell for it. He gets a lot anyway.

Everything went right and children went to sleep. I opened my bedding, but I was going to wait till they came home. Spreading out the *saterunjee*, I saw a tear in the white bedsheet used for covering–maybe from all pulling and pushing with the ghost–and was going to repair it next morning. I put off the light and lay down just to rest. Then cockroach sounds started. I lay quietly in the dark, first to decide where it was. If you put a light on they stop singing and then you don't know where to look. So I listened carefully. It was coming from the gas stove table. I put on the light now and took my *chappal*. There were two of them, sitting next to cylinder. I lifted my *chappal*, very slowly and quietly, then phut! phut! Must say I am expert at cockroach-killing. The poison which *seth* puts out is really not doing much good, my *chappal* is much better.

I picked up the two dead ones and threw them outside, in Baag's backyard. Two cockroaches would make nice little snack for some rat in the yard, I thought. Then I lay down again after switching off light.

Clock in *bai-seth's* room went twelve times. They would all be giving kiss now and saying Happy New Year. When I was little in Panjim, my parents, before all the money went, always gave a party on New Year's Eve. I lay on my bedding, thinking of those days. It is so strange that so much of your life you can remember if you think quietly in the darkness.

Must not forget rice on stove. With rice, especially Basmati, one minute more or one minute less, one spoon extra water or less water, and it will spoil, it will not be light and every grain separate.

So there I was in the darkness remembering my father and mother, Panjim and Cajetan, nice beaches and boats. Suddenly it was very sad, so I got up and put a light on. In *bai-seth's* their clock said two o'clock. I wished they would come home soon. I checked children's room, they were sleeping.

Back to my passage I went, and started mending the torn sheet. Sewing, thinking about my mother, how hard she used to work, how she would repair clothes for my brothers and sisters. Not only sewing

153

to mend but also to alter. When my big brother's pants would not fit, she would open out the waist and undo trouser cuffs to make longer legs. Then when he grew so big that even with alterations it did not fit, she sewed same pants again, making a smaller waist, shorter legs, so little brother could wear. How much work my mother did, sometimes even helping my father outside in the small field, especially if he was visiting a *taverna* the night before.

But sewing and remembering brought me more sadness. I put away the needle and thread and went outside by the stairs. There is a little balcony there. It was so nice and dark and quiet, I just stood there. Then it became a little chilly. I wondered if the ghost was coming again. My father used to say that whenever a ghost is around it feels chilly, it is a sign. He said he always did in the field when the *bhoot* came to the well.

There was no ghost or anything so I must be chilly, I thought, because it is so early morning. I went in and brought my white bed sheet. Shivering a little, I put it over my head, covering up my ears. There was a full moon, and it looked so good. In Panjim sometimes we used to go to the beach at night when there was a full moon, and father would tell us about when he was little, and the old days when Portuguese ruled Goa, and about grandfather who had been to Portugal in a big ship.

Then I saw *bai-seth*'s car come in the compound. I leaned over the balcony, thinking to wave if they looked up, let them know I had not gone to sleep. Then I thought, no, it is better if I go in quietly before they see me, or *bai* might get angry and say, what are you doing outside in middle of night, leaving children alone inside. But she looked up suddenly. I thought, O my Jesus, she has already seen me.

And then she screamed. I'm telling you, she screamed so loudly I almost fell down faint. It was not angry screaming, it was frightened screaming, *bhoot! bhoot!* and I understood. I quickly went inside and lay down on my bedding.

It took some time for them to come up because she sat inside the car and locked all doors. Would not come out until he climbed upstairs, put on every staircase light to make sure the ghost was gone, and then went back for her.

She came in the house at last and straight to my passage, shaking me, saying wake up, Jaakaylee, wake up! I pretended to be sleeping deeply, then turned around and said, Happy New Year, *bai*, everything is okay, children are okay.

She said, yes yes, but the *bhoot* is on the stairs! I saw him, the one you saw last year at Christmas, he is back, I saw him with my own eyes!

I wanted so much to laugh, but I just said, don't be afraid, bai, he will not do any harm, he is not a ghost of mischief, he must have just lost his way.

Then she said, Jaakaylee, you were telling the truth and I was angry with you. I will tell everyone in B Block you were right, there really is a *bhoot.*

I said *bai,* let it be now, everyone has forgotten about it, and no one will believe anyway. But she said, when I tell them, they will believe.

And after that many people in Firozsha Baag started to believe in the ghost. One was *dustoorji* in A Block. He came one day and taught *bai* a prayer, *saykaste saykaste sataan,* to say it every time she was on the stairs. He told her, because you have seen a *bhoot* on the balcony by the stairs, it is better to have a special Parsi prayer ceremony there so he does not come again and cause any trouble. He said, many years ago, near Marine Lines where Hindus have their funerals and burn bodies, a *bhoot* walked at midnight in the middle of the road, scaring motorists and causing many accidents. Hindu priests said prayers to make him stop. But no use. *Bhoot* kept walking at midnight, motorists kept having accidents. So Hindu priests called me to do a *jashan,* they knew Parsi priest has most powerful prayers of all. And after I did a *jashan* right in the middle of the road, everything was all right.

Bai listened to all this talk of *dustoorji* from A Block, then she said she would check with *seth* and let him know if they wanted a balcony *jashan.* Now *seth* say yes to everything, so he told her, sure sure, let *dustoorji* do it. It will be fun to see the exkoriseesum, he said, some big English word like that.

Dustoorji was pleased, and he checked his Parsi calendar for a good day. On that morning I had to wash whole balcony floor specially, then *dustoorji* came, spread a white sheet, and put all prayer items on it, a silver thing in which he made fire with sandalwood and *loban,* a big silver dish, a *lotta* full of wate., flowers, and some fruit.

When it was time to start saying prayers *dustoorji* told me to go inside. Later, *bai* told me that was because Parsi prayers are so powerful, only a Parsi can listen to them. Everyone else can be badly damaged inside their soul if they listen.

So *jashan* was done and *dustoorji* went home with all his prayer things. But when people in Firozsha Baag who did not believe in the ghost heard about prayer ceremony, they began talking and mocking.

Some said Jaakaylee's *bai* has gone crazy, first the ayah was seeing things, and now she has made her *bai* go mad. *Bai* will not talk to those people in the Baag. She is really angry, says she does not want friends who think she is crazy. She hopes *jashan* was not very powerful, so the ghost can come again. She wants everyone to see him and know the truth like her.

Busy eating, bai-seth are. Curry is hot, they are blowing whoosh-whoosh on their tongues but still eating, they love it hot. Secret of good curry is not only what spices to put, but also what goes in first, what goes in second, and third, and so on. And never cook curry with lid on pot, always leave it open, stir it often, stir it to urge the flavour to come out.

So *bai* is hoping the ghost will come again. She keeps asking me about ghosts, what they do, why they come. She thinks because I saw the ghost first in Firozsha Baag, it must be my speciality or something. Especially since I am from village–she says village people know more about such things than city people. So I tell her about the *bhoot* we used to see in the small field, and what my father said when he saw the *bhoot* near the well. *Bai* enjoys it, even asks me to sit with her at table, bring my separate mug, and pours a cup for me, listening to my ghost-talk. She does not treat me like servant all the time.

One night she came to my passage when I was saying my rosary and sat down with me on the bedding. I could not believe it. I stopped my rosary. She said, Jaakaylee, what is it Catholics say when they touch their head and stomach and both sides of chest? So I told her, Father, Son, and Holy Ghost. Right right! she said, I remember it now, when I went to St. Anne's High School there were many Catholic girls and they used to say it always before and after class prayer, yes, Holy Ghost. Jaakaylee, you don't think this is that Holy Ghost you pray to, do you? And I said, no *bai*, that Holy Ghost has a different meaning, it is not like the *bhoot* you and I saw.

Yesterday she said, Jaakaylee, will you help me with something? All morning she was looking restless, so I said, yes *bai*. She left the table and came back with her big scissors and the flat cane *soopra* I use for winnowing rice and wheat. She said, my granny showed me a little magic once, she told me to keep it for important things only. The *bhoot* is, so I am going to use it. If you help me. It needs two Parsis, but I'll do it with you.

I just sat quietly, a little worried, wondering what she was up to now. First, she covered her head with a white *mathoobanoo,* and gave me one for mine, she said to put it over my head like a scarf. Then the two points of scissors she poked through one side of *soopra* really tight, so it could hang from the scissors. On two chairs we sat face to face. She made me balance one ring of scissors on my finger, and she balanced the other ring on hers. And we sat like that, with *soopra* hanging from scissors between us, our heads covered with white cloth. Believe or don't believe, it looked funny and scary at the same time. When *soopra* became still and stopped swinging around she said, now close your eyes and don't think of anything, just keep your hand steady. So I closed my eyes, wondering if *seth* knew what was going on.

Then she started to speak, in a voice I had never heard before. It seemed to come from very far away, very soft, all scary. My hair was standing, I felt chilly, as if a *bhoot* was about to come. This is what she said: if the ghost is going to appear again, the *soopra* must turn.

Nothing happened. But I'm telling you, I was so afraid I just kept my eyes shut tight, like she told me to do. I wanted to see nothing which I was not supposed to see. All this was something completely new for me. Even in my village, where everyone knew so much about ghosts, magic with *soopra* and scissors was unknown.

Then *bai* spoke once more, in that same scary voice: if the ghost is going to appear again, upstairs or downstairs, on balcony or inside the house, this year or next year, in daylight or in darkness, for good purpose or for bad purpose, then *soopra* must surely turn.

Believe or don't believe, this time it started to turn, I could feel the ring of the scissors moving on my finger. I screamed and pulled away my hand, there was a loud crash, and *bai* also screamed.

Slowly, I opened my eyes. Everything was on the floor, scissors were broken, and I said to *bai,* I'm very sorry I was so frightened, *bai,* and for breaking your big scissors, you can take it from my pay.

She said, you scared me with your scream, Jaakaylee, but it is all right now, nothing to be scared about, I'm here with you. All the worry was gone from her face. She took off her *mathoobanoo* and patted my shoulder, picked up the broken scissors and *soopra,* and took it back to the kitchen.

Bai was looking very pleased. She came back and said to me, don't worry about broken scissors, come, bring your mug, I'm making tea for both of us, forget about *soopra* and ghost for now. So I removed my *mathoobanoo* and went with her.

Jaakaylee, O Jaakaylee, she is calling from dining-room. They must want more curry. Good thing I took some out for my dinner, they will finish the whole pot. Whenever I make Goan curry, nothing is left over. At the end seth always takes a piece of bread and rubs it round and round in the pot wiping every little bit. They always joke, Jaakaylee, no need today for washing pot, all cleaned out. Yes, it is one thing I really enjoy, cooking my Goan curry, stirring and stirring, taking the aroma as it toils and cooks, stirring it again and again, watching it bubbling and steaming, stirring and stirring till it is ready to eat.

Bharati Mukherjee

The Management of Grief

A woman I don't know is boiling tea the Indian way in my kitchen. There are a lot of women I don't know in my kitchen, whispering, and moving tactfully. They open doors, rummage through the pantry, and try not to ask me where things are kept. They remind me of when my sons were small, on Mother's Day or when Vikram and I were tired, and they would make big, sloppy omelets. I would lie in bed pretending I didn't hear them.

Dr Sharma, the treasurer of the Indo-Canada Society, pulls me into the hallway. He wants to know if I am worried about money. His wife who has just come up from the basement with a tray of empty cups and glasses, scolds him. "Don't bother Mrs Bhave with mundane details." She looks so monstrously pregnant her baby must be days overdue. I tell her she shouldn't be carrying heavy things. "Shaila," she says, smiling, "this is the fifth." Then she grabs a teenager by his shirttails. He slips his walkman off his head. He has to be one of her four children, they have the same domed and dented foreheads. "What's the official word now?" she demands. The boy slips the headphones back on. "They're acting evasive, Ma. They're saying it could be an accident or a terrorist bomb."

All morning, the boys have been muttering, Sikh Bomb, Sikh Bomb. The men, not using the word, bow their heads in agreement. Mrs. Sharma touches her forehead at such a word. At least they've stopped talking about space debris and Russian lasers.

Two radios are going in the dining room. They are tuned to different stations. Someone must have brought the radios down from my boys' bedrooms. I haven't gone into their rooms since Kusum came running across the front lawn in her bathrobe. She looked so funny, I was laughing when I opened the door.

The big TV in the den is being whizzed through American networks and cable channels.

"Damn!" some man swears bitterly. "How can these preachers carry on like nothing's happened?" I want to tell him we're not that important. You look at the audience, and at the preacher in his blue robe with his beautiful white hair, the potted palm trees under a blue sky, and you know they care about nothing.

The phone rings and rings. Dr Sharma's taken charge. "We're with her," he keeps saying. "Yes, yes, the doctor has given calming pills. Yes, yes, pills are having necessary effect." I wonder if pills alone explain this calm. Not peace, just a deadening quiet. I was always controlled, but never repressed. Sound can reach me, but my body is tensed, ready to scream. I hear their voices all around me. I hear my boys and Vikram cry, "Mommy, Shaila!" and their screams insulate me, like headphones.

The woman boiling water tells her story again and again. "I got the news first. My cousin called from Halifax before six A.M., can you imagine? He'd gotten up for prayers and his son was studying for medical exams and he heard on a rock channel that something had happened to a plane. They said first it had disappeared from the radar, like a giant eraser just reached out. His father called me, so I said to him, what do you mean, 'something bad'? You mean a hijacking? And he said, behn, there is no confirmation of anything yet, but check with your neighbours because a lot of them must be on that plane. So I called poor Kusum straightaway. I knew Kusum's husband and daughter were booked to go yesterday."

Kusum lives across the street from me. She and Satish had moved in less than a month ago. They said they needed a bigger place. All these people, the Sharmas and friends from the Indo-Canada Society had been there for the housewarming. Satish and Kusum made homemade tandoori on their big gas grill and even the white neighbours piled their plates high with that luridly red, charred, juicy chicken. Their younger daughter had danced, and even our boys had broken away from the Stanley Cup telecast to put in a reluctant appearance. Everyone took pictures for their albums and for the community newspapers–another of our families had made it big in

Toronto–and now I wonder how many of those happy faces are gone. "Why does God give us so much if all along He intends to take it away?" Kusum asks me.

I nod. We sit on carpeted stairs, holding hands like children. "I never once told him that I loved him," I say. I was too much the well brought up woman. I was so well brought up I never felt comfortable calling my husband by his first name.

"It's all right," Kusum says. "He knew. My husband knew. They felt it. Modern young girls have to say it because what they feel is fake."

Kusum's daughter, Pam, runs in with an overnight case. Pam's in her McDonald's uniform. "Mummy! You have to get dressed!" Panic makes her cranky. "A reporter's on his way here."

"Why?"

"You want to talk to him in your bathrobe?" she starts to brush her mother's long hair. She's the daughter who's always in trouble. She dates Canadian boys and hangs out in the mall, shopping for tight sweaters. The younger one, the goody-goody one according to Pam, the one with a voice so sweet that when she sang bajans for Ethiopian relief even a frugal man like my husband wrote out a hundred dollar check, she was on that plane. She was going to spend July and August with grandparents because Pam wouldn't go. Pam said she'd rather waitress at McDonald's. "If it's a choice between Bombay and Wonderland, I'm picking Wonderland," she'd said.

"Leave me alone," Kusum yells. "You know what I want to do? If I didn't have to look after you now, I'd hang myself."

Pam's young face goes blotchy with pain. "Thanks," she says, "don't let me stop you."

"Hush," pregnant Mrs Sharma scolds Pam. "Leave you mother alone. Mr Sharma will tackle the reporters and fill out the forms. He'll say what has to be said."

Pam stands her ground. "You think I don't know what Mummy's thinking? Why her? that's what. That's sick! Mummy wishes my little sister were alive and I were dead."

Kusum's hand in mine is trembly hot. We continue to sit on the stairs.

She calls before she arrives, wondering if there's anything I need. Her name is Judith Templeton and she's an appointee of the provincial government. "Multiculturalism?" I ask, and she says, "partially," but that her mandate is bigger. "I've been told you knew many of the people on the flight," she says. "Perhaps if you'd agree to help us reach the others. . . ?"

She gives me time at least to put on tea water and pick up the mess in the front room. I have a few samosas from Kusum's housewarming that I could fry up, but then I think, why prolong this visit?

Judith Templeton is much younger than she sounded. She wears a blue suit with a white blouse and a polka dot tie. Her blond hair is cut short, her only jewelry is pearl drop earrings. Her briefcase is new and expensive looking, a gleaming cordovan leather. She sits with it across her lap. When she looks out the front windows onto the street, her contact lenses seem to float in front of her light blue eyes.

"What sort of help do you want from me?" I ask. She has refused the tea, out of politeness, but I insist, along with some slightly stale biscuits.

"I have no experience," she admits. "That is, I have an MSW and I've worked in liaison with accident victims, but I mean I have no experience with tragedy of this scale–"

"Who could?" I ask.

"–and with the complications of culture, language, and customs. Someone mentioned that Mrs Bhave is a pillar–because you've taken it more calmly."

At this, perhaps, I frown, for she reaches forward, almost to take my hand. "I hope you understand my meaning, Mrs Bhave. There are hundreds of people in Metro directly affected, like you, and some of them speak no English. There are some widows who've never handled money or gone on a bus, and there are old parents who still haven't eaten or gone outside their bedrooms. Some houses and apartments have been looted. Some wives are still hysterical. Some husbands are in shock and profound depression. We want to help, but our hands are tied in so many ways. We have to distribute money to some people, and there are legal documents–these things can be done. We have interpreters, but we don't always have the human touch, or maybe the right human touch. We don't want to make mistakes, Mrs Bhave, and that's why we'd like to ask you to help us."

"More mistakes, you mean," I say.

"Police matters are not in my hands," she answers.

"Nothing I can do will make any difference," I say. "We must all grieve in our own way."

"But you are coping very well. All the people said, Mrs Bhave is the strongest person of all. Perhaps if the others could see you, talk with you, it would help them."

"By the standards of the people you call hysterical, I am behaving very oddly and very badly, Miss Templeton." I want to say to her, I wish I could scream, starve, walk into Lake Ontario, jump from a bridge. "They would not see me as a model. I do not see myself as a model."

I am a freak. No one who has ever known me would think of my reacting this way. This terrible calm will not go away.

She asks me if she may call again, after I get back from a long trip that we all must make. "Of course, " I say. "Feel free to call, anytime."

Four days later, I find Kusum squatting on a rock overlooking a bay in Ireland. It isn't a big rock, but it juts sharply out over water. This is as close as we'll ever get to them. June breezes balloon out her sari and unpin her knee-length hair. She has the bewildered look of a sea creature whom the tides have stranded.

It's been one hundred hours since Kusum came stumbling and screaming across my lawn. Waiting around the hospital we've heard many stories. The police, the diplomats, they tell us things thinking that we're strong, that knowledge is helpful to the grieving, and maybe it is. Some, I know, prefer ignorance, or their own versions. The plane broke into two, they say. Unconsciousness was instantaneous. No one suffered. My boys must have just finished their breakfasts. They loved eating on planes, they loved the smallness of plates, knives, and forks. Last year they saved the airline salt and pepper shakers. Half an hour more and they would have made it to Heathrow.

Kusum says that we can't escape our fate. She says that all those people–our husbands, my boys, her girl with the nightingale voice, all those Hindus, Christians, Sikhs, Muslims, Parsis, and atheists on that plane–were fated to die together off this beautiful bay. She learned this from a swami in Toronto.

I have my Valium.

Six of us "relatives"–two widows and four widowers–choose to spend the day today by the waters instead of sitting in a hospital room and scanning photographs of the dead. That's what they call us now: relatives. I've looked through twenty-seven photos in two days. They're very kind to us, the Irish are very understanding. Sometimes understanding means freeing a tourist bus for this trip to the bay, so we can pretend to spy our loved ones through the glassiness of waves or in sun-speckled cloud shapes.

I could die here, too, and be content.

"What is that, out there?" She's standing and flapping her hands and for a moment I see a head shape bobbing in the waves. She's standing in the water, I, on the boulder. The tide is low, and a round, black, head-sized rock has just risen from the waves. She returns, her sari end dripping and ruined and her face is a twisted remnant of hope, the way mine was a hundred hours ago, still laughing but inwardly knowing that nothing but the ultimate tragedy could bring two women together at six o'clock on a Sunday morning. I watch her face sag into blankness.

"That water felt warm, Shaila," she says at length.

"You can't," I say. "We have to wait for our turn to come."

I haven't eaten in four days, haven't brushed my teeth.

"I know," she says. "I tell myself I have no right to grieve. They are in a better place than we are. My swami says I should be thrilled for them. My swami says depression is a sign of our selfishness."

Maybe I'm selfish. Selfishly I break away from Kusum and run, sandals slapping against stones, to the water's edge. What if my boys aren't lying pinned under the debris? What if they aren't stuck a mile below that innocent blue chop? What if, given the strong currents. . .

Now I've ruined my sari, one of my best. Kusum has joined me, knee-deep in the water that feels to me like a swimming pool. I could settle in the water and my husband would take my hand and the boys would splash water in my face just to see me scream.

"Do you remember what good swimmers my boys were, Kusum?"

"I saw the medals," she says.

One of the widowers, Dr Ranganathan from Montreal, walks out to us, carrying his shoes in one hand. He's an electrical engineer. Someone at the hotel mentioned his work is famous around the world, something about the place where physics and electricity come together. He has lost a huge family, something indescribable. "With some luck," Dr Ranganathan suggest to me," a good swimmer could make it safely to some island. It is quite possible that there may be many, many microscopic islets scattered around."

"You're not just saying that?" I tell Dr Ranganathan about Vinod, my elder son. Last year he took diving as well.

"It's a parent's duty to hope," he says. "It is foolish to rule out possibilities that have not been tested. I myself have not surrendered hope."

Kusum is sobbing once again. "Dear lady," he says, laying his free hand on her arm, and she calms down.

"Vinod is how old?" he asks me. He's very careful, as we all are. Is, not was.

"Fourteen. Yesterday he was fourteen. His father and uncle were going to take him down to the Taj and give him a big birthday party. I couldn't go with them because I couldn't get two weeks off from my stupid job in June." I process bills for a travel agent. June is a big travel month.

Dr Ranganathan whips the pockets of his suit jacket inside out. Squashed roses, in darkening shades of pink, float on the water. He tore roses off the creepers in somebody's garden. He didn't ask anyone if he could pluck the roses, but now there's been an article about it in the local papers. When you see an Indian person, it says, please give him or her flowers.

"A strong youth of fourteen," he says, "can very likely pull to safety a younger one."

My sons, though four years apart, were very close. Vinod wouldn't let Mithun drown. Electrical engineering, I think, foolishly perhaps: this man knows important secrets of the universe, things closed to me. Relief spins me lightheaded. No wonder my boys' photographs haven't turned up in the gallery of photos of the recovered dead. "Such pretty roses," I say.

"My wife loved pink roses. Every Friday I had to bring a bunch home. I used to say, why? After twenty odd years of marriage you're still needing proof positive of my love?" He has identified his wife and three of his children. Then others from Montreal, the lucky ones, intact families with no survivors. He chuckles as he wades back to shore. Then he swings around to ask me a question. "Mrs Bhave, you are wanting to throw in some roses for your loved ones? I have two big ones left."

But I have other things to float; Vinod's pocket calculator; a half-painted model B-52 for my Mithun. They'd want them on their island. And for my husband? For him I let fall into the calm, glassy waters a poem I wrote in the hospital yesterday. Finally he'll know my feelings for him.

"Don't tumble, the rocks are slippery," Dr Ranganathan cautions. He holds out a hand for me to grab.

Then it's time to get back on the bus, time to rush back to our waiting posts on hospital benches.

Kusum is one of the lucky ones. The lucky ones flew here, identified in multiplicate their loved ones, then will fly to India with the bodies for proper ceremonies. Satish is one of the few males who surfaced. The photos of faces we saw on the walls in an office at Heathrow and here in the hospital are mostly of women. Women have more body fat, a nun said to me matter-of-factly. They float better.

Today I was stopped by a young sailor on the street. He had loaded bodies, he'd gone into the water when–he checks my face for signs of strength–when the sharks were first spotted. I don't blush, and he breaks down. "It's all right," I say. "Thank you." I had heard about the sharks from Dr Ranganathan. In his orderly mind, science brings understanding, it holds no terror. It is the shark's duty. For every deer there is a hunter, for every fish a fisherman.

The Irish are not shy; they rush to me and give me hugs and some are crying. I cannot imagine reactions like that on the streets of Toronto. Just strangers, and I am touched. Some carry flowers with them and give them to any Indian they see.

After lunch, a policeman I have gotten to know quite well catches hold of me. He says he thinks he has a match for Vinod. I explain what a good swimmer Vinod is.

"You want me with you when you look at photos?" Dr Ranganathan walks ahead of me into the picture gallery. In these matters, he is a scientist, and I am grateful. It is a new perspective. "They have performed miracles," he says. "We are indebted to them."

The first day or two the policemen showed us relatives only one picture at a time; now they're in a hurry, they're eager to lay out the possibles, and even the probables.

The face on the photo is of a boy much like Vinod; the same intelligent eyes, the same thick brows dipping into a V. But this boy's features, even his cheeks, are puffier, wider, mushier.

"No." My gaze is pulled by other pictures. There are five other boys who look like Vinod.

The nun assigned to console me rubs the first picture with a fingertip. "When they've been in the water for a while, love, they look a little heavier." The bones under the skin are broken, they said on the first day–try to adjust your memories. It's important.

"It's not him. I'm his mother. I'd know."

"I know this one!" Dr Ranganathan cries out suddenly from the back of the gallery. "And this one!" I think he senses that I don't want to find my boys. "They are the Kutty brothers. They were also from Montreal." I don't mean to be crying. On the contrary, I am ecstatic. My suitcase in the hotel is packed heavy with dry clothes for my boys.

The policeman starts to cry. "I am so sorry, I am so sorry, ma'am. I really thought we had a match."

With the nun ahead of us and the policeman behind, we, the unlucky ones without our children's bodies, file out of the makeshift gallery.

From Ireland most of us go on to India. Kusum and I take the same direct flight to Bombay, so I can help her clear customs quickly. But we have to argue with a man in uniform. He has large boils on his face. The boils swell and glow with sweat as we argue with him. He wants Kusum to wait in line and he refuses to take authority because his boss is on a tea break. But Kusum won't let her coffins out of sight, and I shan't desert her though I know that my parents, elderly and diabetic, must be waiting in a stuffy car in a scorching lot.

"You bastard!" I scream at the man with the popping boils. Other passengers press closer. "You think we're smuggling contraband in those coffins!"

Once upon a time we were well brought up women; we were dutiful wives who kept our heads veiled, our voices shy and sweet.

In India, I become, once again, an only child of rich, ailing parents. Old friends of the family come to pay their respects. Some are Sikh, and inwardly, involuntarily, I cringe. My parents are progressive people; they do not blame communities for a few individuals.

In Canada, it is a different story now.

"Stay longer," my mother pleads. "Canada is a cold place. Why would you want to be all by yourself?" I stay.

Three months pass. Then another.

Vikram wouldn't have wanted you to give up this!" they protest. They call my husband by the name he was born with. In Toronto he'd changed to Vik so the men he worked with at his office would find his name as easy as Rod or Chris. "You know, the dead aren't cut off from us!"

My grandmother, the spoiled daughter of a rich zamindar, shaved her head with rusty razor blades when she was widowed at sixteen. My grandfather died of childhood diabetes when he was nineteen, and she saw herself as the harbinger of bad luck. My mother grew up without parents, raised indifferently by an uncle, while her true mother slept in a hut behind the main estate house and took her food with the servants. She grew up a rationalist. My parents abhor mindless mortification.

The zamindar's daughter kept stubborn faith in Vedic rituals; my parents rebelled. I am trapped between two modes of knowledge. At thirty-six, I am too old to start over and too young to give up. Like my husband's spirit, I flutter between worlds.

Courting aphasia, we travel. We travel with our phalanx of servants and poor relatives. To hill stations and to beach resorts. We play contract bridge in dusty gymkhana clubs. We ride stubby ponies up crumbly mountain trails. At tea dances we let ourselves be twirled twice round the ballroom. We hit the holy spots we hadn't made time for before. In Varanasi, Kalighat, Rishikesh, Hardwar, astrologers and palmists seek me out and for a fee offer me cosmic consolations.

Already the widowers among us are being shown new bride candidates. They cannot resist the call of custom, the authority of their parents and older brothers. They must marry; it is the duty of a man to look after a wife. The new wives will be young widows with children, destitute but of good family. They will make loving wives, but the men will shun them. I've had calls from the men over crackling Indian telephone lines. "Save me," they say, these substantial, educated, successful men of forty. "My parents are arranging a marriage for me." In a month they will have buried one family and returned to Canada with a new bride and partial family.

I am comparatively lucky. No one here thinks of arranging a husband for an unlucky widow.

Then, on the third day of the sixth month into this odyssey, in an abandoned temple in a tiny Himalayan village, as I make my offering of flowers and sweetmeats to the god of a tribe of animists, my husband descends to me. He is squatting next to a scrawny sadhu in moth-eaten robes. Vikram wears the vanilla suit he wore the last time I hugged him. The sadhu tosses petals on a butter-fed flame, reciting Sanskrit mantras and sweeps his face of flies. My husband takes my hands in his.

You're beautiful, he starts. Then, What are you doing here?

Shall I stay? I ask. He only smiles, but already the image is fading. You must finish alone what we started together. No seaweed wreathes his mouth. He speaks too fast just as he used to when we were an envied family in our pink split-level. He is gone.

In the windowless altar room, smokey with joss sticks and clarified butter lamps, a sweaty hand gropes for my blouse. I do not shriek. The sadhu arranges his robe. The lamps hiss and sputter out.

When we come out of the temple, my mother says, "Did you feel something weird in there?"

My mother has no patience with ghosts, prophetic dreams, holy men and cults.

"No," I lie. "Nothing."

But she knows that she's lost me. She knows that in days I shall be leaving.

Kusum's put her house up for sale. She wants to live in an ashram in Hardwar. Moving to Hardwar was her swami's idea. Her swami runs two ashrams, the one in Hardwar and another here in Toronto.

"Don't run away," I tell her.

"I'm not running away," she says. "I'm pursuing inner peace. You think you or that Ranganathan fellow are better off?"

Pam's left for California. She wants to do some modelling, she says. She says when she comes into her share of the insurance money she'll open a yoga-cum-aerobics studio in Hollywood. She sends me postcards so naughty I daren't leave them on the coffee table. Her mother has withdrawn from her and the world.

The rest of us don't lose touch, that's the point. Talk is all we have, says Dr Ranganathan, who has also resisted his relatives and returned to Montreal and to his job, alone. He says, whom better to talk with than other relatives? We've been melted down and recast as a new tribe.

He calls me twice a week from Montreal. Every Wednesday night and every Saturday afternoon. He is changing jobs, going to Ottawa. But Ottawa is over a hundred miles away, and he is forced to drive two hundred and twenty miles a day. He can't bring himself to sell his house. The house is a temple, he says; the king-sized bed in the master bedroom is a shrine. He sleeps on a folding cot. A devotee.

There are still some hysterical relatives. Judith Templeton's list of those needing help and those who've "accepted" is in nearly perfect balance. Acceptance means you speak of your family in the past tense and you make active plans for moving ahead with your life. There are courses at Seneca or Ryerson we could be taking. Her gleaming leather briefcase is full of college catalogues and lists of cultural societies that need our help. She has done impressive work, I tell her.

"In the textbooks on grief management," she replies—I am her confidante, I realize, one of the few whose grief has not sprung bizarre obsessions—"there are stages to pass through: rejection, depression, acceptance, reconstruction." She has compiled a chart and finds that six months after the tragedy, none of us still reject reality, but only a handful are reconstructing. "Depressed Acceptance" is the plateau we've reached. Remarriage is a major step in reconstructing (though she's a little surprised, even shocked, over how quickly some of the men have taken on new families). Selling one's house and changing jobs and cities is healthy.

How do I tell Judith Templeton that my family surrounds me, and that like creatures in epics, they've changed shapes? She sees me as calm and accepting but worries that I have no job, no career. My closest friends are worse off than I. I cannot tell her my days, even my nights, are thrilling.

She asks me to help with families she can't reach at all. An elderly couple in Agincourt whose sons were killed just weeks after they had brought their parents over from a village in Punjab. From their names, I know they are Sikh. Judith Templeton and a translator have visited them twice with offers of money for air fare to Ireland, with bank forms, power-of-attorney forms, but they have refused to sign, or to leave their tiny apartment. Their son's money is frozen in the bank. Their son's investment apartments have been trashed by tenants, the furnishings sold off. The parents fear that anything they sign or any money they receive will end the company's or the country's obligations to them. They fear they are selling their sons for two airline tickets to a place they've never seen.

The high-rise apartment is a tower of Indians and West Indians, with a sprinkling of Orientals. The nearest bus stop kiosk is lined with women in saris. Boys practice cricket in the parking lot. Inside the building, even I wince a bit from the ferocity of onion fumes, the distinctive and immediate Indianness of frying ghee, but Judith Templeton maintains a steady flow of information. These poor old people are in imminent danger of losing their place and all their services.

I say to her, "They are Sikh. They will not open up to a Hindu woman." And what I want to add is, as much as I try not to, I stiffen now at the sight of beards and turbans. I remember a time when we all trusted each other in this new country, it was only the new country we worried about.

The two rooms are dark and stuffy. The lights are off, and an oil lamp sputters on the coffee table. The bent old lady has let us in, and her husband is wrapping a white turban over his oiled, hip length hair. She immediately goes to the kitchen and I hear the most familiar wound of an Indian home, tap water hitting and filling a teapot.

They have not paid their utility bills, out of fear and the inability to write a check. The telephone is gone; electricity and gas and water are soon to follow. They have told Judith their sons will provide. They are good boys, and they have always earned and looked after their parents.

We converse a bit in Hindi. They do not ask about the crash and I wonder if I should bring it up. If they think I am here merely as a translator, then they may feel insulted. There are thousands of Punjabi-speakers, Sikhs, in Toronto to do a better job. And so I say to the old lady, "I too have lost my sons, and my husband, in the crash."

Her eyes immediately fill with tears. The man mutters a few words which sound like a blessing. "God provides and God takes away," he says.

I want to say, but only men destroy and give back nothing. "My boys and my husband are not coming back," I say. "We have to understand that."

Now the old woman responds. "But who is to say? Man alone does not decide these things." To this her husband adds his agreement.

Judith asks about the bank papers, the release forms. With a stroke of the pen, they will have a provincial trustee to pay their bills, invest their money, send them a monthly pension.

"Do you know this woman?" I ask them.

The man raises his hand from the table, turns it over and seems to regard each finger separately before he answers. "This young lady is always coming here, we make tea for her and she leaves papers for us to sign." His eyes scan a pile of papers in the corner of the room. "Soon we will be out of tea, then will she go away?"

The old lady adds, "I have asked my neighbours and no one else gets angrezi visitors. What have we done?"

"It's her job," I try to explain. "The government is worried. Soon you will have no place to stay, no lights, no gas, no water."

"Government will get its money. Tell her not to worry, we are honourable people."

I try to explain the government wishes to give money, not take. He raises his hand. "Let them take," he says. "We are accustomed to that. That is no problem."

"We are strong people," says the wife. "Tell her that."

"Who needs all this machinery?" demands the husband. "It is unhealthy, the bright lights, the cold air on a hot day, the cold food, the four gas rings. God will provide, not government."

"When our boys return," the mother says. Her husband sucks his teeth. "Enough talk," he says.

Judith breaks in. "Have you convinced them?" The snaps on her cordovan briefcase go off like firecrackers in that quiet apartment. She lays the sheaf of legal papers on the coffee table. "If they can't write their names, an X will do–I've told them that."

Now the old lady has shuffled to the kitchen and soon emerges with a pot of tea and two cups. "I think my bladder will go first on a job like this," Judith says to me, smiling. "If only there was some way of reaching them. Please thank her for the tea. Tell her she's very kind."

I nod in Judith's direction and tell them in Hindi, "She thanks you for the tea. She thinks you are being very hospitable but she doesn't have the slightest idea what it means."

I want to say, humour her. I want to say, my boys and my husband are with me too, more than ever. I look in the old man's eyes and I can read his stubborn, peasant's message; I have protected this woman as best I can. She is the only person I have left. Give to me or take from me what you will, but I will not sign for it. I will not pretend that I accept.

In the car, Judith says, "You see what I'm up against? I'm sure they're lovely people, but their stubbornness and ignorance are driving me crazy. They think signing a paper is signing their sons' death warrants, don't they?"

172

I am looking out the window. I want to say, In our culture, it is a parent's duty to hope.

"Now Shaila, this next woman is a real mess. She cries day and night, and she refuses all medical help. We may have to–"

"–Let me get out at the subway," I say.

"I beg your pardon?" I can feel those blue eyes staring at me.

It would not be like her to disobey. She merely disapproves, and slows at a corner to let me out. Her voice is plaintive. "Is there anything I said? Anything I did?"

I could answer her suddenly in a dozen ways, but I choose not to. "Shaila? Let's talk about it," I hear, then slam the door.

A wife and mother begins her new life in a new country, and that life is cut short. Yet her husband tells her: Complete what we have started. We, who stayed out of politics and came halfway around the world to avoid religious and political feuding have been the first in the New World to die from it. I no longer know what we started, nor how to complete it. I write letters to the editors of local papers and to members of Parliament. Now at least they admit it was a bomb. One MP answers back, with sympathy, but with a challenge. You want to make a difference? Work on a campaign. Work on mine. Politicize the Indian voter.

My husband's old lawyer helps me set up a trust. Vikram was a saver and a careful investor. He had saved the boys' boarding school and college fees. I sell the pink house at four times what we paid for it and take a small apartment downtown. I am looking for a charity to support.

We are deep in the Toronto winter, gray skies, icy pavements. I stay indoors, watching television. I have tried to assess my situation, how best to live my life, to complete what we began so many years ago. Kusum has written me from Hardwar that her life is now serene. She has seen Satish and has heard her daughter sing again. Kusum was on a pilgrimage, passing through a village when she heard a young girl's voice, singing one of her daughter's favourite bhajans. She followed the music through the squalor of a Himalayan village, to a hut where a young girl, an exact replica of her daughter, was fanning coals under the kitchen fire. When she appeared, the girl cried out, "Ma!" and ran away. What did I think of that?

I think I can only envy her.

173

Pam didn't make it to California, but writes me from Vancouver. She works in a department store, giving make-up hints to Indian and Oriental girls. Dr Ranganathan has given up his commute, given up his house and job, and accepted an academic position in Texas where no one knows his story and he has vowed not to tell it. He calls me now once a week.

I wait, I listen, and I pray, but Vikram has not returned to me. The voices and the shapes and the nights filled with visions ended abruptly several weeks ago.

I take it as a sign.

One rare, beautiful, sunny day last week, returning from a small errand on Yonge Street, I was walking through the park from the subway to my apartment. I live equidistant from the Ontario Houses of Parliament and the University of Toronto. The day was not cold, but something in the bare trees caught my attention. I looked up from the gravel, into the branches and the clear blue sky beyond. I thought I heard the rustling of larger forms, and I waited a moment for voices. Nothing.

"What?" I asked.

Then as I stood in the path looking north to Queen's Park and west to the university, I heard the voices of my family one last time. Your time has come, they said. Go, be brave.

I do not know where this voyage I have begun will end. I do not know which direction I will take. I dropped the package on a park bench and started walking.

Uma Parameswaran

How We Won the Olympic Gold

Three stories stand out from the scores of events and experiences that made up my recent visit back home to India: Bunto getting toilet trained; I almost breaking up two schoolchums' marriages and my own; and us winning Olympic Gold.

I'll start with the last one first because that's the way I am; after a trip back, everything is topside down, there being such mountains of things–material and memory–and nothing gets put away because the moment one gets back, the waiting routine of the rat race chomps away at us thirty two hours a day, and weekends fly by.

How we won the gold. You know your end of the story already but this is what happened at mine.

It is not that T is a village far from civilization. Seat of maharajahs, it is a city all right, with its Central Avenue ending in the great big temple, and its three palaces and cantonment and what have you.

But when it comes to telephone exchanges and long-distance calls, we are on another planet altogether. I should have realized it but when one is halfway around the world in Canada, one forgets that T is not Delhi or Madras. So when the travel agent phoned to say that all flights were confirmed and I turned to Seenu and asked should I really really go, would he be all right? and he said of course I should and of course he would be I made the mistake of saying, Promise you'll phone me once in a while. He said he would phone me every Tuesday and Friday night and I said, That would be lovely, I'll live for Tuesdays and Fridays. You'd think he'd be flattered and give me a

175

fond pat but what he said was, "Darn, don't get confused. It means Wednesday and Saturday mornings for you. And listen, I don't want to hear all about your day, what you bought and where you went or whom you met. I want to be told all about Bunto and nothing but. Write it down so you don't forget when I call; every new word he picks up, everything. And if he falls ill, for godssake keep me informed of everything. I mean it, abso everything. And don't think to spare me the worry. Promise you won't hold back any details, promise?"

I heard that speech, with minor variations, about one hundred forty seven times between then and the time I walked through the security gates at Winnipeg Airport with Bunto in my arms. Even though I often enough felt like hitting him over the head, I also felt sorry for him. That husband of mine loves his son, abso dotes on him, and I felt awfully guilty about separating them for two months.

Those phone calls became a major exercise in timing and patience mainly because the telephone was three doors away from ours, at Aunt Kamu's (no relation of ours, needless to say), and every Wednesday and Saturday morning became a large-scale production effort that involved many people.

Bunto and I reached my parents' house on a Tuesday morning. What with the overnight train journey and jet lag and friends and relatives dropping in to welcome Bunto, I forgot to tell anyone about the telephone-call arrangements for seven o'clock on Wednesdays and Saturdays.

Wednesday morning I was awakened by mother. "It is a phone call," she said in that ominous whisper we reserve for bad news. I jumped out of bed. "Is it seven o'clock already?" It was still dark outside. "No, hardly four, but hurry." I was about to lift the baby but she motioned me out of the room. Groggy with interrupted sleep, I did not register her worry and so didn't think to tell her it was a routine call and I followed the servant maid to Aunt Kamu's.

"Listen, woman!" Uncle Ramu was bellowing into the phone as I reached their front door. "No, I am not Sita but I want to speak to Seenu, I mean Dr Srinivasan," but clearly the operator was not to be shaken out of her procedural exactitudes. I took the receiver, and on identifying myself, the call went through.

Uncle Ramu, satisfied after the first thirty seconds that all was well with Seenu and that the call was just part of a routine arrangement, stopped hovering protectively over me, and dismissed with a sweep of his hand the half dozen heads that already converged at the door.

Seenu was obviously practising what he had preached about preparing written notes before phoning. He marshalled out his questions, and wanted only one-word answers judging by the time he gave me between questions. Was the flight on time? Had there been enough milk or had they run out as usual the . . . (four-letter words)? Had his brother met us at Bombay Airport? Did Customs give me a hassle about all those cartons of diapers and baby food? How was Bunto's stomach reacting to the change of water? Was I insisting on boiled water? Did I have mosquito netting for his bed? etc. etc.

When I could get in a question of my own, I asked why he was calling at this unearthly hour. Because Rita had invited him over for dinner and he wanted to check that we'd reached safely. But why at four o'clock for godssake? Because sometimes it took forever to get the connections and hell, the day starts early in India so why was I hollering? You've woken up the whole street, for godssake, and was it Rita or Neela? It was Neela and I should know it took close to an hour driving out there but geez he was sorry for calling so early but how could he enjoy Neela's famous samosas unless he knew for sure we'd reached okay, and did Bunto miss him? Yes, I said, Bunto missed him. And how about me, did I miss him? Yes, I said, but please don't call before five o'clock. What, he said, what did I say? Yes, I shouted, I missed him too, very very much, and would he take care? What? he said, he couldn't hear me at all, what?

And just then, Pichai our servant maid came in, carrying Bunto who was howling his head off. Seenu heard it, could have heard it even without the phone it seemed, and started shouting all uptight about his baby and would I please please take good care of him, and I kept saying the baby was fine and he went on about boiled water and diaper rash and going easy on medication, until we suddenly got cut off.

Meanwhile, other heads had joined the cluster at the door, and my end of the conversation had been relayed along with creative reconstruction of Seenu's side of the exchange. And the baby was still screaming because he was being passed from hand to hand, the darling wasn't he exactly like his grandpa? the gold nugget what a voice he had! Ammamma, poor child, he misses his daddy. And did you hear how she misses him? chuckle chuckle. Hardly a day since she's arrived and already, wink wink. That poor man, our Seenu Ayya, left all alone. Un unh, didn't you hear he's dining with some white woman, Rita's the name.

Where Rama is shouldn't be Sita's Ayodhya, Aunt Kamu said, with a disapproving shake of her head, continuing the stance with which she had greeted me–about how it was bad enough that I's had my baby in some heathen land but it was downright inauspicious that I should come without my husband on this my first visit after my first baby.

So that's what happened on the first Wednesday. Seenu did not call me before six o'clock after that but all too often the call came through only after ten o'clock, which meant that I often had to spend half the morning hanging out at Uncle Ramu's under Aunt Kamu's colourful but crude tirade against the world at large. And, more disconcerting, half the colony waited with me.

Just why they did is one of those inexplicable aspects of community living. On Wednesdays and Saturdays, the day's routine was paralysed for many of us in the lane until I'd got my telephone call. The vegetable vendor went so far as to take it as an omen; if I got it close to six o'clock, it would be a good day for her and if it did not come by seven, she had to break a coconut for special protection from the malignant fates that so loved to torture her.

I could tell you a story for every one of those Wednesdays and Saturdays (which mercifully changed to just Saturdays after my return from a visit to my in-laws) that I spent at my parents' house in T.

But the Olympic gold has been kept waiting in the wings too long. So let me get on with it.

It happened the day before I was to leave for Bombay and on to Winnipeg. Saturday, September 24, 1988.

By now I had got into a routine. I left Bunto sleeping, in charge of Pichai, and started out for Uncle Ramu's. Pichai, as usual, was sweeping the front veranda and yard before sprinkling water and making the kolam design. I had the usual harangue with her about keeping within hearing distance of Bunto and washing her hands of all this dust before attending to him. She gave her usual lecture about how I had changed, all snooty and bossy using words no one could understand when all along she, and I, knew what a messy kid I had been, always falling into fresh cowdung (it had happened once, when I was four) and I wasn't any the worse for having been carried all the time in her unwashed arms, was I?

I did my usual chores while I waited. I cut vegetables for Aunt Kamu, and churned the cream into butter; I read aloud from the vernacular newspaper to Uncle Ramu's aunt who was now old and half-blind; Bunto was brought over around eight o'clock and I gave him his breakfast. Nine o'clock and still no phone call. I had dozens of packing details to attend to but I knew Seenu well enough to know that if I did not confirm my travel plans with him, I would have to pay for his two-day worry with two years of rebukes. There had been a slight change in my itinerary; our flight would reach Montreal two hours earlier than the one marked on the copy posted on our frig door back in Winnipeg, and I thought I would ask him to arrange a visit to Balwant's who lived close to Dorval. It would be nice to shower and relax so we could be fresh and dressed up when he received us back home.

It was about 9:45 when the phone rang. Instead of the usual questions about Bunto, Seenu was roaring jubilantly and the words echoed and reechoed against each other but I caught the contagion of his excitement even before I untangled his words, WE'VE WON THE GOLD!

I yelled back. Fantastic! WE'VE WON OLYMPIC GOLD!

The cry was picked up by Aunt Kamu's grandson, Nari, and spread quickly down the length of the lane. We've won a gold.

Seenu said, Ben Johnson did it for us. 9:79 seconds! 9:79!

PT Usha's done it, someone shouted at the door. I told you bad heel or no PT would go for it!

Usha my foot, she shouldn't have been there in the first place, all that mumbo jumbo about not competing in the prelims. Usha's just a lame duck.

O yeah?

Yah.

The slanderer and knight errant took their fists outdoors.

I waved NO NO with my hand. Not Usha? Nari asked. No, I motioned, as Seenu shouted on, Carl Lewis was a whole. . .

It isn't Usha, it is Mercy Kuttan in the 400 metre, Nari shouted.

Mercy has got us the gold, word went down the lane.

No, no, it is Shiny Abraham in the 400 metre relay. Hip hip hurray for Shiny!

Yippee doo.

Hey listen, the women's track events are all over anyway. Must be Vijay Amritraj who got a tennis gold.

Yippee doo. Olympic Gold!

Listen, I said, I've got to tell you about our connection in Montreal.

It's the best Carl Lewis has run, you know, Seenu said. He ran 9:93 at both Zurich and Rome but got in at 9:92 now.

Hurray, we've won a gold, some kid was clanging a stainless steel plate with a spoon.

Seenu was saying, Our Ben actually slowed down a bit because he knew he had it all wrapped up. You should have seen the look on his face. Boy oh boy.

Listen, I said, can you hear me? because just then other voices came over crossed wires.

Sell off the rubber shares. Just trust me and sell them. But how about the paper stocks? Hang on to those, the market's going to change.

While the speculators carried on their business talk, Seenu went on with other statistics starting from Sudbury in 1980 when Ben was sixth with 10:88 and Lewis first with 10:43 to Seoul and 1988; the cheering human chain of neighbours and passersby embellished their own speculations about the feats of the 69 members of the Indian team.

What about Montreal? Seenu said at one point. Any changes in your schedule?

No, I said, nothing at all. Bunto and I will be in Winnipeg exactly as scheduled, Tuesday evening.

Which was just as well because the flight into Montreal was three and a half hours late and what with having to clear customs and what not, we barely made it aboard the Winnipeg flight for which we had been scheduled.

Bunto, who had been awake and fidgeting all the way from London to Montreal and had thrown a royal tantrum at the Customs officer and driven the stewardesses up the wall during the last lap of our trip, suddenly fell asleep as I stepped off the plane at Winnipeg.

As I stood on the escalator going down to the baggage carousel and the cluster of people waiting to receive passengers, I had my first sight of Seenu. He had grown a beard, or was trying to. He looked quite ghastly. I cursed Don Johnson, prophet of the unshaven look. Seenu looked quite quite ghastly, and as he ran his hand through his hair I

180

noticed that his hair too was quite wildly ill groomed. But still and all, breathes there a woman with soul so dead who to herself hath never said this is my own my much loved spouse. . .

But something was wrong for sure. He patted Bunto's cheek and asked about the flight etc in a tone that said he didn't really want to know.

"Is anything wrong?" I asked hesitantly.

"Oh, you haven't heard the bad news, then?"

"My mouth got all dry and my stomach went into a cramp. "What news?" I asked urgently.

He calmed me with his hand. "Don't worry. I'll tell you later. You've had a long journey. I thought you'd have heard already."

With that he went off to get a cart to load the suitcases.

Father, I knew it had to be father because mother had always had all kinds of ailments but father was the fit one, and it is always the fit ones who go first. I felt ill and empty.

We walked to the car. The baby seat was not in its usual place. I sat in the front with Bunto cradled in my arms.

"Your parents okay?" he asked, drawing the car out of the parking spot.

So it wasn't father or mother, thank god. Which meant it was someone else. Who? Who? I wanted to ask but was tongue-tied.

"I've had a terrible day," he said, switching on the radio. Meech Lake, Free Trade, the newsman was droning out the usual pronouncements.

The silence between us was deafening. I pinched Bunto so we could have the distraction of his voice. But he refused to wake up.

I remembered that Seenu's Uncle Sami was visiting the US. He had looked after Seenu through his teens, when Seenu's father had been posted in little places far from any good schools. He had built up a thriving business; a year ago he had a massive stroke that just about did him in; on returning from the hospital, he had announced he was going to live it up during the days left him and had sold his business. Last I'd heard of him was during my visit to my in-laws' when they'd got a letter from his granddaughter that he had taken every ride in Disneyland and had wanted more. Montezuma's Revenge at Knottsbury Farm had probably got him, I thought. And what did one do now? Would they fly his body back home to Madras? If we were to die tomorrow would we want our bodies flown back? Not me, I knew, but no one else knew that about me. God, god, we should talk about these things some time or another before it is too late. Poor Uncle Sami, poor Seenu who probably loved him more than he loved his father.

On the radio, some panelists were talking about the Olympics, about the pressure that drove athletes to drugs, and the commercial greed of sponsors who were willing to pay a million dollars to whoever could set right their athlete's torn ligaments or whatever.

"Now you know," Seenu said moodily.

Yes, the suspense was over, sad though it was that poor Uncle Sami was gone.

"He was a good man," I said commiseratingly, placing my hand on Seenu's knee.

"I am not so sure," he replied gloomily, "no matter what the pressure from others, oneself alone is responsible for one's actions.",

What a harsh thing to say, I thought, there's always hoards of secret resentments in every close relationship that others don't know about.

But suddenly it struck me that maybe it wasn't Uncle Sami. O god, of course it wasn't. It was Seenu's brother whose suicidal streak I thought had been set straight years ago. He now had a wonderful wife and two great kids but he had at one stage of his life tried to . . . oh god, how terrible!

We reached home in silence. What a sad homecoming, I thought. Poor Seenu, And now I suppose he's have to go off to Chicago for the funeral. I felt tired, sick, empty.

Seenu brought in the suitcases from the car and the newspaper from the mailbox. He flung the paper across the room. "Dammit," he shouted, "it's not just his funeral, it is ours, all of ours, dammit. Every Canadian's."

Which is when I saw the banner headlines.

The relief was so great that hugging Bunto to my heart, I switched on all the lights in the house and then condoled wholeheartedly with my husband and our country and our poor Ben for having lost the Olympic Gold.

182

Nazneen Sadiq

Ice Bangles

Naila Siraj glanced over her shoulder. He was looking at her quite openly. A perplexed wrinkle snaked across his forehead, breaking the ivory perfection of his Chinese face. Yards of silk slithered around in her lap, the soft edge continually missing her desperate fingers. She was trapped, half-undressed, in a plane which was threatening to descend in five minutes. Underneath the plaid wool airline blanket draped over her lap, the detached pleats of her silk sari swirled in a riot of confusion. Now the trick was to get them folded and tucked back without drawing the attention of the man seated next to her. He had been a silent fixture at her side until her feverish activity had started beneath the blanket. Then the magazine in his hands had become very still. He wanted to get involved but remained silent. She could feel her face heat up with embarrassment. Four rows of seats ahead, the toilet faced her, tantalizing and close, yet out of reach. She gripped at least one end of her sari firmly. Six yards of fabric seemed to have multiplied to a hundred, and the Chinese man was oozing curiosity. Even turning slightly away from him did not work. Perhaps she could rise half naked, leaving behind six yards of her crumpled silken cocoon. Then the stillness would be broken.

The blue clad stewardess advanced down the aisle. "Warm enough?" she mouthed to Naila. The Chinese man shot the stewardess a quizzical look. He looked pointedly as the blanket which had momentarily suppressed all signs of activity beneath it. Naila nodded at the stewardess who wound her way languidly down the aisle. Naila looked with envy at the gentle roll of her buttocks encased securely in blue serge.

"You have a seat belt problem?" It was a whisper rising beside her elbow, but coiling around her like a serpent. Grabbing what she thought was the right amount of fabric she rose abruptly and stumbled across the wool-clad legs of the Chinese man. She felt the flurry of hands and knees making a fleeting contact as she lurched down the aisle. For a moment she was catapulted into her schooldays. The egg and spoon race and the sack race rose as a murky, dusty vision, and a hysterical giggle fought its way through her. The ghostly faces of the Sisters of St Joseph rose wraithlike in the dimly-lit aisle of the plane: the Austrian nuns who had undertaken to deliver countless Muslim girls with faultless school diplomas and cumbersome virginities to their doting parents. The convent was a stone-walled garrison, patrolled by the sweeping hush of white habits, which she had fought for nine years, only to be reminded by her implacable mother that it was the best school in Pakistan.

She had been a convent girl, which had meant that even in the 110 degree swelter of a Karachi summer she could not unbutton the collar of her school uniform. Untying the drawstring of her sari petticoat was her ultimate act of revenge against Mother Superior, who regularly impaled her with the glacial disapproval of her grey eyes. The mirror in the toilet of the CP jet threading its way through alien space confirmed that the women who had supervised her dressing fourteen hours ago had got the better of her. Two sets of mothers, Hers and His, making certain that a Pakistani bride and not some tourist got off the plane at Toronto.

The crackling static cling of her orange Benaras silk sari and the brazen clump of her gold bracelets were new signatures Naila wasn't used to. Not yet anyway. Of course it was just going to be this for a short while, until she got to the country where her outdated school books had assured her everyone spoke French. Canada, where Daud, her hawk-eyed husband would wear a flannel shirt and she would play doll's house in a log cabin.

. . . .

Journalism I. The word jumped off the green board in white chalk letters. The tall, lean instructor stood relaxed. It was seven in the evening, but his casual scrutiny held a degree of alertness. The class seated in front of him was a ragtag group of nightschoolers. Somebody's grandmother felt she had memoirs to compile, and a member of the metropolitan Toronto police force was indulging a schoolboy dream. There was even a chemist flanked by two post-pubescent females seated on the hardback chairs. The classroom, with its appropriately scuffed vinyl floor hummed with expectancy. The collective emotional stance was paws up, waiting for a biscuit. All the teacher had to do was find the Hemingway in the group.

Naila had managed to bag a ride with Kathleen's husband, who taught accounting classes. She had stumbled into the sprawling maze-like college with sharpened pencils and a notebook. She pressed her knees together, tugging at the hem of her miniskirt. The holes of her fishnet stockings grew wider across her thighs, and she knew she was incorrectly dressed. There were only four women in the class of eighteen people, and the other three were wearing pants. The man seated next to her had edged his chair a little too close for comfort. The instructor had observed this and rescued her by insisting that everyone spread out.

The instructor, who was a sports writer, asked each person to introduce himself. He also wanted to know why they had signed up for his course. The response was a chorus of mumbled confessions. She thought it was unnecessary for him to subject the class to this. She couldn't even begin to think of what to say. Unfortunately, her reticence drew his attention. He dipped his head to study the registration list.

"Naila Siraj, is that correct?" He pronounced her name slowly.

"Yes, that is right," she replied, feeling eyes swivel at her.

"And what are your expectations?" The tone was soft, curious.

"I want to learn how to write." Her reply was meant to be light, dismissive, but it hung in the air between them.

"Write what? For newspapers, magazines?" he wasn't through with her.

"I don't know, maybe to get a job one day." She wasn't ready to exchange this confidence with a stranger.

. . . .

"Look, just over the hill," said her father, his face flushed with excitement as he leaned away from the steering wheel.

"For God's sake, keep your hands on the wheel," snapped her mother with a show of ill humour.

"I see it, nana-abba," piped up her six-year-old daughter rising on the seat of the car.

Her father shot her a triumphant look. It said the lives of her children would not be different if he could help it. He was determined to change all that, and he had two months to do it in.

The car wound its way along the mountainous road in northern Hazara, carrying them to her parent's retirement home. The only air traffic which coasted Hazara skies were army helicopters. The mid-sized German car her father drove carried them comfortably over the winding mountainous road. Her mother sat in the front seat, with a picnic basket at her feet. She sat in the back with the two children and the tall sturdy woman who would become surrogate mother to her younger child. She had already staked her claim by holding the baby possessively in her lap. The lower half of her face was concealed by the traditional "burqa" veil. Her self-assured six-year-old, raised on Sesame Street and Beatrix Potter, had decided that the Pakistani nanny was smarter than Mary Poppins. She had come all dressed up to play peek-a-boo.

Her father ran a rambling tour guide conversation for the benefit of his older granddaughter. The small northern province thundered with a history he concocted at each turn of the road. She knew his desperation, and was familiar with the capricious alertness of his six-year-old audience. He would win on that front, and she supposed he had every right to it. He had recently retired from Government Service and had created an idyllic retreat in the mountains complete with roses and flowering almond trees. Nothing, he maintained, would induce him to leave it, not even the subtle entreaties of her active social mother, who repeatedly said that she felt somewhat marooned.

There had been a stockpile of blue aerogrammes in her home in New York. Her presence, especially with the new grandchild, was demanded, and so she had arrived for a two-month vacation. The company had decided to send her husband for some global bounty hunting. She wouldn't be missed. So far everything had worked out, except the shock at the airport over the American passport of her younger daughter.

The car crept along the tiny cantonment. When they left the commercial area and sped along the silver birch-lined road towards the valley, she saw clusters of army cadets raise their hands to greet her father. He was part of a small group of retired civilians who had bought land in the valley, and had actually built a retirement home to live in. The Military Academy and the local residents provided mutual diversion for each other. They were removed from civilization by seventy miles of winding mountainous roads, and a telephone exchange which operated on sheer whimsy. She had been informed by her father that it was the next best thing to paradise.

The white concrete bungalow, with its red brick portico, sat like a picture-postcard at the end of a dirt road. It swam in a deep front lawn dotted with young fruit trees and flowering rose shrubs. In the background, a range of dark mountains with patches of spring snow looked close enough to walk to. There wasn't another house in sight. She watched her daughter skip out of the car and race towards the fruit trees. The nursemaid knelt and rolled the baby towards the grass like a billiard ball on emerald-green felt.

"This," whispered her father, "is their home, their land."

Naila smiled at her father.

. . . .

I am praying for you, her mother wrote in the blue aerogrammed missile. She had stopped saying when are you coming home. Instead she wrote frank disarming letters about loneliness and the need to get enough Vitamin C. Naila dashed off to buy bottles of Vitamin C, swallowing one each morning as an antidote for guilt. She hadn't reached the point where she could tell her mother she was now consigning her life into phases, and not countries. The pressed folds of saris in her closet were muted ghosts of a phase. Her outer skin was more resilient, interchangeable, and losing a definition which had rubber stamped her for ages.

"I'm never going to live here when I grow up," announced her seventeen-year-old daughter.

"But you were born here." Naila sensed the storm brewing from another shore, wondering how it had landed on her doorstep.

"I don't care. It's not half as much fun as Mexico, and I hate the cold," said her daughter.

"It's your home." Naila felt the outrage lancing her, thinking of the apple tree they had planted together. It was supposed to have rooted them in a lifelong apple-pie conspiracy. The outburst was just the recent product of a Mexican vacation, but the betrayal unexpected.

"We never see you," complained Devi, luring her to an Asian women's group.

"I'm on a long break today," Naila warned Devi, wanting only to stay for an hour.

"How do you like it here?" asked a newly-arrived Devi protegé.

Naila looked at the woman with the slightly off-centre red dot on her forehead. Her crackling muslin sari, bordered with handblocked paisleys, was damp at the hem.

"It's home," she replied, shocked at the rush of pity she felt for the young woman.

"My husband and I, we don't know what it's going to be like," shrugged the woman, bangles jingling as she fearfully plucked at her sari.

"It's all right," Naila murmured, thinking about bachelor apartments at Yonge and St Clair where saris with damp hems dried on radiators.

"I think we old timers have to teach the others how to adjust," Devi intoned solemnly, ready for new projects.

"Don't worry," Naila whispered soothingly to the younger woman, wanting desperately to find some short cut for her.

"What are you writing about now?" Devi gave her a searching look.

"I'm writing about her." Naila gestured to the woman with the off-centre forehead dot, who had glided away to another corner of the room.

"Seriously?" Devi yelped, giving her a comical look.

"Seriously," Naila replied, slipping away forever.

Samuel Selvon

The Harvester

It sounded as if a giant hand was crunching a giant newspaper when they fired the canefield in Wilderness in the evening. As the flames rushed through the dry trash, the crackling sound intensified or diminished to the caprice of the wind. Sometimes there was no sound at all, as if the hungry flames had been diverted to the opposite direction. Black smoke rose to merge with grey clouds, and charred wisps of burnt trash fell in the village streets. Children caught them as they fell and rubbed one another's faces with their blackened hands.

Where before was greenery and the pale brown of dry leaves hiding the ripened cane, the sooty stalks now stood naked like a field of thin stakes, a straggly tassel of burnt leaves capping the taller ones here and there.

The firing of a canefield is a responsible job calling for care and experience. Much heed is paid to wind speed and direction, and it has to be under constant supervision, with men around the field controlling the flames. It has to be done when the cane is full and ripe, and the crop should be harvested not longer than 72 hours after, for the sweet juice is likely to start drying up or losing quality.

Sometimes a labourer with a grudge, or some malcontent, would fire a dry field maliciously, and unless the flames were brought under control quickly and prevented from spreading, this could cause great loss and damage. On the plains, the company had a lookout post for such outbreaks, keeping an alert watch for any signs of unauthorized fires.

Early the next morning, with dew spangling silver across the fields, the harvester came lumbering like a cumbersome juggernaut from the company station. It was accompanied by a Land Rover, in which were company personnel, a special loading truck which worked in conjunction with the harvester, and a mobile welding unit. Wherever the harvester operated, the welding unit had to be standing by for emergency repairs.

There were some people in Wilderness who believed that when the harvester came, it would disgorge eighty men, like some metal Trojan horse, who would quickly cut the cane and jump back and hide in the harvester, trying to fool them that only the driver and operator and machine were responsible. And by the time the operation was about to start, almost the whole village had turned out to see the magic machine.

The driver of the harvester, high up on his perch, surveyed the silent spectators like a lord, aware of his own importance. There were not many like him in Trinidad, though the company had started to train a few men in the hope that they would be allowed to import and use more machines in the near future.

Teeka was among the labourers and villagers who were all standing a respectful distance away, as if they were not sure what the crazy machine might get up to: perhaps it might charge into the crowd and send them scattering if they came too close. He had heard about the harvester from a friend in Orange Valley, another estate, but this was the first time he was ever so close to one. It had two of the largest wheels he had ever seen. The tires looked as thick as if they would last forever, and there was a third smaller one out front on an extended bracket of the machine.

As it approached the first ridge of burnt cane, Teeka saw why they had had to lay out the land that way: the wheels fitted in the drains between the ridges.

The harvester went to work noisily, two shiny spiral cutters at earth level, while another blade at the top lopped off the heads of the cane.

Teeka blinked his eyes, not sure of what he was seeing. The machine was just moving relentlessly down the lines of cane, leaving behind only the roots for the next crop. Now the loading truck drove alongside it, and the lengths of cane, already cut into pieces, were chuted into the truck. In a short time the harvester was clattering and jogging halfway down the ridge, spilling the cut cane into the loader.

Teeka wondered how many men it would have taken to reach that far and do so much work. Maybe Balgobin could tell him. He looked around, suddenly thinking that he had not seen his uncle all morning. He asked the others, but they shrugged or shook their heads. They were too busy watching the miracle.

When half the field was reaped the company supervisor decided to call a halt and invited the labourers to inspect it. But none of them wanted to go any nearer. He explained that though the machine did the work of many men, it was not true that only two were employed on the operation. Workers were needed to clear the fields properly after it had gone through, maintenance men were necessary, there were two shifts of work during crop time, and altogether, it required more labour than they thought or had heard about. And in any case, the harvester could only be used on suitable terrain, they would still have to use the old reaping methods in several parts of the island.

They listened to him in silence, for now they had seen with their own eyes that Wilderness was suitable terrain, as he called it and they felt that he was only soft-soaping them for the day when mechanization took over all their jobs. Some of them imagined one man (white) sitting in a room before a panel of knobs and meters pressing buttons and producing instant sugar.

They drifted back to the village in little gloomy clusters of argument and gesture, leaving a silence in the field, and the harvester, which was going to be removed the next day.

Blackbirds descended on the exposed ridges looking for worms and insects in the freshly turned earth.

It was full moon that night. The fields of green were covered by a silver light and an almost ghostly hush. Further north, old man Caroni's murky brown turned to shimmering gold as it meandered across the plains between fields of rustling cane, Orange Grove on one side, Orange Valley on the other; the domineering Northern Range to the north, the gentler, less ambitious Central Range to the south. Up here by the river, cane was majesty; down south oil was the ruler. Up here the royal palms–palmiste–aged scores of years on their way to the sky, thick trunks soaring up a hundred feet to an umbrella of green leaves. There are avenues of them in every sugar area, planted from the old days, perhaps with the first ratoon of cane, and they are seldom, if ever, felled, even for the purpose of development on the estates.

When Balgobin left the rumshop, it was close on midnight. He had spent most of the day in his hut brooding over the presence of the harvester in Wilderness, talking to his cutlass.

"Poya," he said–it was the Indian word for cutlass, but he used it like a name–"what you going to do now? The white people send a big machine with eighty-eight men to cut the cane. What you going to do about that? You going to stand for that?"

All day he pottered about the hut, muttering imprecations on the company as he did odd chores, moulded the tomato plants or mended a leak in the carat roof.

"Poya," he said, "they think we getting old. But that is a mistake, because we old already. You remember the old days, Poya? You remember when it only had barracks for the people to live in? You remember when it didn't have no school? You remember when we used to work for a shilling a day and cut more cane than any blasted machine? And you remember that big strike in nineteen . . . when we march from San Fernando to Port of Spain?"

It was good to talk to Poya because Poya could not reply or interrupt, and he could break the conversation whenever he wanted. This he did often, his thoughts scattered and unconnected over the past. Of late it was becoming difficult and tiresome to remember everything.

"We can't strike no more," he muttered. "The government and them stop we from striking. Otherwise you and me would of gone on strike, and what would happen to all that cane that have to cut? The company would catch their arse."

In the evening when Popo came with his food, the boy found him sitting on the back steps, just recovered from a bout of coughing.

"Uncle!" Popo was excited. "You seen the harvest machine? It look like a big invention!"

"Well, why you don't go and play with it? Poya not good enough for you now, eh?"

"All of we went to see it after school." Popo did not listen to the old man in his excitement. "And I climb up which part the driver sit down. Up there so high, you could see across the field!"

"What your mother send this time?"

"I don't know." Popo handed him the paper bag to see for himself, but Balgobin only rested it on the step.

"You still sick?" The boy became aware of his mood. "You been taking the medicine I get from the doctorshop for you?"

"Yes."

But when Popo took the food inside, he saw the bottle of cough mixture on the shelf, just as full as the day he had bought it. He took it up and carried it outside.

"It don't look as if you had any," he accused, "and I buy it with my own money, too besides."

"That is another bottle, " Balgobin lied. "I finish what you bring and it was so good I went for another dose myself."

The boy knew his uncle was lying, but it warmed his heart. "You know something, Uncle? I didn't like that harvest machine. It ugly. It resemble a monster. And I hear it can't go fast at all. and you know another thing? It break down all the time, and they have to have a welder there to repair it. When you cutting cane, you don't need no welder!"

"Where you hear all that, from your father?"

"No. He gone to town since yesterday and he ain't coming back yet."

"How he could go to town when the company people was coming with this machine?"

"I don't know. Teeka must of been in charge." Popo paused. "You going to let me practice the cutlass today? We don't have to if you don't want to." He would have preferred to be up in that high seat on the harvester. He asked, "You ever see a machine cutting the cane?"

"How much I got to tell you, boy, that when it come to cane, it ain't having nothing I don't know?"

"You ever sit down on the seat like me? You ever drive one?" Popo could not know he was aggravating Balgobin's gloomy mood. "I think maybe now, instead of the cutlass, you could teach me to drive a harvester! Then you and me could do the work of eighty-eight men!"

"You seen the machine working?"

"No. It was just there in the field."

"Then how the arse you know it could do work like eighty-eight men?" Balgobin vented his anger on the boy. "You trying to teach your uncle how to suck eggs?"

"Everybody say so, who see it working in the field this morning. You wasn't there?"

"What I know I know with my own brain, I don't need no machine to teach me. It must of had men who cut that cane in the night and put them back to stand up, and then that machine just pass and fool people that it cutting the cane."

"I hear Teeka tell ma that you wasn't there. Why you wasn't there? You was feeling sick?"

"Yes."

"Because you would have seen with your own eyes."

"Well you wasn't there either, so keep quiet."

Popo did so for a few moments, then, "Why you 'fraid that harvester?"

Balgobin blinked. "Me?" He coughed, clutching his sides as if to keep his body from falling apart.

"Romesh say it will cut the work in half."

"So! It does cut work, too, eh?"

"Yes." The boy was wrapping one ankle around the other restlessly, and his hands fidgeted as if they wanted something to do. As last he summoned up enough courage to speak his mind.

"I can't stay to play and talk today. I want to go and have another look before it get dark."

Balgobin said nothing. The boy waited for a minute, and then he began to inch himself out of the yard, although his uncle's face was turned from him.

"All right then," he called when he was some distance away, "I will make up for it tomorrow." As soon as the hut came between them he quickened his pace, then ran.

The harvester represented a space machine, a trip to the moon, a glimpse of the world outside Wilderness and Trinidad. He was sorry for the old man, but how could he expect a small cutlass to hold competition against a big thing like that?

Balgobin had not known when the boy left. Later, he went to the rumshop, choosing a late hour when he thought most of the men would have finished their drinking and talking. The shop was closed, but there was a light in the adjoining shed where the shopkeeper kept an old table and a few benches for lingerers, and where customers came to buy after shop hours.

Balgobin sat by himself, ignoring three men who were finishing off a bottle of rum and making their final pronouncements on the topic of the day. As they were leaving, one of them stopped and said, "Ah, like you doing a night shift with the harvester, Balgobin!" And they laughed themselves out.

He did not drink a lot. He had two, and nursed this third until it was time to lock up.

Wilderness was asleep or going to sleep when he left. A gentle breeze, cane scented, blew down the village street, and he walked with it, his cutlass glinting in the moonlight.

He spoke now for the first time since Popo had left him .

"Popo says we 'fraid, Poya." His voice was soft, tempered by the night. "Let we show him who 'fraid and ain't 'fraid. You want to see it?" He lifted the cutlass above his head. "What you think, eh?"

He could make out no distinguishing features from so far, even with the moonlight.

"They might have a watchman looking out. We best hads circle slowly, and come round from behind."

He walked around the field, treading softly, his eyes sharp for any sign of movement. Only the wind swayed the remaining canes, and burnt as they were, there was no rustle. When he got nearer he walked faster: he did not want those eighty-eight men to think he was afraid. It seemed to him as if the machine came to meet him, towering like a giant monster. He went right up to it, and stood up and lifted his head.

"All right!" he shouted. "Come on out! One by one, or the whole eighty-eight of you at one time! I don't care how you come, I will chop every manjack down like how you chop the cane!"

He waited for them, and when nothing happened he chuckled and said to Poya, "Look at all them scamps and cowards, they so 'fraid they playing as if they sleeping!"

He walked around the machine, beating it with his hand. "Come on, wake up in there! All-you come to take away my work, eh? Come on, we have a fair fight, is only Balgobin and Poya waiting out here. If you win, is because I dead. And when you lose, is because you laying down like cane lay down when Poya pass!"

All this time, he did not examine or look closely at the machine, he did not want to know what it looked like; it was only an overwhelming presence which he was going to hack into small pieces before the night was out.

The breeze was freshening and a dark cloud, as shapeless as the harvester but not as angular, moved over the moon, switching off the light.

"Ah! You want to fight in the dark, eh? I don't mind. I cut cane day and night, year after year." He raised his voice to a scream. "Wake up, all-you only full of mouth! Talking about how much cane you could reap and frighten for one man!"

The effort brought his cough on, he tried to curb it, shaking silent-ly, blood wanting to burst out of his skin.

Recovered, he told Poya, "I don't want them to hear me cough. They might feel I getting old and sick, and use that as a excuse." He chuckled again. "These people funny, yes. You mean they frighten of the two of we? Or maybe they peeping out and can't make out who it is?" He raised his voice. "Is me, Balgobin who here talking. I cut cane all over Trinidad, in Felicite, in Waterloo in Perseverance, in La Gloria, in La Fortune. It ain't have a sugar estate I ain't work on. I plant more ratoons than any man, and I throw nitrogen and potash and phosphate with my hand and a bucket, no blooming machine. And I kill weeds and froghoppers with a knapsack sprayer on my back, not from no blooming aeroplane. All-you listening? You mean not even one of you brave enough to come out and fight man to man?"

Walking to and fro as he talked, Balgobin struck hid toe on a large cane root on the reaped ridge, and cursed.

"That is the way you reap cane?" He shook Poya at the harvester. "You left big stump here to break men foot? It look like I will have to give you-all a lesson here tonight. Poya," he stroked the blade, "they want me to show them how to do the work. You think we should? Yes?"

He went up to a line of cane as the moonlight came pouring down, the cloud sailing off to the horizon.

"This is the way." He began cutting, his arm arcing the air with Poya in a grace of movement. It did not seem as if he hurried, and yet cane after cane fell swiftly. Every move he made had purpose and ef-fect, and after a minute or so he became engrossed with the rhythm of the work and almost forgot the harvester. It was always so with him in the fields. He was like a machine himself, performing automatical-ly without pause, incorporating the action of wiping beads of sweat off his face as part of the general movement. Once occupied this way, no one could interrupt him. Sometimes other labourers rushed their cut-ting, taunting him as they went by with their cutlasses flying, but he paid them no mind, and when they were exhausted and paused for breath, he would be working steadily forward, as if he were unable to stop even if he wanted, each stroke completing its intention without repetition.

And then his cutlass struck at a hard root. It was not a jarring blow, and in fact, the stroke went on to completion and the cane fell, but it was sufficient to put him off his stride. It was the first time in living memory that Poya had ever let him down, and he was so taken aback that his body stretched out of its working stance and he straightened up and looked around him as if recalled from a dream.

But it was no dream. The eighty-eight coward vagabonds had crept out of the machine while his back was turned, and now they had him surrounded. He could see them all around him, trying to pretend they were just standing there like cane.

"Oho!" he cried. "That's the way you-all fight, creeping up on a man when he not looking!" He kissed the cutlass. "Poya, is not your fault with that last cane we cut. Is these good-for-nothing scamps who must of set a trap for you. Is only eighty-eight of them we got to slaughter."

And he slashed out at the cane. There was no more rhythm or method in his actions. Wild with fury, all his pent-up rage and frustration went into the fight. He struck left and right savagely in a crisscross sweep, panting now, no more regulation or discipline in his body, except to twist the blade slightly as he swung it from one side to the other.

"Start counting, Poya. One! Two! Three!" He tossed the bodies aside in the furrow for burial. The moonlight cast the shadows of the man and the cane and the cutlass in a mingled confusion: it doubled him and his cutlass but it also doubled the remainder of the eighty-eight, and in his frenzy he attacked both shadow and reality.

"Fifty, fifty-one, fifty-two!" The cutlass itself seemed to have a life of its own. For years it had been accustomed to certain patterns of the movement, obedient to the call of particular muscles, to a fixed routine of action. From the moment the hand of its master touched it, the fingers meshing into the worn grooves of the handle, Poya knew what it had to do. If a stranger held it, it rebelled, and once, in La Gloria, as a labourer made fun of it, it dropped from his hand and split his big toe in two, through nail and bone. Poya had longed to test itself in a variety of ways. It had descended from a strain of buccaneers; its ancestors had tasted real blood. Poya knew that several of his friends and relatives kept the buccaneering spirit alive, particularly on the banks of the Caroni, and in the Indian villages: the boys who played table-tennis even had a joke about any player who chopped the ball. "Call a policeman for him, he is a chopper!" Cutting cane was tame work in comparison.

"Seventy-five, seventy-six, seventy-seven!"

Tonight Poya was delighting as it responded to a different angle, a new turn or twist, an unusual pull or thrust. All the years it had longed to prove to its master that given the opportunity it could move in any direction and perform any task under his skilful guidance. But it never got the chance before. It only had to threaten and men would run from its master like cowards, leaving it disappointed and still yearning for the flow of red blood on the decks of a field or a village street. And though it knew its master was only pretending these opponents were real men, it gained some satisfaction playing the game with him, and even hummed as it worked. Poya did not know where the humming came from: it may have happened when it struck that hard root two minutes or so ago, and hesitated for a fraction of a second. Or it may have been that in the pretension of a fight employing latent talent, the buccaneer in it was stirring. Poya did not know, but what a song it would sing on the banks of the Caroni if it chopped a real man and joined the ranks of its notorious companions and owners!

"Eighty-six, eighty-seven, eighty-eight!"

A deep laugh of triumph started in Balgobin's throat, threatening his cough: in fact, he combined the laugh and cough into a prolonged noise. With the swish and the hum of the cutlass ceased, with the regular thud of bodies falling, the laugh-cough rumbled across the field in a monopoly of sound, ending in a gasping wheeze and a spitting of real blood.

"Any more?" Balgobin hardly waited to catch his breath. "Any of all-you hiding there in the cane? Come on out and fight, might as well, because I ain't taking no surrender!"

He cupped a hand over his ear, listening intently, turning his head this way and that. "Well, Poya, it look like was only eighty-eight of them in truth. But the job ain't done yet! We kill all the ants, but we got to kill the nest, too!"

He walked in the furrow, trampling and kicking the slain bodies, heading back to the source. He circled the harvester warily, suspicious of a trap, because it had been too easy, maybe he had not counted correctly–it had been years since he reached to eighty-eight –and they had a few more men on guard. Or they might have set some trip wire or coiled spring to blow him to smithereens, in case he escaped them in the cane.

At length he was near enough to touch it. Balgobin did not wait to see if the monster had a soft spot or any vulnerable section, nor was he interested in the mechanical detail or shape and design of the thing. He just leaped forward, holding the cutlass with both hands, and wielding it like an axe, he brought it down with all his strength against the side of the machine.

To his utter amazement, instead of sinking into the monster in that stroke of destruction, Poya ricocheted, springing backward with a whine, and a quiver ran up the length of his arm. He stumbled back a step and almost fell. So there was a trap after all! He had to proceed with caution and cunning, though his original intention had been to slash and hack in a frenzy of rage until the whole nest was crumbled into pieces.

He clambered up the front of the machine as quietly as he could. He tripped over the fuel connections and went sprawling flat on his face. The cutlass fell from his hand. It was the first time in the battle that they had had him down. His astonishment was such as to make him lie as if stunned for a moment or two. Then he jumped up in a rage as towering as the monster itself and, grabbing the cutlass, he smote at the pipelines as if hacking his way out of a jungle of lianas. This time something gave, but even so Poya whined in protest and rebounded, and again that jolting shock ran up Balgobin's arm and he also toppled from the machine as he fought hard to keep his balance. He was about to bring a slanting blow down when he felt something cold and wet on his feet.

"Aha!" he paused to cry. "I hit you on a vein, eh? This is your soft spot?"

And in the pause, his sensitive fingers felt that something was wrong with the cutlass. It was such a slight sensation that it might have been more intuition than physical contact, but he lowered his hands and passed a testing thumb carefully along the edge of the blade. His thumb encountered a jagged six inches where the force of his blows had concentrated. He cursed loudly in the moonlight as he examined it. He would have to hone Poya down a quarter inch at least before it could be serviceable again. It was an honourable wound received in battle, but the battle was not ended. He went to wipe the wetness from his feet, and a box of matches fell from his shirt pocket. As he took it up, he smelt the oil.

In the morning, the combine harvester was still smouldering and smoking, but from a distance it was hardly possible to tell that anything was wrong with it. It was only on a closer look that it was discovered it had been destroyed beyond repair, still towering above the cane, but now a wreck of twisted metal.

M G Vassanji

No New Land

"When does a man begin to rot?" Gazing at the distant CN Tower blinking its signals into the hazy darkness, Nurdin asked himself the question. He sat in his armchair, turned around to look out into the night. Through the open balcony the zoom of the traffic down below in the valley was faintly audible, as was the rustle of trees. Pleased with the sound of his silent question, he repeated it in his mind again, this time addressing the tower. The lofty structure he had grown familiar with over the months, from this vantage point, and he had taken to addressing it. "When does a man begin to rot?" he asked. Faithful always, it blinked its answers, a coded message he could not understand.

He liked to keep the room darkened when alone. Somewhat vaguely he was aware of the photograph on the wall, on his right. Vaguely, because he rarely looked at it, and when he did, by accident, he tried as much as possible to block his father's face on it from his mind. Something had changed, he did not know what, perhaps new ideas, like the question he was asking, not knowing why. Some inner reserve was creaking, shifting its weight. The photograph on the wall, its face, intruded into his consciousness at this moment, eyes boring into him from the side, and he shuddered.

His father's photograph, taken in the 1940s, was one of the prized possessions Zera had brought from Dar. Other things had seen the dustbins–photographs, old books, souvenirs–but not this. It was the first object to go up on the walls. Sometimes when she lighted incense sticks and went around the apartment consecrating it, she would stand before the photograph and hold the incense to it–as one would to a real person–thus giving it a real presence in the home. The fez on the small head, the bushy eyebrows, the hard eyes, the small mouth: relentless in judgement here as the real person had been in Africa. . .

For Nurdin Lalani a new life had begun with his job at the Ontario Addiction Centre. With it he had accepted a station in life–not one he believed he deserved, a son of a prominent elder and businessman, but one which would have to do. At least he could say, in mosque and at Sixty-nine, that he had a job downtown. He didn't have to say precisely what job. "Say manager," Zera told him. "You do manage supply rooms."

Romesh's companionship made the work more tolerable, sometimes even enjoyable, although he had to get used to the man. Romesh had a way of edging into his confidence, assuming a familiarity, that had startled him at first. That, and his different idiom and accent.

One day they were having their lunch together. Nurdin noticed something on Romesh's plate and asked, "Is that a hot dog?"

How could he not have known. Surely that was Satan speaking through him. Romesh cut it in two, neatly, and gave him half. "Like hot dog, but better. Try it."

He ate a piece and it was good. Even before he had finished swallowing it, as it was going down his gullet, everything inside him was echoing the aftertaste, crying, "Foreign, foreign." Yet it did nothing to him.

When Romesh returned with a second helping, he had finished his half. Romesh nodded approvingly. "That was sausage."

"Beef, I hope."

"No."

He pretended shock, and Romesh comforted him. "See, you're the same. Nothing's happened to you. Forget pork, man, I was not supposed to eat *meat*. Even egg. I'm supposed to think you're dirty. You think *they* are dirty. Who is right? Superstitions, all."

The pig, they said, was the most beastly of beasts. It ate garbage and faeces, even its babies, it copulated freely, was incestuous. Wallowed in muck. Eat pig and become a beast. Slowly the bestial traits–cruelty and promiscuity, in one word, godlessness–overcame you. And you became, morally, like *them*. The Canadians.

There were those, claiming to be scientific, who said it's the diseases the pig carries and the quality of meat, which has long-term effects, which are the reason for the prohibition: the Book has all knowledge for all time. And there was Nanji–who himself drank wine, Nurdin knew, and probably ate pork–who said it's the discipline that's important, you've been forbidden to do it for whatever reason, and that's that.

In any case, he, Nurdin had eaten *it* –he could not make himself name "it" yet–and perhaps that is where the real rot began, inside him. . .

Ever since that first act of serious incontinence–tasting a bit of pork sausage and then proceeding to consume a sizeable chunk of it– Nurdin's sins, it seemed to him, had multiplied. Thinking back on a statement Nanji had made, he could find some explanation for his predicaments and even a little comfort for his inner turmoils. Nanji, he said to himself, had hit the nail right on the head! Well, they didn't give out degrees for nothing. You've got to have something up here. You are already changed when you think about eating pork. Think about that. There must be something in the Canadian air that changes us, as the old people say. The old people who are shunted between sons and daughters and old people's homes–who would have thought that possible only a few years ago. It's all in the air: the divorces, crimes you could never have imagined before, children despising their parents. An image of his own arrogant Fatima came to his mind and he pushed it back.

There was this nice young couple at number Seventy-one: respectable, pious. They had met in mosque doing voluntary service, married, and were expecting their first child. What could be more gratifying to watch and reflect upon: the couple strolling back from mosque, parents of a new generation. Then baby was born, but it had blue eyes. It took some doing by the young man's family before he would believe what his own eyes told him, and the wife confessed to the truth. The couple were divorced now, and the girl was living with the father of the baby. What is more, it had all been accepted as the way the world is. What was once unthinkable became acceptable. Roshan, Zera's sister, continued to be battered at home. Already in the last few months twice she had come with puffed-up face to spend the night. Nurdin was all for calling the police: "Let them lock up the pig" (yes, pig, he had said). But the women said no, hush-hush, don't wash your dirty linen in public. Well, hadn't they heard, that is precisely what you do, there are laundromats here. This is Canada, he told Roshan, giving back her own. She had returned home the following day, after being nursed by Zera, as for the next round at boxing. Wait till her son grows older, two or three years from now, he'll beat the shit out of his father. . .

He looked at Zera. No carnal sin from that quarter, he thought, eyeing the ample hips move under her favourite sack dress as she dusted the table. She was in the greatest of spirits because, after long entreaties, several years of pleading, the Master, Missionary himself, had decided to come and settle in Canada. The arrival was several months away, the dusting and vacuuming today was only to make the place look like it should for the Master. Nurdin was pleading earache and resting on his favourite chair. And looking at Zera.

Even though she had grown fat, there *was* still an attraction about her. There was that friendliness, the soft-heartedness, and the sense of humour. Those breasts were still ripe mangoes and the large hips were yet firm. But she did not let him come close. Blocking his intentions, in bed, turning against his desires that mountain of a haunch, behind which he felt rather helpless and small. Do you want me to come from behind? If you want to. With this Kilimanjaro facing me? Go to sleep.

Zera was married to God, the idea of Gods. Not that she was otherworldly or excessively devotional. Her obsession was to discuss God and religion, and she liked nothing better than to sit at the feet of her teacher, Missionary, and to hear him discourse on God, the Prophet, the sages. A little like listening to expert commentary on sports. If there was any devotion, it was to the Master. There had been in the past, on one or two occasions, innuendoes at this unhealthy worship of Missionary by his female followers. Nurdin knew his wife, not to say Missionary, and was never bothered. And, after all–thinking back on those innuendoes–who could know the innermost secrets of the heart, even if they were your wife's . . . or husband's . . . or your own. . .

They had not been physically really close for years. Not had sex–what a nice legitimate way of putting it. He had resigned himself to this celibacy. There was so much to do, to worry about. And now this late reawakening, a blossoming in middle age of a youthful obsession. Will it pass? He shuddered, felt the almost physical impact from the steely eyes he knew were staring at him from the picture on the wall–

should I let it pass?

Romesh had observed it. Romesh with the roving eye had observed his roving eye, and his shyness with women.

"That big wife of yours not letting you have it?"

It rather shocked Nurdin at first, this open remark about his wife. "She is very pious, very religious, you know."

Romesh had a simple solution, an idea Nurdin was not quite ignorant about, especially in his youth. So he tried just taking her one night, but she had given such a scream, a yelp, that Fatima and Hanif came running, Fatima lumbering in the lead. Zera did not help him with explanations, she let him go to sleep with the knowledge that the kids already guessed what had happened.

To be young in this land free of inhibitions. What did he care of morality, can you change the way the world is going? He regretted his innocent youth somewhat. Once, when he was a boy, the picture of a beauty-contest winner had been printed in the newspaper, a white girl in a swimsuit, and they had all looked at it gravely in his home, at dinner, his father first. The picture had gone round the table. Then Nurdin had secretly cut it out and hid it among the pages of his exercise book. Later someone had removed it, he didn't know who, presumably to protect him from his father's wrath. In place of the picture of Angela (that was the girl's name), there was the traditional peacock feather. That was the extent to which he had let his desire run away, more or less, barring moments in the bathroom. He wished sometimes he had gone fornicating with the boys in the alleys and byways, in the huts with Arab and African prostitutes. Or in the quarters where Indian women ran the same trade more furtively and at higher price. He had even accompanied his friends on such expeditions. All, or most, respectable men now. Like Jamal, who had done everything in his youth. Now he was respectable and rich. Then there was that Nanji. Difficult to make out what Nanji was. A Sufi, you would think, an ascetic. But he had spent three days–and, worse, nights–with three women, drinking and doing God knows what. Zera had not really approved, of course, in spite of her enthusiasm in fixing up Nanji's apartment, though she had blamed not Nanji but the three girls. Pretty girls, all. Pretty and free.

Nurdin's lusty eye, he had discovered, hovered not only on the ample but forbidden body of his wife–which God would surely excuse –but on practically all women, it seemed. Like a boy at puberty he had become aware of Woman, the female of the species, and he found her diverse and beautiful. And what was offered to an eye starved for such visions was simply breathtaking. It was like sending to the hungry of the world not just rations of wheat but whole banquets. Bra-less women with lively breasts under blouses and T-shirts that simply sucked your eyeballs out. Buttocks breaking out of shorts. And when you saw these twin delights nuzzling a bicycle seat, doing a gentle rhythmic dance of their own in the dazzling heat and among the trees and flowers and the smells of nature in the park–why, you had to be sure you were dressed right. And Zera marching along ahead. "Hurry up, Nurdin, stop loitering like a boy." Boy, indeed. His head would be pounding, his body aching with desire.

Later, after witnessing such a vision, he would be overcome by bouts of guilt. The picture on the wall fixing him with its eyes, reminding him of that hymn, "Lust and anger, those two you shall avoid." Anger was not his problem, that was his father's. Let him pay for it. Nurdin's problem was lust. Don't covet another man's woman. Well, what if yours doesn't give? The punishment for backbiting was to be hung by your tongue, and for listening to backbite, to be hung by your ears. And for fornicating? A gruesome image of himself hanging by his balls intruded into his mind. He stifled a giggle. He didn't remember who had listed those punishments, probably one of his father's cronies during their interminable sessions. Hell will have scorpions as large as camels. And the sinful will cry in anguish, mercy, mercy.

One day Romesh and he had got out early from work, a little after lunch. It was election day. They stood outside, hands in their pockets, looking, feeling, small next to the impressive broad building from which they had emerged.

"Well, what do you intend to do for the rest of the afternoon," Romesh said.

"Go home, I think." The bus stop was a block away on Spadina.

"Tell you what, Nur. Let's go for a walk."

"Here?" A casual, aimless walk in the streets was not something he had done for a long time.

"Let's go to Yonge Street."

"Yeah, let's go to Yonge Street." He liked driving on it on Friday nights with the family, to see the gaiety and lights, and hear the noisy crowds on the streets and music at each corner. Pretending not to see the prostitutes in tight skirts and heavy makeup. He had walked on Yonge Street perhaps once. He could now see why. The daytime crowd made walking difficult. The street was littered and congested with noisy traffic, many of the shops were dingy if not outright disreputable. There was nothing much to see.

They sat down at a rather fashionable-looking outdoor cafe. "This is the life, man," said Romesh with a sigh. "I could sit here forever, just watching the people go by."

"And life go by, eh?" Sometimes he never knew how to talk to this man.

"And life go by, alas."

The waitress was young and pretty, attentive. "Well, what can I do for you gentlemen today."

"Plenty. But for now. . ." Romesh said with a grin.

Nurdin had a coffee, Romesh a beer. They sat and watched in silence. At work there was enough to talk about, they saw each other all the time, had lunch in the cafeteria together.

"Hey, would you like to taste my beer?"

"Oh, no."

"There is nothing wrong with tasting, you know. From what I know of the Quran, only getting intoxicated is forbidden."

Nurdin knew the argument. It was the latest among the educated Dar crowd before they too relented.

"You could have three or four beers easily without getting drunk."

That Nurdin had also heard. "Let me try a sip." His coffee cup was empty, in any case. He concentrated his mind on drinking that sip, so that it would not wander off and summon guilt from somewhere. That accomplished, he sat back and watched Romesh finish the drink. Finally he had a glass of his own, to accompany Romesh's second. He did not know why he was doing what he was doing, did not think about it, though a vague consciousness of his deed lay somewhat heavily on his heart. The beer was refreshing, the bitter taste he got used to. His eyes were soon glazing over, he only hoped that no one walking by on Yonge Street would recognize him. They were sitting at a most conspicuous spot. The beer mug before him could not be mistaken for anything else.

"There's nothing to see on Yonge Street, eh," he said.

"Ah, if you want to really see something. . ." Romesh grinned. "Let's corrupt you some more." They got up.

They walked two blocks south to a part of the street where the pedestrian traffic thinned. They stood outside a place called Dar es Salaam, The Heaven of Love. It was a name you couldn't miss–not if you came from a place called Dar es Salaam. The name of this heaven was printed on an oriental-style red canopy with a nude drawing to highlight it.

"Where do you say you come from, eh, Nur? This should feel quite like home to you."

"What is it?"

"Follow me."

Romesh went in, he followed. What promised opulence from out-side turned out to be, inside, a narrow corridor: unswept, oil-painted yellow walls now grimy. On the walls some framed photos of nude girls, pubic hair conspicuous. There was a window just inside the entrance, from which Romesh got some change and counted half of it into Nurdin's hand. "Enjoy. It's all on me, man. All on me."

There were six booths inside, two of them taken, each with a pair of viewers–like binoculars–to see through. You put a quarter into a slot–no, first you put your eyes on the viewer, instinctively, then you looked for the slot and put a quarter there, and you leaned forward on the viewer and pressed home the coin.

Nurdin's heart pounded violently against a chest that seemed to have contracted. He had never seen anything like it, not in ads, not in movies, nor even the girlie magazines of his youth. Sex scenes beyond his wildest dreams: dirty, depraved, exciting–how much the flesh was capable of! It was enough to destabilize you forever, question all the inhibitions and prohibitions of childhood and youth–do this, don't do that: who had thought them up? Reluctantly he looked up from the viewer, worked up to quite a state. He had used up all his coins.

As they were walking out two very young prostitutes in tight leather miniskirts stood around, vigorously chewing gum. "How about the real thing now, boys?" said one.

"Sorry. We are booked, ladies," grinned Romesh.

"Fags."

"Now to go home for the fun, eh, Nur. Why pay when you can get it free. Your big woman obliges now, I hope? My trick worked, I bet. What did I tell you. They like it."

He went home oppressed with guilt. "What's the matter, Nurdin?" Zera asked. "Oh, a headache." He kept well away from her, his eyes averted, two cardamom pods in his mouth to sweeten his breath. To punish himself, he looked full square at Haji Lalani's photograph, eye to eye. Do to me what you will: twenty-five, fifty, a hundred strokes of hippohide whip, dipped in salt. When he died, his father would be waiting for him with the whip, God's personal executioner. . .

III. Drama

Rana Bose

On the Double

(The inspiration for this play was a theatre performance by a group of New Delhi women players, but in form and content the play reflects Montreal and Canadian reality. The play should be performed in a space carved out of the audience area, rather than on a proscenium stage. The players are dressed in black clothes with colourful sashes and head bands. They require cubes or boxes for sitting. In the original production, the Montreal Serai players provided live music.)

Cast:

Woman 1	Man 1
Woman 2	Man 2
Woman 3	Man 3

SCENE 1

(*Three women come in, with jerky movements–two freeze, the other mimes switching on a TV. With each flick of the channel she makes the sound "click" with her mouth -- the other two verbalize the channel changes and mime the rectangular screen with their hands framed around their faces. They switch accents and physical mannerisms. In another version of the play the three women start the play by singing a parodied version of the old Beatles favourite "If I fell in love with you, would you promise to be true?"*)

(*Click*) WOMAN 1: J.R., if you still haven't found out what I have been up to, hey! rest assured I'm stoking your goose in my oven, honey! Ewing stocks and all!

(*Click*) WOMAN 2: (*Puts on shades.*) Hi! the name's Sonny Crockett–this muh buddy Rico–the word's out–you got 9/10ths of a second to clear out of this strip–or me and my buddy gonna make mince meat patty out of you and sell it to the sharks. Yeh! (*Pretends holding a handgun, while she takes an aggressive kneel down stance.*)

(*Click*) WOMAN 3: Why do I insist on Preparation H? I insist on Preparation H because I can go golfing, I can go swimming, and there is no pain. It's true, with Preparation H, there's no pain. Preparation H–with Biodine.

(*Click*) WOMAN 1: (*Sound of the* Journal's *theme tune and woman starts speaking with Barbara Frum accent and body movements.*) We will now talk to Mr Larry Smith, a hog farmer in Mudhead Creek, Oregon.

(*Click*) WOMAN 2: "As far as I'm concerned, the Canadian government is too damn far to the left, with all those subsidies that it is giving to the Canadian hog farmer. We 'merican farmers think that's a bit of un-American activity going on out there–like the socialist stuff–next thing you know they's gonna stuff the Das Kapital down your throat."

(*Click*) WOMAN 3: As a woman, I like to feel secure–anywhere I go, anything I do and with ultra thin baby powder scented maxi pads–why, they even fit into my purse!

(*Click*) WOMAN 1: (*Male style.*) I use speed stick by Mennen. Goes on smooth, goes on dry and stays dry. Wide enough for a man, heck, made for a man! Speed Stick. By Mennen.

(*Small musical riff. Blues boogie style. Can be done live by male in black, with guitar, wearing shades and a fedora style hat. When man finishes the 3 women come back.*)

WOMAN 1: (*Rolling up sleeves, fake cigar in mouth.*) Hi, I'm a single woman. I came to Montreal twenty years ago to do a Ph.D. in Biochemistry. It didn't work out. I drive a snow plough for the city and I love to hang out at single bars–lots of heat and action there. Got to relax you know. I put in a hard day–9 to 3–sometimes the night shift. It's a dog eat dog world–but I can be soft–sometimes I put on milkbone underwear. (*Winks, spits and walks away. Turns around.*) And, by the way I hate Tampons that have a baby powder perfume on them. (*Walks back.*)

WOMAN 2: Hi, I'm a mother–mother of three–I own the depanneur on the corner of Pine and St Urban. I am demanding, opinionated, contemporary, and I love that Rico–love the way he licks the Sealtest yogourt under a mean blue haze.

WOMAN 1: (*Different accent.*) Hullo, I am a wife and a social worker (*clears her throat*). I am presently studying the psychological ramifications of sociological alienation on the siblings of second generation South Asian teenage girls living in Brossard with their parents in semi-detached condominium cottages with 2 car garages.

WOMAN 3: (*Looks lost.*) Hi, I am a sister, and I'm working the late shift at Dairy Queen. I had to struggle with my parents to take this job. My mum says–she is all for woman's liberation–that's why she is saving money to send me to university (*gap*) so I can find the right man. My father does not beat up my mother–that's not our style–he beats on the TV set instead–to stop the image from slipping up constantly. (*She mimics her father.*)

WOMAN 1: Now a woman can mean different things in different places, right? Here we are thousands of miles away from the country of our birth, right? Thousands of miles away from Baroda, right? From Beliaghata, right? From Ghat Kopar, from Sangrur, right?

ALL THREE: Wrong!

WOMAN 1: We are only a few feet away. Because Baroda is just around the corner–you make a left on Mountain Sights, and there you are. Sangrur is right next to the Metropolitain–you take the l'Acadie exit–Ghat Kopar is on Taschereau Sud–keep going till the fork on the road–and Beliaghata is . . .

ALL THREE: Brossard!

(*All three women turn around and put colourful shawls around their shoulders. Two men appear from either side, like they are scrutinizing the women, head to foot. This section may be done in a Hip Hop style, intermittently.*)

WOMAN 1: (*Subdued.*) I am a woman.

WOMAN 2: I am a mother.

WOMAN 3: I am a wife.

WOMAN 4: I am a sister

MAN 1: Yo sis, talk to me, talk to me.

MAN 2: But a broad is a broad, yaar.

MEN: What it is, what it is!

ALL WOMEN: Yes, we are all broads.

MAN 1: You broads have been told several times over.

MAN 2: Not to hoop and not to holler.

MAN 1: Not to cackle like a bunch of geese.

MAN 2: And not to check us out, like we were sex objects or something.

MAN 1: And besides, your body is weak . . .

MAN 2: Your world is bleak . . .

MAN 1: You pace is timid.

MAN 2: Your life is insipid . . .

WOMAN 3: . . . So smother your desires.

WOMAN 2: . . . And jail your minds.

WOMAN 1: . . . And shatter all your hopes.

ALL THREE: In lonely days and lonely nights.

(*Change of style to more positive.*)

WOMAN 1: But we do know a few things.

WOMAN 2: And we do know a good fight.

WOMAN 3: And as such we present our play.

ALL THREE: *On the Double,* Tonight!

(*Black out.*)

SCENE 2

(*All characters turn their backs to the audience. MAN 1 comes to the front of the stage. He is in the process of getting ready to go to work. WOMAN 2 is busy, pretending to comb a child's hair.*)

HUSBAND: (*Nervous wreck. Looks for tie, then realizes it is around his neck. Mimes looking for socks in drawers–throws everything out.*)
Kamla, Kamla, where the hell are you?

KAMLA: Where the hell do you think I am–would you like to try getting Munnie ready for school?

HUSBAND: I cannot find my socks, dammit.

KAMLA: Have you looked in your shoes, dammit.

HUSBAND: Shit, There's a button missing from my shirt . . .

BOTH TOGETHER: Shit! Why didn't I/you fix it last night?

HUSBAND: May I give my humble, yet important opinion? Was I to dream at night that I'd have a button missing in the morning?

KAMLA: All right, don't shout so much. I'll fix it after I've done Munni's hair.

216

HUSBAND: What else do you think I do but get up early? But I can never find anything where I left it. Now I can't find my handkerchief.

KAMLA: It was lying on the floor. I washed it. Take another one from the closet.

HUSBAND: (*In utter frustration.*) Oh gee, How many times have I told you not to touch my things . . . but of course you love to be the typical Indian woman . . . always picking up everything behind me . . .

KAMLA: Oh, yes, of course–now it's my fault that I've washed your dirty handkerchief. On reaching the office, you would have told your male cohorts: "Such a drag she is, nosing into everything."

HUSBAND: Forget it. I don't want to listen to your nonsense first thing in the morning. Where is my cornflakes? (*Walks to the back of the stage.*)

KAMLA: Where is his cornflakes? Where are his dirty socks? Where is his dirty handkerchief? How many times have you washed my socks? I mean it's ok with me that your problems are my problems, but why can't my problems be your problems too . . . instead of yours being ours and mine being only mine. (*Freeze and black out.*)

SCENE 3

(*Woman 1 and Man 1 have returned from work. He sits down and turns on the TV. Woman 1 is reading a letter. Man watches TV and mimes taking off his socks, tie, sweater and throwing them in all different directions*).

KAMLA: There is a notice from the school.

HUSBAND: Hummm!

KAMLA: There is a parent-teacher meeting.

HUSBAND: Hummm!

KAMLA: Try to come back early on Thursday.

HUSBAND: Are you going to do something about supper, or are you just going to order me around?

(*Turns off TV and walks away. There is a knock on the door. Kamla rushes around and gets the place in order.*)

Kamla, Kamla, where the hell are you? Somebody's at the door . . . Here, put these keys on the dresser.

(*Kamla opens the door. Woman 2 and Man 2 enter. Man 2 has his shoulder up in a funny posture.*)

HUSBAND: Hi Vicky, how's it going?

KAMLA: I will go into the kitchen to make tea.

WOMAN 2: And I will follow you into the kitchen, naturally.

HUSBAND: I'm glad you dropped by, 'cos I tell you, I was getting dead bored here all by myself.

KAMLA: All by yourself? Wasn't I here with you?

MAN 2: Heh, Heh, Your wife, she has a sharp tongue!

HUSBAND: Yeah, sometimes. She is usually very quiet. Now watch this. Kamla, Kamla!

KAMLA: Yes, I'll be with you in a minute!

HUSBAND: See, I told you. Kamla, bring some tea!

MAN 2: Just tea? (*Like a jerk.*)

KAMLA: (*Entering.*) Well! Start with these, I'll have supper ready soon.

MAN 2: You make delicious pakoras! Hah hah!

(*The women bring a tray with tea and snacks. Both men turn their backs and start talking in gibberish, very serious, prolonged gibberish. Occasionally you hear "Reagan," "Mulroney," "Challenger," "Marcos," "Canadian dollar," "Rajiv Gandhi," "computers," "New blood." Gradually the two women come to the front. The men recede to the back.*)

WOMAN 1: (*To Woman 2.*) You know, when they talk politics, if you listen carefully, they basically always agree with each other.

WOMAN 2: But they always find something obscure to rave and rant about . . .

(*Both women now put on papier mache masks that have striking resemblance to the two men. Woman 3 passes by with a placard. Placard has a drawing of a naked bum with water dripping on it from a "lota" (a brass pitcher used in India, with water, in lieu of toilet paper). Sign says "Ancient Indian device to cleanse the soul."*)

WOMAN 1: Without the lota . . . we would never have made it to where we are now . . . which civilization has the lota . . . which? . . . none Because when we don't use water we become unclean and when you have an unclean body you have an unclean mind.

WOMAN 2: Bullshit . . . Lota means we remain backward . . . to the field, early in the morning, in the a middle of winter . . . it's an absurd, indecent practice . . . it is outdated . . . The mass use of toilet paper is the only answer.

WOMAN 1: What about pollution? Have you ever thought of that aspect . . . we cannot afford toilets . . . so you will have the whole landscape littered with toilet paper . . . who will pick it up, rag pickers? Never! . . . You need a new caste for that . . . and none exists. So what will you do? And besides, toilet paper is not even reusable.

WOMAN 2: Arey, shut up . . . technology has always solved these problems . . . technology is the answer . . . With the new prime minister we will be stepping into the 21st century before it is here.

WOMAN 1: Your 21st century is a disaster and a debacle for the great Indian spiritual and philosophical tradition.

WOMAN 2: Toilet paper, my dear, is a sleeping giant. India must wake up to this sleeping giant and history will unfold itself . . . full of new dreams, new lifestyles, new successes . . .

WOMAN 1: Without the lota all will be lost. The glorious tradition of our forefathers, of our spices, of our mythology . . . Even a sadhu going to the Himalayas always carries no worldly belongings except a walking stick and a lota.

WOMAN 2: Oh, come on! In fact . . . in fact . . . without our penchant for the appropriate use of technology maybe we can find a happy medium to combine the latest with the future . . . and discard the ancient . . . With the proliferation of computers all over the land . . . maybe we can produce a specially textured printout that will also find use as toilet paper . . . as an end use!

(*The two scream at each other "lota" and "toilet paper" alternately and then stop abruptly.*)

WOMAN 1: But politics is politics.

WOMAN 2: Yes politics is politics . . . and whisky is whisky. (*They pretend drinking whisky and make the sound glug glug glug.*)

(*End with these words; freeze. Man with guitar plays another quick riff.*)

SCENE 4

WOMAN 2: The dude's back from work, dog tired . . . mumbling about office intrigue . . . now who cares?

WOMAN 1: She comes back from work, dead beat, keeping her sorrows to herself.

WOMAN 2: He flops down on the love seat: "Sweetheart, can I have a bourbon?"

WOMAN 3: His friends come, they discuss politics, and real estate.

She makes the food.

WOMAN 1: He stomps out with this friends, she stays home to listen to the whine of the vacuum cleaner on the rug.

WOMAN 2: He returns home late, she stays up for him.

WOMAN 3: He drinks and pukes all over, she cleans up after him.

WOMAN 1: He has a deep sleep, she wakes up in a cold sweat.

WOMAN 2: And she wakes up before he does in the morning and makes tea for him.

WOMAN 1: He runs helter skelter, looking for his socks.

WOMAN 3: She finds then in his shoes.

WOMAN 2: And this is the way the wheel keeps on rotating.

WOMAN 1: One two, one two . . . (*As in a ship's galley. The two other women arch their hands in opposite directions and pull the oars.*)

WOMAN 2: The wheel of day.

WOMAN 3: The wheel of night.

WOMAN 2: The wheel of morning.

WOMAN 3: The wheel of evening.

WOMAN 2: The wheel of Karma.

WOMAN 3: The wheel of Dharma.

WOMAN 2: The wheel of tradition.

WOMAN 3: The wheel of life.

One, two, one two, one two . . . (*Fade out.*)

SCENE 5

(*Man with shades and fedora playing with a yoyo, at up stage left.*)

WOMAN 1: Ram's brother is a writer, he flirts with the mind, with the written word–he is a progressive.

WOMAN 2: He lends his voice to the mute . . . outside the house that is!

WOMAN 1: It is past 10 o'clock, my daughter has not returned home as yet. (*Worried.*)

MAN 1: (*Always to the audience, in a nervous manner.*) Maybe she has an important rendezvous set up with a possible employer.

WOMAN 1: (*Pacing.*) She should have returned by now, it is getting very late.

MAN 1: Maybe she got held up on the "Metropolitain."

WOMAN 1: But she is very young, and she is a girl, also her brother and father should come in any moment now. (*Man 2 walks in, city slicker, shirt buttons open etc.*)

MAN 2: Ma, I don't see Bani, where is she?

Woman a: I don't know . . . normally she is here by now.

MAN 2: You are very indulgent with her. Some day she will get herself into trouble.

MAN 1: He means she will be pregnant by a white man.

WOMAN 3: (*Entering.*) Will you quit worrying on my account for God's sake. I won't be the cause of any disgrace to the family.

MAN 2: Where have you been so late at night?

MAN 1: (*Nervously for her.*) Nowhere, nowhere, just here and there.

WOMAN 3: Who are you to ask me? Do you ever tell me where you go?

MAN 3: Exactly, does he ever tell her where he goes?

MAN 2: You see that Ma, you see that, see the way her tongue flies.

MAN 1: He means she talks like a Canadian girl.

WOMAN 1: Don't say anything to her. I will do the asking myself.

WOMAN 3: I went to see Jack's father. He said I could do some graphic design for his consultancy on a freelance basis.

WOMAN 1: You left at 10 in the morning and you are returning now after 8. Don't you realize what you are saying?

WOMAN 2: I wanted to come back earlier, but I missed the 6 o'clock bus.

MAN 2: What a lame excuse, you missed the bus, shit! When you knew you would miss the bus, why did you leave the house in the first place. Working for Jack's father! Bullshit! All you needed was a pretext to leave the house and loaf around Crescent and Bishop . . . I'm fed up with all these lies . . . anyway, Ma! I'll be late for dinner, don't wait up for me. I'm going to Vijay's. He's got the new Madonna video. (*Wicked eyes. He leaves.*)

WOMAN 2: Bunch of yuppy jocks . . . sit around and swig budweisers and hum and haw.

MAN 1: And wait for Madonna's nipples to pop out, but they never do.

WOMAN 1: It is different with him Bani. You are a young girl. You should come back home before dark.

MAN 1: Women are hopeless in the dark. (*Eyes twittering.*)

WOMAN 2: Ma! I only went to see somebody for a job . . . I want to come up with some of the money for school . . . don't you see that?

WOMAN 1: Yes, but back home it was easier ... anyway I have something to tell you ...

WOMAN 2: (*Starts backing out. Man 1 says "Oh Oh!"*) Not another proposition from a tall, handsome, fair-complexioned, Kayastha business executive, is it Mum? ... and who, it just happens does not have an immigrant visa.

MAN 1: Or a tall, handsome Jab Sikh from Jullundur, with several video stores. Hmm hmm, but the Sikhs are in the dog house these days.

WOMAN 1: Do not pretend to be ignorant Bani. These people have been approached by your brother. One of the brothers went to Doon School with Rajivji.

WOMAN 2: But I want to complete my Masters.

WOMAN 1: Masters! You've got to be kidding! What for ... These people are not going to wait.

WOMAN 2: So why don't you find another young virgin bride for them?

WOMAN 1: What's that? You know damn well that your father and brother have been negotiating this match for you. How can you dare say that we break this arrangement? Your brother feels the same way—if it's not going to help you any further, what is the point in going through a Masters, and once you do your Masters, you will want to do a Ph.D.

MAN 1: And once she does her Ph.D. ... it is too late ... she's out of the marriage market ... Indian men only study up to M.B.A.

(*Mother leaves in a huff.*)

WOMAN 2: Yes, I know my brother feels the same way as well! Professionally, he is a writer of progressive fiction. He writes of love and turmoil and revolution in unknown republics. He writes of the revolt of the working class intermingled with the sweet aroma of romance in a far away Middle East Sheikhdom. At home he is just a brother—an upholder of decadent male patriarchy.

MAN 1: He is just protecting the little sister.

(*Blackout.*)

SCENE 6

WOMAN 1: My husband is a writer ... What are you writing, husband?

MAN 2: (*Sitting on a cube, pretending to write.*) A story, wife.

WOMAN 1: What kind of a story is it, husband? (*Looking at the audience.*)

MAN 2: The story of a young woman during the days of the British Raj in India, wife.

Man 3: (*With yoyo.*) Ah yes! The raj is hot (*counts on his fingers*) Passage to India, Heat and Dust, Jewel in the Crown, Ghandi, Edwina and Nehru (*bites his tongue*).

WOMAN 1: What is the theme of the story, husband?

MAN 2: The woman goes to her husband's home with great desire and expectation in her heart. But her dream never comes true. He has taken a vow of perpetual celibacy. She quietly accepts everything that comes her way.

WOMAN 1: Why does her dream not come true?

MAN 2: Because her husband cannot understand her feelings.

MAN 3: He has very little of his own. There is numbness in his vitals.

WOMAN 1: Does her husband try to understand her feelings?

MAN 2: Why are you pestering me with all your dumb questions?

WOMAN 1: Tell me, does her husband try to understand her feelings?

MAN 2: You will not understand all this. You are a woman and this is literature.

MAN 3: Exactly, here is a fish, and there is a bicycle.

WOMAN 1: Why? Is not literature a reflection of life, of reality?

MAN 2: Look, quit hassling me, will you? Literature is simply . . . (*Lost in creative looks.*) Literature . . . an experiment with the unknown.

MAN 3: Bullshit that sells!

WOMAN 1: Alright I understand. Here drink your milk, I am leaving.

MAN 2: Shit! Now she's gonna be mad again . . . Don't get upset please . . . I promise you that we will make that trip to Europe this summer.

WOMAN 1: This is to say as tho' the destination of our emotions is a trip to Europe . . . And my husband has written a story about a woman's emotions. Here I am a woman, serving milk to my husband and revving my engines on the runway to an emotional high . . . (*She stops with glazed eyes . . . breaks into a smile and rushes over to her husband.*)

Hey! What do you say, why don't we go out and do something crazy tonight? Maybe rattle the old cage a little, you know. Shake down your tree a little. What do you say, eh, eh, eh (*She wraps herself around him. He gets nervous, drinks milk and splits.*)

MAN 3: This was another scene from the play. But the subject is not covered as yet. As usual we are hammering home the issues. As usual we are being political. After all anything that is not silly as shit is political. Anything that is not sheer mindless entertainment is political. Anything that takes sides is political. Anything that is not sold at Perrette's is political.

Freeze, blackout

SCENE 7

(*The three women appear again. When one speaks, the other two mime the scene.*)

WOMAN 2: Hi, I'm the sister. It's that time of my life when the rest of the family starts giving me those looks which mean "this house is not going to be yours for much longer now . . . " I must look "prospective". Even the women giggle and poke me with their fingers . . . "Guddi, it is time you got hitched!"

WOMAN 1: (*Chewing gum.*) She was born in Canada, she grew up in Canada, she went to CEGEP in Quebec. Her father is Vice-President of URANUS 2000–a Canadian holding company. Her father attends receptions at the Ritz with Yvon LaMarre, Pierre Des Marais, gives $20 tips to the doorman. He wears Giorgio Armani. Her mother wears a Banarasi brocade sari– There she is in the "Living" section of *The Gazette* giving mean shitty looks to the wife of the Pakistani ambassador. Her father travels all over the world.

WOMAN 2: Her mother worries. God only knows what he does during his jaunts. But he must be hot 'cos he's got the bucks coming.

WOMAN 1: Now the girl is in Concordia. She hangs out on the 4th floor. That's where all the kids hang out–make the connections, flirt a little, where the lockers are. She's got a guy she's been seeing for a while–they're pretty close–but so what! Her mother says she's got someone big set up for her.

WOMAN 2: Someone from Faridabad. He's got a cement factory, a bicycle factory, and an export brand dal-moth factory. And he chews pan. (*All three of them pretend to chew pan and scratch their groins, in a typically male fashion*.) He visits here often. Last time he was here there was a heated discussion in the living room on the exact percentage of extra-marital sex amongst Indians living in Montreal. Now who really did a survey of this? Anyway the point is that she's gotto go through this ritual. Her parents are gonna tie her to a chair in the living room and she will be discussed, examined, measured, and then she will do kathak.

WOMAN 1: Yes, all Indian girls growing up in Montreal must learn Kathak or Gharat Natyam. And they must do Kathak in front of their "prospective" in-laws. Her father who is the V.P. of URANUS 2000, a Canadian holding company, who attends receptions at the Ritz, and who pays $20 tips to the doorman, who travels all over the world, who wears Giorgia Armani suits will screw up his eyes and say, "Tradition must be maintained." (*All three say it together.*)

SCENE 8

(*Woman 1 sits down on the cube, chin in palm, disgusted looks. Man 1 comes in and announces "Prospective in-laws'." Man 1 goes out, brings in son. He holds a placard which says, "I am the man from Faridabad who owns cement, bicycle and dal-moth factories." Son has back problems. (Slumped, unsmart posture. He comes in, clears throat to attract attention. Daughter visibly disturbed by appearance.*)

WOMAN 2: (*To audience.*) I am her future mother-in-law. I have come to look at my future daughter-in-law.

MAN 1: She seems good looking.

MOTHER: You always like everything at first sight. Rush, rush, rush–always rushing around. In New York, you rushed around and bought a JVC cassette deck without even looking around. It has only one deck. Everybody in Faridabad is now buying Sony cassettes with two decks. Now everybody will say we came to New York and could not find a 2 cassette deck. All these charmars and low castes going to Kuwait are also coming home with 2 cassette decks. Always rush, rush, rush. And you, son of an engineer . . .

FATHER: Will you shut up and look at her closely. I think she is a shade darker than they told us. What do you think, Ricky (*son*)?

MOTHER: What can he think?–stand up straight–he will do exactly whatever I tell him to do. It is my kitchen she will inherent not his. Ha!

SON: Everytime you give your opinion, the girl decides she needs more time to think over it. This is our third trip to Canada . . .

MOTHER: You keep quiet. Nobody has asked you for your opinion. Don't open your mouth without permission. I haven't even seen her figure. You do aerobics my dear? All the girls are doing aerobics in Faridabad these days.

WOMAN 1: I do work out once in a while.

MOTHER: Work out? What work out? What does she mean by work out?? (*All go into consultation. After a while she goes back to the daughter.*)

I haven't checked her height as yet–

SON: She looks tall enough for me . . .

MOTHER: You shut up. Nobody asked you for your opinion.

FATHER: How can you tell when she is sitting?

SON: By now I am experienced. A always see them sitting. I always see you two arguing, I always am told to shut up. I always like them, I always am ready to marry, but you must always weigh them, you must always measure, you always argue and then you negotiate, and it always breaks down and on to the next one who is always sitting and I must always shut up until I get your permission and I never get your permission. (*He starts bawling.*)

WOMAN 1: And the hollowness of the whole thing . . .

MOTHER: Oh my God! She speaks!

(*The whole family cowers, while the young woman rises to stage front.*)

WOMAN 1: . . . is it right that here now in the midst of a quiet hilltop residence overlooking downtown Montreal, or in Flushing in New York for that matter, I will be examined, scrutinised, dehumanised and chastised because my parents believe in the upkeep of tradition while his parents believe in obtaining a thoroughly modern, English-speaking, "phoren" import to install in the already large acquisition list his family has. And for all this the poor boy and the poor girl must wait for the gentle nod from the parents that signifies permission. Permission is religion–permission is the last straw that our parents have. That's why they have given it religious sanctity.

(*The in-laws rush out. They say they will go to Florida where there are more "prospective in-laws."*)

MAN 1: (*Stops playing with his yoyo.*) When an Englishman has an emotion, his first instinct is to repress it. When an American has an emotion, his first instinct is to express it. When a Canadian has an emotion, his first instinct is to ask for a government subsidy, and earn the wrath of the American. And when an Indian has an emotion, he must look for permission.

(*Lights slowly fade out.*)

Rahul Varma and Stephen Orlov

Isolated Incident

(This play commemorates the first anniversary of Montreal's most tumultuous racial incident, the 1987 slaying of an unarmed black teenager, Anthony Griffin, by a Montreal police officer.)

Characters

Ustad	story teller
Jamura	Ustad's assistant
Matilda	waitress
police chief	
Savage	police officer
Hobly	police officer
Dexter Gibson	young black youth
Ravenol Roach	landlord
Balwinder Singh	a sikh tenant
moving-van driver	
police sergeant	
Mugger 1	
Mugger 2	
Rockhead Potter	judge
Giscard	prosecuting attorney
Grace	Dexter's mother
Joyce	Grace's friend

Alfred   Dexter's father
Five members of the chorus
Three police officers
uncle of Dexter Gibson

The play can be performed with 10 actors

Isolated Incident was first staged by Teesri Duniya in December of
1988 at McGill University's Morrice Hall theatre.

The set design is simple. The stage is divided into distinct zones.
Upstage right is a Dunkin Donut shop: a coffee machine sits on a
counter, behind a table and chairs, with a menu board tacked on the
back wall. Upstage left is a police station with a city police department
logo displayed. Papers, files, miniature Quebec and Canadian flags
and other paraphernalia clutter up a police chief's desk. Behind the
desk is the policemen's locker room with a dartboard tacked on a
locker. A complaints-report counter, with headphones, microphones
and radio is located at the entrance of the station area. Downstage
right with two square wooden blocks is a multiple location area vary-
ing from scene to scene. Downstage centre, the main playing area,
also varies as a metro station, park, apartment and courtroom. Props
around the rectangular wooden block in the middle of this area vary
to help identify the different locations.

For the most part cross-fades rather than blackouts will open and
end the scenes. Only the downstage centre light remains on
throughout the play. Jamura enters the stage.

JAMURA: Hi, my name is Jamura and my partner's name is Ustad.
Some people call us Ustad and Jamura and some call us Jamura and
Ustad. Others call us even worse names, but you choose what you
like. Ustad is my boss. But she's late. (*Looks towards the wings.*) She's
probably stuck at the airport. You know the problems with . . .

(*Some noise is heard, Jamura looks into the wings.*)

I guess she's here. Yes, it's her. So ladies and gentlemen, here I
present, the woman small in size but big in heart–my boss the one and
only, Ustad.

(*Ustad rushes in; she is out of breath.*)

USTAD: I made it. The customs, the immigration, the security and above all the traffic jam. But here I am, just in time.

(*Jamura checks his watch and smiles sarcastically.*)

JAMURA: Isn't she incredible folks–give her a big round of applause.

USTAD: (*Trying to gain control.*) Come off it Jamura. Let's get on with the show.

(*Jamura doesn't move. Ustad pulls him towards the rectangular block. Jamura sits down on the block and ustad takes control of the stage.*)

Well ladies and gentlemen, now for the show. (*To Jamura.*) Jamura, you will talk, hear and see only on my command. (*To the audience.*) Jamura will show you exotic magic directly imported from the land of diversity–India. He can fly without wings, walk barefoot on fire, eat raw nails, gulping them down with a mouth full of acid. But tonight, Jamura will do something that no human has ever done in Canada . . .

(*Ustad blindfolds Jamura with great flourish.*)

Anyone of you from the audience can come up to the stage and slap Jamura, who as you can see, is blindfolded, and he will describe the person. So how many of you would like to slap Jamura? Raise your hand.

(*Ustad looks into the audience, shouts from the wings. Few raised hands.*)

What an audience! I knew I could count on you tonight.

(*Ustad calls to the stage an actor from the audience.*)

Jamura, I'm sure you know what's coming.

JAMURA: Right.

(*Ustad slaps Jamura.*)

USTAD: Who was that?

JAMURA: You Ustad.

USTAD: I told you folks. Take a bow Jamura.

(*Jamura bows.*)

USTAD: Some other volunteers, please?

(*Man sits down. Police officer and handcuffed prisoner come on stage from the audience.*)

How about these two fine gentlemen. But I will give you a hint, Jamura. The first gentleman is a police officer and the second is his prisoner.

(*Cop slaps Jamura.*)

There. Now what colour is his shirt?

JAMURA: Blue.

USTAD: What colour are his pants?

JAMURA: Blue.

USTAD: What colour is his skin?

JAMURA: White. Come on Ustad, these questions are too easy.

USTAD: O.K. O.K. We'll go on to the second gentleman.

(*Prisoner handcuffed to cop slaps Jamura.*)

What colour is his underwear?

JAMURA: His underwear? You expect me to see through two layers of clothes?

USTAD: How about the colour of his T-shirt?

JAMURA: Be serious Ustad.

USTAD: I knew I should have stuck to the easy questions. Alright then, what's the colour of his skin?

JAMURA: Black, of course.

USTAD: Now isn't he incredible folks?

(*Ustad sends the two men back and whacks Jamura on the head.*)

How about an encore, Jamura?

(*Jamura rips off the band from his eyes.*)

USTAD: What do you think your doing?

JAMURA: I'm leaving.

USTAD: What?

JAMURA: You heard me. I'm quitting. First you blindfold me, then you slap me, then you slap me again. And for all that, you pay me peanuts. I can't take it any more. I quit. Yes, I quit.

USTAD: Are you out of your mind? What will you do?

JAMURA: Find another job.

USTAD: Huh! That's what you said the last time.

JAMURA: Well, my luck is about to change.

USTAD: Your luck is about to change? What can do anyway? Can you count?

JAMURA: No.

USTAD: That's a problem. If you did, you could be an accountant. Can you programme?

JAMURA: No.

USTAD: That's a problem. If you did, you could be a programmer. Can you type?

JAMURA: No.

USTAD: That's a problem. If you did you could be a typist. Can you kill?

JAMURA: No.

USTAD: That's also a problem. If you did you could be a police officer.

JAMURA: Hey, watch it Ustad. You don't mean that our clean-shaven officers in blue-white cars with red flashers, sipping coffee and nibbling on donuts are killers? New.

USTAD: (*Pathetic expression.*)

JAMURA: All I know is that they catch druggies, give parking tickets, escort politicians and protect scabs. But murder . . . New. They aren't above the law, they are the protectors of the law.

USTAD: Seeing is believing. (*Points to come along.*) Wait a moment Jamura. (*Steps towards audience.*) Ladies and Gentlemen, step right up and don't be shy. Come one and come all–as Teesri Duniya presents Isolated Incident.

Ustad and Jamura, dance off stage. Four police officers enter, chattering away. Chief rushes in.

CHIEF: Squad! I said, squad!

(*Squad quickly lines up at attention.*)

Are you listening?

SQUAD: Yes sir!

CHIEF: I didn't hear you.

SQUAD: (*Louder.*) Yes sir!

CHIEF: What does the "P" of police stand for?

SQUAD: "Pee" of police?

Puzzled expressions. One officer checks his groin.

CHIEF: P stands for polite, O for obedient, L for lenient, I for intelligent, C for confident, and E for efficient. Are you polite, obedient, lenient, intelligent, confident and efficient?

SQUAD: Yes sir.

CHIEF: Good. (*Chief points to an imaginary wall map.*) There are four crime sensitive areas in the city: A, B, C and D. Learn them well.

(*Inspects one officer after another, lecturing them on their duties.*)

You be a terror to smugglers, you be a cocaine drug buster. Be nice to all elders, don't give them the cold shoulder. Fine traffic violators, check all parking meters. Clean the city of hookers and pimps. Flush out all the city's whims. Learn it all, it's your duty. And above all, show mercy to all minorities.

SQUAD: (*Yawns.*)

CHIEF: Good, now you are ready to perform your duties. Dismissed!

(*Squad, bumping into each other, marches off stage. Lights fade-in on the donut shop. Matilda is pouring coffee as officers Savage and Hobly enter.*)

MATILDA: Good morning Officer Savage.

SAVAGE: How are you doing Matilda?

MATILDA: Fine Officer.

SAVAGE: Say, you are looking real pretty today.

MATILDA: (*Ignoring the compliment.*) What will it be today, the usual?

SAVAGE: No, let me see. Why don't you give me a chocolate glazed donut and a coffee. No, make it "le super."

MATILDA: Same for you Officer Hobly?

HOBLY: No, just a donut will be fine.

SAVAGE: So what's new in the neighbourhood, Matilda?

MATILDA: Oh, just a couple of crazy skinheads running loose.

HOBLY: Three officers have been attacked by those lunatics.

MATILDA: When are you guys going to do something about those—

SAVAGE: Ya, ya. Listen, we got a tip that black gangs are moving into this area. Have you seen any of them around?

MATILDA: No, for every 100 whites, maybe I see a couple of blacks.

SAVAGE: That's still too many. The Metro stations are packed with them. Why every time Hobly and I try and arrest them, they scoot like rabbits into the metro cars. Those darkies are always dancing up a storm, with those noisy ghetto-blasters. Christ, they drive me up the wall.

HOBLY: Dancing is in their blood.

MATILDA: Well, I never see them dancing in the metros. You must be dreaming.

SAVAGE: Ya, I'm dreaming alright . . . dreaming about flushing them out and making our metros civilized again.

MATILDA: So, it seems like an election is in sight, eh?

HOBLY: And how would you know?

MATILDA: Whenever the city gears up to clean up the metros, you can bet it's election time. I hear this year, Officer Savage will be leading the clean-up crew.

SAVAGE: You just love to play social worker, don't you Matilda?

MATILDA: And you, Officer Savage, just love to brag about crimes you've solved. Tell us officer, what crimes have you solved lately?

SAVAGE: Ah, lay off.

MATILDA: Come on officer. Don't be so humble.

HOBLY: Him humble?

(*Savage hesitates but Matilda and Hobly insist.*)

MATILDA: Why, you should have had your picture in the newspaper after you broke up that teenage gang stealing car radios.

SAVAGE: It wasn't a gang, just a couple of dumb, spoiled Westmount brats. But those black gangs roaming the metro stations. (*Shakes his head.*) Now there's a bunch of pimps, dope addicts and rapists for you. Forget about school -- the only thing they want to learn about is what's below their belly buttons. No wonder they have babies every year.

HOBLY: Thank God no reporters hang out here. A line like that could put your face on the front page of *The Gazette.*

SAVAGE: Hey, should I worry about a story or a gang of blacks taking over the metros?

MATILDA: What makes you think blacks are taking over the metros?

SAVAGE: Because you just don't know what's on their minds, that's why.

MATILDA: I'll tell you what's on their minds. It's fear that's on their minds. That's why you never see them alone.

SAVAGE: What are you talking about? Don't you know what colour most criminals are?

HOBLY: There you go again! Front page head-line, "racist cop."

MATILDA: (*To Hobly.*) I think you'd better tape his mouth.

(*She leans over the counter and takes Savage's coffee cup.*)

SAVAGE: (*Sarcastically.*) The way you two talk, you'd think I got something against blacks.

HOBLY: Really!

SAVAGE: I just ain't colour blind.

(*Matilda gestures in disbelief. Lights fade-out on the donut shop and fade-in on a metro station. Several people saunter in and line up, backs to the audience, as they wait for the subway train on the platform. Some read newspapers and others carry briefcases or shopping bags. Sound of a subway train is heard, as Savage and Hobly walk their beat inside the subway station. The sound of the subway train coming to a stop, cues people to mime boarding the subway car holding the support bar inside. A black youth struts by savage in rhythmic steps and nods. He is about to board the train, as Savage shouts rudely.)*

SAVAGE: Hey, Mister . . . you!

DEXTER: *(To the audience.)* No cop ever called me mister.

SAVAGE: Ya, you. Step over here.

DEXTER: What can I do for you officer?

SAVAGE: I'll ask the questions. You got a job or are you just bumming around?

DEXTER: I'm an accountant. I'm not working now, but I should be soon.

(Puts on sunglasses.)

SAVAGE: Are you drunk boy?

DEXTER: No, I ain't drunk . . . just fed-up . . . fed-up with you stopping me. If you got something to say officer, please hurry up because I don't have much time . . . got a million things to do.

SAVAGE: Take off those glasses . . . I said take off those glasses!

(Savage rips off the sunglasses, arm locks on Dexter and frisks him.)

What do you got in your pocket?

DEXTER: You got a warrant officer?

(People from inside the train, lean their bodies to exaggerate their stares at Savage and Dexter.)

SAVAGE: What's this? *(Pulls out pill vial.)* Are you on drugs?

(Savage gets rougher.)

DEXTER: Yes officer. I'm on drugs. I got my tooth pulled out and those are my pain killers.

(Dexter opens his mouth wide & shows his teeth. Savage gets more aggravated. As he is about to club Dexter, Hobly breaks them up.)

HOBLY: Let me see those. *(Inspects the vial.)* Negative Savage. Let him go.

SAVAGE: What! *(Savage releases Dexter.)*

DEXTER: *(Boarding the metro car.)* Hey officer, your shoe laces are untied.

(Savage charges at Dexter, but Hobly stops him, as Dexter saunters into the subway train.)

HOBLY: Savage, one day you're really going to get us into trouble.

(*Savage stares at Hobly. Sound of train leaving is heard. Officers exit, as Jamura and Ustad enter to the main playing area.*)

JAMURA: Ustad.

USTAD: Come out, it's safe.

JAMURA: I'm hungry.

USTAD: Why don't you go to Dunkin Donuts?

JAMURA: No, officer Savage is probably there.

USTAD: Then you should go to Balwinder Singh's place.

JAMURA: Who is he?

USTAD: A very kind-hearted man from India. Here in Canada he is called an Indo-Canadian. He wears a checkered jacket, goes to all Indian functions to catch up on the real estate prices and latest tax shelters and to talk about Rajivji's politics. One of those kind.

(*As Indian classical music plays, Ustad points towards Balwinder Singh, who enters wearing a turban. He walks downstage and greets the audience with a namaste and then sits on a chair with legs crossed as if meditating. Ustad and Jamura enjoy watching him go through the motions.*)

JAMURA: Does he know me?

USTAD: He doesn't have to know you. Just go in. He'll treat you well. He's Indian.

(*Ustad exits, smiling with the knowledge that she has set Jamura up for an experience. Jamura knocks at an imaginary door and walks in.*)

JAMURA: Assalam–Wale–kum Balwinder Singhji.

BALWINDER: Do I know you stranger?

JAMURA: I'm your neighbour.

BALWINDER: I have no neighbours.

JAMURA: I met you in the shopping centre.

BALWINDER: I don't go shopping.

JAMURA: I mean I'm an Indian.

BALWINDER: In that case, why don't you have some lunch.

JAMURA: If you insist.

BALWINDER: Vegetarian?

JAMURA: Naturally.

BALWINDER: Then sit down. I will go and cook some onion bhaji. (*Baldwinder exits.*)

JAMURA: (*To audience.*) Ustad, was right. This man is incredible. (*There is a knock at the door.*)

Mr Singh, somebody's at the door.

BALWINDER: (*Off stage.*) How so very strange. I wasn't expecting anybody else.

(*Jamura opens the door and before he can say anything, the landlord, Mr Ravenol Roach, barges in.*)

ROACH: Is this Mr Singh's house?

JAMURA: Yes, it is. And whom shall I say has intruded?

ROACH: I'm Mr Ravenol Roach, the landlord.

(*Balwinder enters.*)

BALWINDER: How so very nice to see you Mr Landlord. What can I do for you?

ROACH: I've come to inform you that your apartment is about to be bulldozed.

BALWINDER: So you finally decided to do something about the broken balcony.

ROACH: Not quite. We are converting your apartment into a luxury condo. I presume you aware of the eviction notice?

BALWINDER: Eviction notice?

ROACH: In the sealed envelope–my secretary mailed it to you, exactly 90 days ago. And since today is the 90th day notice, you'll be, how should I say, let go.

JAMURA: Let go?

ROACH: Quite right. The bulldozer is at the door now.

(*Roaring noise of a bulldozer is heard.*)

BALWINDER: I presume you are aware of the stay order I got from the court. Feast your eyes on that.

(*Balwinder hands him the court order.*)

ROACH: You think you can stop me with a little piece of paper? (*Throws court order on the floor.*) You think I'm a fool?

BALWINDER: Listen, I have not complained once in five and a half years about the loose windows, the clogged plumbing or anything else. And now you want throw me out?

ROACH: Are you calling me a cheat?

JAMURA: (*Aside.*) You got that right.

ROACH: No man ever calls me a cheat, and certainly not a coloured man. Why, I have never cheated one of your kind. Not one. I'm not one of those landlords who won't take in coloured people. But I have to evict you, just like the other 10 families I evicted yesterday. For years landlords like me have gone out of their way to beautify this city to what it is today. . . (*Motions outside.*) . . . what do you see?

(*Jamura looks outside.*)

JAMURA: A bulldozer.

ROACH: You better pack up fast.

JAMURA: And when will your exit take place?

ROACH: Who are you?

JAMURA: Nobody that you know.

ROACH: I don't suppose you live here.

JAMURA: No, I'm homeless, thanks to landlords like you. Now why don't you give us a break.

ROACH: I'm trying to give you a break, but you are too dumb to take it.

(*Jamura winds up to punch Roach in the groin, but stops half way through. Roach still jumps in the air, covers his groins and screams as if actually hit.*)

If you're not leaving the easy way, I can find other means. I know a thousand and one ways to get rid of a tenant . . . especially when they come between me and my project to revitalize downtown neighbour-hoods. (*To Jamura.*) As for you, I know you snuck up the fire escape and you don't have any right to be here. (*Jamura gives him the finger, Roach squeals and turns to Balwinder.*) I'm going to charge you with illegally keeping a tenant, or should I say, refugee.

(*Jamura gives him the finger again.*)

Now you did it!

(*Roach rushes upstage and picks up an imaginary phone and starts talking.*)

Hello police, if you come to 420 B, B for basement, Roach Lane right now, you can catch an alien. He came up the fire escape and won't leave my house . . . he is an illegal refugee . . . he has to be . . . I don't have a name and keep this call confidential.

(*He slams the imaginary phone and turns towards Jamura.*)

Well you asked for it.

(*Jamura gives him the finger again. Roach exits cursing them.*)

BALWINDER: I need some peace and quiet.

(*Lights fade-out on Balwinder, who sits with his back to the audience. As a beeper sound is heard, Savage and Hobly dash into a spot-lit area of the stage. They stand back to back, as if talking on walkie talkies.*)

SAVAGE: Officer Savage here, over.

HOBLY: Illegal alien named Jagminder Singh gone underground at home of Balwinder Singh, over.

SAVAGE: Got you. Some Singh is underground at some other Singh's, over.

HOBLY: Emergency . . . search . . . action . . . immediate. Over.

SAVAGE: Got you, over.

(*They hop on two wooden blocks, as if jumping into a police car. Hobly drives while Savage coaxes him to step on the gas.*)

SAVAGE: Hurry up, Hobly. Step on it.

HOBLY: That's as fast as I can go.

SAVAGE: I don't want that alien to get away.

(*Hobly jams on the breaks to a screeching sound, forcing both officers to lunge forward and run across the stage into the opposite wings. Lights cross-fade from the police car (blocks) to Balwinder who sits quietly with his back still to the audience. He hears banging at his door and turns around slowly.*)

BALWINDER: How so very strange. I wasn't expecting any more visitors.

SAVAGE: (*Off stage*) Open up. Police.

(*The officers break down the door, and barge in with pistols aimed. Somewhat surprised, Balwinder remains composed.*)

SAVAGE: Police . . . That's it for you alien.

(*Searches around.*)

We know you're here . . . come out with your hands up . . . or I'll level this place.

(*Balwinder looks up.*)

BALWINDER: Would someone tell me what's going on in my own house?

(*Savage, aiming his gun, moves in on Balwinder.*)

SAVAGE: This is your house?

BALWINDER: And you have broken in.

(*Balwinder rises and pushes the gun in another direction.*)

SAVAGE: Hey, watch it, we are the police. Now hand over the alien.

BALWINDER: Alien? From where, outer space?

SAVAGE: You talk pretty funny for your kind?

BALWINDER: You're not bad either, for your kind?

SAVAGE: I'm warning you hand over the alien.

BALWINDER: And I'm telling you, this is my family home, I work at me ... It's as though I was in a trance ... I could see the past in front of my eyes ... I saw Buddy Evans shot in 1978 ... I saw Albert Johnson shot in 1979 ... I saw Anthony Griffin shot in 1987 ... I saw J.J. Harper and Michael Wade Lawson shot in 1988 I saw *Dexter* ... and now *Dexter* is dead.

USTAD: The officer says he's sorry, but his gun went off accidentally. Who does he expect to convince with a line like that?

JAMURA: The all-white jury, that's who.

USTAD: At least the crown has charged him with manslaughter. Yea, everyone I know is talking about the trial.

JAMURA: That's what makes us different from whites.

USTAD: Wait a minute, Jamura. You can't blame all whites, for what one cop did.

JAMURA: Why not? You saw what happened! From the moment our people first set their eyes on white men, we have had to fight racism.

USTAD: Sure, but most people have changed their ways. And if you don't realize that, then you are no better than those cops in the brotherhood crying reverse racism.

JAMURA: Why should I be better? And better at what? Being shot in cold blood?

USTAD: (*Pointing towards the audience.*) Look over there. See, whites marching with blacks ... denouncing racism ... and look at all the TV cameras everywhere.

JAMURA: Oh, yes. Suddenly there is media attention. But where was it before? How many of us had to be shot dead to get all this media attention now?

USTAD: Jamura, give them credit for understanding our pain.

JAMURA: Understanding our pain? (*Points towards the audience.*) You can understand (*Glances back at Grace holding Dexter.*) this mother's pain?

(*Lights dim slightly, as the chorus lifts Dexter's stiffened body on their shoulders and circles the stage in a funeral march. The chorus puts down the body downstage centre, near the audience. Two members of the chorus mime shovelling dirt on the grave while others cross their chest. The body lies at that spot, throughout the remainder of the play. The chorus along with grace and Joyce exit.*

Lights fade-in on the police station as chief enters from the wings. He satisfied, he bends down, his rear end protruding up, grabs the legs and tries unsuccessfully to lift the heavy couch by himself. Jamura pretends to help Savage, by mocking Savages's motions and groans. Savage, puzzled, looks up squarely at Jamura.)

SAVAGE: Who the hell are you?

JAMURA: Nobody, just visiting.

(*Savage grabs Jamura.*)

SAVAGE: It's him, he's the alien.

(*Savage throws Jamura to the floor and starts roughing him up.*)

How long have you been underground here?

JAMURA: I don't live here.

SAVAGE: He confessed!

(*Savage continues to beat up Jamura.*)

BALWINDER: Why are you treating him like that. He's my guest.

HOBLY: Your guest, eh! Then, you'll be charged, too, for shielding an alien.

JAMURA: Wait a minute officer. I'm not an alien. I'm a human. My name is Jamura Singh.

HOBLY: Ya, Let's see some proof.

(*Savage lifts him high off the ground. Jamura frantically opens his wallet.*)

JAMURA: Look here. This is my driver's license, my social insurance card, my citizenship card.

(*The two officers after checking his identification cards shrug their shoulders.*)

HOBLY: Then who is Jagminder Singh?

BALWINDER: There are at least 500 Jagminder Singhs in Montreal. Which one do you want?

HOBLY: How am I supposed to know? You're all either Singhs or Patels. And you turban-heads all look alike. It ain't our fault if we got a bit mixed up.

JAMURA: Sure, it's not your fault. It's my fault that my bones are broken.

(*Savage is about to open his mouth but Hobly stops him.*)

HOBLY: Don't start in again Savage. This was another fumble.

(*The officers exit, shaking their heads. Jamura watches them go, as Balwinder looks after his bruises.*)

JAMURA: I must leave.

BALWINDER: Why so soon? Won't you take some dinner?

JAMURA: I would rather take some pain killers . . . and a trip to the Human Rights Commission.

(*They say goodbye and exit as the lights fade-in on the Dunkin Donuts shop. Matilda is tidying up the place. She turns on the radio and picks up the newspaper.*)

RADIO: Good morning. This is Terry Austin reporting for the nine o'clock news. Yet another complaint of police misconduct against ethnic minorities. A police officer assaulted a suspected alien, in what turned out to be a case of mistaken identity. The Human Rights Commission charges insensitivity on part of the police officer, while the officer is said to have blamed the victim. He says they all look alike, thus hard to distinguish from one another. In sports news, the Expos are set for game five of the World Series with the Boston Red Sox . . .

(*Matilda shuts off the radio in disgust, as Savage and Hobly enter.*)

MATILDA: Good morning officer. (*Neither officer answers.*) I said good morning, officers.

SAVAGE: Ya, Ya, Ya.

(*Matilda holds up the newspaper.*)

MATILDA: Well officers, you are the talk of the town today. Your adventure, or should I say misadventure, made the front page.

SAVAGE: Those bastards.

MATILDA: (*Reads the newspaper.*) Police assaulted wrong man. Racism charged. What's your chief got to say about all this?

SAVAGE: The chief! That son of a bitch. He wants to take me off street duty because of charges . . . charges . . . charges of . . .

HOBLY: Charges of racial misconduct against minorities. He called them Pakis and bashed them up.

SAVAGE: And the chief treats me like I'm already guilty . . . says I'm an embarrassment to the entire force.

MATILDA: At least he hasn't fired you.

SAVAGE: Fire me? He can't fire me. At least not on charges of racial misconduct. No sir! Not as long as brotherhood is around. Ah, those minorities are all the same. Something happens to one of them and they all cry racism. But they better wise up, or they'll end up back where they were born.

MATILDA: And where were you born officer?

SAVAGE: Me? Why in a hospital, of course.

MATILDA: (*Sarcastically.*) The man's got quite a sense of humour, doesn't he?

(*She hands them cups of coffee. Savage sips some coffee and laments.*)

SAVAGE: Christ Hobly, over 10 years on the force. I should have been superintendent by now.

HOBLY: Before you start dreaming promotion, the review board still has to clear you.

SAVAGE: Ah, there's more loonies on that review board then on the corner of St. Catherine and St. Laurent. And the city pays those big-name, thick-headed ass holes a hell of a lot of money to make recommendations, but they never do. And now they are calling me a racist! Hey, you are my partner, why don't they call you a racist, too?

HOBLY: Because I ain't a racist. I just hate everybody equally.

SAVAGE: This is getting on my nerves. I'm going to talk to Chief, right now.

(*Savage ignores Hobly and stands up to go as lights cross-fade from the donut shop to the police station. Chief appears at his desk. Savage straightens his tie and heads straight for the chief who glances up from his desk but then gets on with his work. Savage waits impatiently until the chief finally talks.*)

CHIEF: (*Without looking up.*) What's your problem Savage?

SAVAGE: Uh, no problem chief.

CHIEF: Nobody comes here without a problem.

SAVAGE: Chief, all these years I've been playing by the book and now they are talking of taking me off street duty. It ain't fair. I ought to be promoted.

CHIEF: Calm down. I want to ask you some serious questions. OK?

SAVAGE: I'll try.

CHIEF: What's this mean?

(*A line of officers marches on to the stage. They stomp their feet and stand in a row, holding a placard which reads "Brotherhood."*)

SAVAGE: (*Motioning towards the Brotherhood.*) I said I'll try.

CHIEF: Let me get your file (*Opens file.*) You have been charged five times for beating up minorities. You raided some Balwinder Singh's apartment to catch an alien Jagminder Singh, who turns out to be a citizen. You bashed him around.

SAVAGE: That ain't true.

CHIEF: It's not true?

SAVAGE: Well, he was a bit jumpy, so I used a bit of muscle and broke his arm . . . but the rest of him is fine.

CHIEF: The rest of him is fine?

SAVAGE: Well, he was slipping away, so I bruised his leg . . . but his other faculties are intact

CHIEF: His other faculties are intact?

SAVAGE: Well, he was giving smart answers, so I bashed his skull . . . but everything else is OK–really.

CHIEF: What about our image?

SAVAGE: What about it chief?

CHIEF: You brutalized a wrong man. How can I keep you on street duty with your record?

SAVAGE: Chief, I'm a man of the people. I have to work with people. You can't expect me to work behind some desk in the station.

(*Chief imitates Savage's lip movement.*)

CHIEF: You are unsuitable for street duty.

(*Brotherhood officers stomp their feet and shout "hupp" in unison.*)

(*To audience.*) Now don't overreact. (*To Savage.*) You threw racial slurs at him.

SAVAGE: Like what?

CHIEF: Like you called him a Paki.

SAVAGE: Chief, the guy is a Paki.

CHIEF: These days, people aren't going to put up with that kind of crap from a police officer.

SAVAGE: Chief, after 10 years of service, I know a Paki when I see one.

(*Chief imitates Savage's lip movement.*)

CHIEF: You are insensitive.

(*Brotherhood officers stomp feet and shout "hupp" in unison.*)

(*To himself*) No, I'm overreacting . . . think about morale of the force. (*To Savage*) The report says you just sit in the donut shop, when you are supposed to be improving relations with the ethnic community groups.

SAVAGE: It's a free country. A man has a right to hang out where he wants to.

CHIEF: A man has a duty to do his job.

SAVAGE: I wasn't on duty then. I wasn't, I wasn't.

CHIEF: You are lying. Savage, you have a strange habit of repeating yourself when you lie.

SAVAGE: I'm not lying. I'm not, I'm not.

CHIEF: You are not lying? You are not, you are not?

SAVAGE: Well, maybe I had a cup of coffee (*Pause.*) . . . and a donut . . . some soup and a sandwich and a bit of chit-chat. But that was all. No reason to call me a liar.

(*Chief imitates Savage's lip movement.*)

CHIEF: You are unworthy.

(*Before the brotherhood officers can stomp their feet, chief motions them to stop.*)

I'm not overreacting.

SAVAGE: So what's the verdict, Chief?

CHIEF: In order to keep you on the force, I can't promote you. But I won't demote you from street duty, either. That's a fair exchange. As for this complaint, we'll work on an out-of-court settlement. But this is the last time I listen to the stomping of the brotherhood. Enough of it!

SAVAGE: Right Chief.

CHIEF: Dismissed. I said, Dismissed!

(*Savage doesn't leave. Chief exits shaking his head. The brotherhood marches off stage. Savage checks around. Now alone, he jumps up suddenly, talks jive and then dances to soul song "midnight hour" music. The sergeant enters unnoticed and slowly claps his hands. Savage now embarrassed, exits quickly. The sergeant sits at the complaints desk and puts on the headphones. Moving van driver of an ethnic origin enters.*)

DRIVER: (*Looks around as sarge ignores him.*) Officer, I was in my moving van, when someone broke in and stole . . . (*Shouting.*) officer! (*Sarge looks up.*) Someone STOLE A BIKE.

SARGE: *Move a Kike?* No, no Outremont's on the other side of town.

DRIVER: That's not *what I said.*

SARGE: *Hampstead?* Oh, you are taking him to *Hampstead.* That's not far from here.

DRIVER: (*Shouting.*) This is the place (*Looks around.*) *To report a crime, eh?*

SARGE: *Transport a Hymie.* Right, that's what I thought you said.

DRIVER: Officer, I've been robbed!

SARGE: (*Takes off headphones.*) Why didn't you say so. What did the guy look like? (*Puts on headphones again.*)

DRIVER: Well, I'm think he was, eh . . .

(*Sergeant mimes typing the driver's report, but constantly interrupts.*)

SARGE: His height?

DRIVER: Well . . . he was about my height . . . say . . . 5 feet 9 inches . . . or may be . . .

SARGE: His weight?

DRIVER: About . . . one hundred and . . . sixty . . . no . . . seventy . . . or may be . . .

SARGE: (*Voice rising with impatience.*) His clothes?

DRIVER: He, uh, had a green jacket and . . . a . . . I don't know . . .

SERGE: (*Very loud.*) His race?

DRIVER: (*Blurts out.*) He was black.

SARGE: (*Types and shouts one letter at a time.*) b . . . l . . . a . . . c . . . k. OK, we'll get some officers on the case right away.

DRIVER: (*Walking away.*) So, you'll get the bike back, right?

(*Sergeant smiles and nods his head as the driver exits. Sergeant calls Savage and Hobly on a radio-mike.*

SAVAGE: (*Off stage with Hobly.*) Shit, why does this always happen just when we are about to take a break?

HOBLY: Swallow your donut and ask the Sergeant what he wants.

SAVAGE: Savage here, what's up Sarge?

SARGE: (*Transmits garbled message, ending with "black man."*)

SAVAGE: Hit me again Sarge, there's a bit of static on the line.

SARGE: (*Repeats garbled message ending with "black man."*)

SAVAGE: Got it Sarge. We'll cruise the neighbourhood. Over and out.

HOBLY: So where are we off to?

SAVAGE: The Sarge wants us to (*Speaking gibberish.*). . .and a black guy did it.

HOBLY: Oh!

(*Sergeant exits as the lights cross-fade from the police station to the main playing area. Two punks enter fighting over stolen wallet. They don't have a chance to split the ten dollar bill in the wallet. The wallet is flung in the air towards Dexter, who catches it as he enters.*)

MUGGER 1: (*To Dexter.*) You got change for a ten?

DEXTER: I only have a 20 dollar bill.

MUGGER 2: Ain't got anything smaller?

DEXTER: That's it. I don't carry any more than I can afford to loose.

(*Dexter throws back the wallet to them. The muggers are annoyed as they step away.*)

MUGGER 1: Like this park?

MUGGER 2: What?

MUGGER 1: I said, do you like this park?

MUGGER 2: (*Pointing to Dexter.*) Too many of them around.

MUGGER 1: Ya, I'd like to send them all back to the Black Sea.

MUGGER 2: Where?

MUGGER 1: The Black Sea. You know, off the coast of Africa.

MUGGER 2: Oh, ya sure. Well, this is as good a time as any to start.

(*Muggers approach Dexter.*)

MUGGER 1: You ain't got anything smaller than a 20, eh?

DEXTER: You got a problem?

MUGGER 2: You ain't from around here, are you black boy?

DEXTER: Mind your own business, punk.

MUGGER 1: Want to get hurt, nigger?

DEXTER: I wasn't planning on it

MUGGER 2: Bright set of teeth you got in that big mouth of yours.

DEXTER: Mind your own mouth, punk.

(*Mugger 2 throws a punch, but Dexter catches his arm and pushes him down.*)

I don't want to dirty my hands on you (*Spits on Mugger 2.*).

(*Mugger 1 kicks Dexter, who falls down groaning.*)

MUGGER 1: Nothing worse than an ordinary black boy.

(*Both muggers punch and kick Dexter. Dexter manages to get up, grab his umbrella and start swinging it. Both muggers run off stage. Dexter, screaming, runs after them. Officers Savage and Hobly cruise in on the wooden box car.*)

HOBLY: Neighbourhood seems pretty quiet.

(*Dexter walks backwards, looking into the wings. He is screaming furiously at the punks.*)

SAVAGE: (*Spotting dexter.*) Pull over. Looks like another drunken bad-breath. Let's check him out. (*Calls.*) Hey you, stay right there!

(*Eyes Dexter from head to toe.*) Haven't I seen you somewhere before? (*Dexter remains silent.*) What's your name?

DEXTER: Dexter.

SAVAGE: Dexter what?

DEXTER: Gibson. Dexter Gibson.

SAVAGE: So, what are you up to, Dexter?

DEXTER: Nothing.

SAVAGE: What do you mean nothing?

DEXTER: I was on my way home . . . and those punks attacked me.

HOBLY: I'll call the station and have them run a check on him.

(*Hobly returns to car (wooden block*) and mimes talking on walkie talkie.)

SAVAGE: (*To Hobly.*) Ya, you do that. (*To Dexter.*) Some punks attacked you, eh?

DEXTER: (*Pointing with his arm.*) Ya, they ran that way.

SAVAGE: Oh, (*Pointing with his arm.*) they ran off that way, did they?

DEXTER: That's what I said. Don't waste your time on me. Go after them.

(*Hobly returns.*)

HOBLY: Seems like the young man has been in trouble before.

(*Savage shoves Dexter.*)

SAVAGE: So, I'm wasting my time, eh?

(*Savage shoves Dexter towards the car.*)

DEXTER: (*Nervously.*) I was minding my own business . . . Not bothering anybody . . . I get hit and you treat me like I am guilty.

SAVAGE: (*Pushes him violently.*) We are taking you into the station for some questioning.

DEXTER: I haven't done anything wrong . . . I ain't going to the station. Besides my head is bleeding. I'd rather go to the hospital.

(*Turns to go.*)

SAVAGE: You take one more step, and you'll worry about a lot more than a bleeding head.

(*Dexter reaches for his umbrella.*)

Put that weapon down!

(*Savage draws and aims his gun.*)

DEXTER: An umbrella?

SAVAGE: Put it down!

DEXTER: (*Drops the umbrella.*) OK . . . O.K, now can I go? I've got to go to the hospital.

(*Begins to leave.*)

SAVAGE: Stop or I'll shoot–

DEXTER: I haven't done–
SAVAGE: Freeze or I'll–
DEXTER: Don't shoot ... don't shoot. ...
SAVAGE: Stop–
DEXTER: OK–
SAVAGE: Damn it–
HOBLY: Wait Sav–
(*Savage shoots, Dexter drops dead, his body falling backwards. Savage leans over Dexter.*)
SAVAGE: Oh shit! (*Picks up Dexter's limp wrist.*) Oh no, he's dying ... *Hobly!*
HOBLY: (*Rushing over and feels Dexter's pulse.*) He's dead.
SAVAGE: It was an accident.
HOBLY: (*Rises.*) I didn't think you would shoot him.
SAVAGE: (*Hysterically.*) You saw it Hobly, it was an accident.
(*Hobly remains silent.*)
The bastard wouldn't stop! I warned him! Right Hobly?
(*Hobly remains silent.*)
Christ, Hobly, you are my partner, say something ... say something!
HOBLY: Get hold of yourself, Savage ... everything will be alright.

(*Both leave slowly. Jamura, Ustad, Joyce, Dexter's uncle and the members of the chorus gather around the body as an ambulance siren is heard in the background. A loud voice is heard "someone's been killed." The members of the chorus whispering to each other, enter. Jamura is with the chorus.*)

CHORUS 1: What happened?
CHORUS 2: Someone's been shot in broad day light.
CHORUS 3: A black man.
CHORUS 4: I saw two officers here.
CHORUS 5: Emergency, ambulance, hurry up.
JAMURA: (*Shouts at the chorus.*) Call emergency. (*Dead silence.*) And take the dead man to the hospital, where the doctor will pronounce him dead.
(*Chorus freezes around Dexter's body. Joyce, a friend of Dexter's mother, recognizes the corpse.*)
JOYCE: Oh no. I've got to tell Grace. I've got to get to Grace.
(*Spotlight appears on downstage right where Grace sits reading a*

book. *Joyce rushes across the stage towards Grace, as lights dim on the chorus.*)

(*Out of breath.*) Grace! . . . Oh Grace!

GRACE: What's wrong Joyce?

JOYCE: (*Long pause.*) Grace, brace yourself. . . I just heard that . . .

GRACE: (*Takes off her glasses.*) What is it? What happened?

JOYCE: It's your son . . . its Dexter . . . . He's been shot by a police officer. He . . . he's dead.

GRACE: (*Hesitates, then speaks in a tone of denial.*) No . . . no it can't be Dexter. He just left home a few hours ago. It's someone else . . . it's got to be someone else.

(*Pause as the two stare at each other. Joyce looks towards Dexter's body, as Grace takes Joyce's arm and rises.*)

It can't be true.

(*Grace, clinging to Joyce, takes a few slow steps towards Dexter's body, then breaks from Joyce and runs to the body. The chorus stands aside as Grace cries out.*)

Dexter!

(*Grace kneels down, embraces Dexter's head on her lap and rocks back and forth.*)

Oh, Dexter, my poor boy . . . What have they done to you?

(*Grace begins to wail, calling out Dexter's name.*)

Why? Why have you been taken from me?

(*Turns her head towards the chorus.*)

What did he do? (*Chorus is silent.*) Who killed him?

(*Grace looks towards the audience.*)

Who killed my son? (*Pause.*) Who killed my son?

(*Grace freezes with Dexter in her arms. Jamura steps out from the crowd.*)

JAMURA: (*Bewildered, as if in a trance.*) Don't shoot . . . don't shoot (*Pulls his pockets inside out.*) . . . see I am not armed. . . All of you, you must not roll your shifty eyes, and you must pull your pockets out and walk like this (*Hands up.*) . . . it's dangerous . . . please listen to me. . . otherwise . . . .

(*Ustad steps out.*)

USTAD: Now you understand, Jamura.

JAMURA: (*Comes out of the trance.*) I don't know what came over the bank from 9 to 5, watch TV at night like all immigrants and I don't know any alien.

SAVAGE: If I find the bastard, your gonna pay.

BALWINDER: Put your gun down and search for yourself. If you don't mind I'm busy.

(*Balwinder sits down calmly and starts to read a book.*)

SAVAGE: Don't tell us how to do our job.

BALWINDER: You both are wasting your time and mine.

HOBLY: We have reliable information that an alien is underground here.

BALWINDER: I'm positive your information is incorrect.

SAVAGE: Don't give me that bull? I know you Pakis stick together like shit.

BALWINDER: You don't know shit from sauce, officer.

SAVAGE: I'll bust your . . .

(*Savage moves to grab him but Balwinder raises one arm prompting a dumbfounded Savage to step backwards.*)

HOBLY: Stop blabbering Savage and search every damn corner of this house. Look behind the curtains . . . everywhere.

(*Savage bends down on his knees out of sight behind the rectangular block. Household items are flung in all directions from behind the rectangular block. Jamura races after each item. To collect the things.*)

(*To Savage.*) Check in the kitchen.

(*Savage, frying pan in hand, rises from behind the block.*)

SAVAGE: Only pots and pans in here.

BALWINDER: A frying pan is definitely too small for a man to fit in.

(*Jamura finally gives up trying to collect all the items and sits down on the couch. The officers are too excited to notice him.*)

HOBLY: Don't be so cute. (*To Savage who changes direction for each suggestion.*) Check the closets, the drawers . . .

BALWINDER: . . . And the sink, the refrigerator, the toilet.

(*Savage continues to turn the place upside down.*)

You're making a mess here.

(*Savage yanks the book from Balwinder and fans its pages.*)

Nobody inside.

HOBLY: Negative Savage. Nothing to report. Check under the couch.

(*Savage, not realizing that Jamura may be the alleged alien, asks him politely to get off the couch. Savage tries to check under the couch. Not is nervous and frustrated, as he looks back towards the wings, where off-stage reporters relentlessly ask questions about the shooting. Camera bulbs flash, as his phone rings.*)

CHIEF: (*To the reporters in the wings.*) I said I'll make a statement in an hour and not before! (*Picks up telephone.*) Hello. No comment at this time! (*Slams down the receiver.*)

(*Calling.*) Savage . . . Savage, get in here!

SAVAGE: (*Savage enters.*) What is it Chief?

CHIEF: You know, Savage, even before this trial of yours, the whole force had become a punching bag for the Black community and the media. Now even the politicians are on our backs.

SAVAGE: Now you're speaking my lingo, Chief. Those political hacks will do anything for a few votes. All this crap we have been taking . . . makes me mad as hell, too.

CHIEF: (*Chief rises, ignores Savage and addresses the audience.*) They complained about no minority hiring . . . so we even hired a black *woman* on the force.

SAVAGE: Ya, that makes it, how many now? (*Counts using fingers.*) 5 . . . no 6 . . . 6 Black officers. And if you count up all the different coloured cops . . .

CHIEF: The term is visible minorities.

SAVAGE: Oh ya, visible minorities . . . well we have got 18 of them. That's not bad at all. There's only 4500 cops in the city. Christ, they can't expect integration overnight . . . it's not like we play baseball for a living, eh.

CHIEF: (*Towards the audience.*) They said we needed special visible minority *Sensitivity* sessions for the force, so now we have got those workshops.

SAVAGE: You said it chief. And almost half the guys show up, when they are supposed to. I think Hobly went to one of them workshops a while back . . . or maybe it was someone else. Sgt. Tremblay for sure. I distinctly remember him telling me he slept through it. Ya, he went.

CHIEF: (*Towards the audience.*) But these beatings of minorities. They have just got to stop. Think of our image. We can't afford that.

SAVAGE: I totally agree, chief. We can't afford all those out-of-court settlements. Seems like every time one of those dancing darkies trips and falls trying to avoid arrest, he ends up with a few grand in his pocket.

CHIEF: (*Turns towards Savage.*) Out-of-court settlements?

SAVAGE: Keep that up and the city would go broke in no time . . . might even have to do something drastic . . . like raisin' property taxes. Then we'd really have some riots on our hands, eh. See what problems these visible minorities cause.

CHIEF: What are you talking about, Savage? What I'm trying to get to is that we . . . I mean you . . . are in a lot of trouble.

SAVAGE: But chief, the way you talk . . . you know it was an accident. The boy could have been white, too.

CHIEF: Well, you are damn lucky he wasn't. Otherwise you would have been in jail today. Listen Savage, if I were you, I would keep out of sight for a while.

SAVAGE: Why should I hide out?

CHIEF: I wasn't suggesting that. I meant you should go on a long vacation, until the trial either clears you or convicts you. Dismissed!

(*Savage doesn't move.*)

CHIEF: (*Exits mumbling.*) Christ Savage, you are becoming more and more of a burden for the police force every day.

(*Savage staggers backwards into the police brotherhood locker room. Two officers enter.*)

OFFICER 1: Hey, You are looking good Savage.

(*Savage hunches over with a depressed look, as the two officers talk off to the side. A third officer enters.*)

OFFICER 2: Welcome to the police brotherhood. (*Places his arm on Savage's shoulder.*) Men, a round of applause for our buddy Savage. Here's to a restful vacation.

(*The three officers start singing "For he's a jolly good fellow," as Savage rises slowly.*)

Christ Savage, you look like you really need this vacation.

SAVAGE: (*Blinking.*) My wife tells me I'm looking pale these days. What do you think? Is my complexion a bit yellow?

OFFICER 2: No you don't look like a chink. (*Rubs his finger on Savage's face, then looks at it*) You are a white as ever, don't worry. In fact you have put on a few pounds.

SAVAGE: Never weighed this much in my whole life. My wife cooks good meals. You know, I haven't been sleeping too well. But I tell you, if it wasn't for you guys in the brotherhood, I don't know what I would do. Even if a man knows he's going to beat the charges in court, all this trial talk still gets you down.

OFFICER 1: Cheer up Savage. Tell me the last time a cop was convicted of murder, eh? Besides, no coloureds are going to be on the jury.

OFFICER 3: Probably should be though.

OFFICER 1: What did you say?

OFFICER 3: It's only fair.

OFFICER 1: You actually believe that?

OFFICER 3: And so would you, if you had a bit of common sense. Nearly one out of every five people in this country isn't white, or hadn't you noticed.

OFFICER 2: Hallelujah. An outspoken radical in our ranks.

OFFICER 1: Don't you worry SAVAGE. You know the brotherhood supports you.

OFFICER 2: You bet. Men, it's about time we showed Savage where the brotherhood stands. Let's take a vote. All those who support Savage, (*Pause.*) sit down.

(*All four officers are already seated. Office 3 slowly stands up and walks out. Others laugh.*)

OFFICER 2: (*Rises and points in Officer 3's direction.*) He's worse than these blackies.

(*Picks up a photo of a black man and holds it out for the audience to see.*) I don't know what all the fuss is about?

(*Officer 2 pins the photo of the black man onto a dart board, steps back and shoots darts at the picture.*)

You'd think these black welfare bums would have something better to do than bitch about us all the time. Let's face it, the guy could have been shot by another black. (*Shoots another dart.*) They do it all the time. Would anybody be screaming racism then?

OFFICER 1: Racism my ass! It's all politics. Savage is just a scapegoat. (*Savage nods his head in agreement.*) He's taking a bum rap for the whole force.

OFFICER 2: Ya, and what the hell is going to happen to law and order in this city, if a cop can't do his job? As far as I'm concerned, we are getting along just fine with all the other minorities.

(*Lights fade-out on the police station. Three chorus members enter and stand near Dexter's body. They talk facing the audience directly.*)

255

CHORUS 1: "It was more than hurtful–it was shocking," says a black police officer, who testified at the inquiry. Shortly after the shooting death of a black youth, a white policeman photocopied a picture of a black man for target practice. The black officer who testified is apparently being ostracized by fellow officers. He is now on sick leave.

CHORUS 2: A dramatic chapter in the history of police race relations has ended with Toronto police paying a large out-of-court settlement to the widow of a Jamaican immigrant slain by the police in 1979.

CHORUS 3: A black woman, who refused to change out of her night gown in front of two police officers about to arrest her without a warrant, had an assault charge dismissed, because the police officers didn't let her call a lawyer, which is guaranteed by the Charter of Rights.

(The chorus gathers downstage right by the wooden blocks which now represents the visitor's gallery. They are joined by Grace, Alfred and Joyce. Spotlight rises on Dexter's corpse as a clerk enters. As the clerk speaks, he rearranges the stage to represent a courtroom by setting up chairs and converting the wooden block into a judge's table and a witness box. The clerk puts a chair downstage left . . .)

CLERK: *(Facing the audience.)* Would the prosecuting attorney, please step forward?

(Attorney Giscard enters. He bows to the audience and sits down on the chair downstage left. The clerk sets three more chairs just to the side of the rectangular wooden block which is the judge's table.)

Members of the jury, please step forward.

(Three jurors enter wearing white masks. They bow to the audience and sit down on the three chairs facing the audience. The clerk spreads a table cloth on the rectangular block which displays the logo of the institution of justice. He puts a stamp, a few files, a pen-holder, a paper weight and a judge's gavel on the desk to give it the appearance of a judge's desk. He stands with a chair behind it.)

All rise for the Right Honourable Justice Rockhead Potter.

(Everybody rises. Judge Potter enters taking long cartoonish steps and dragging his feet. He pauses to stare, face to face from one person to the next. He steps over Dexter's corpse without taking a note of it and finally reaches his desk. The clerk pulls out the chair for him and he sits

down.)

Please be seated.

(*Everyone sits down. The clerk brings in the front panel of a witness box and places it on an angle between the judge's table and the prosecutor's chair.*)

Would the accused step into the witness box.

(*Savage enters and steps into witness box. There are whispers in the visitor's gallery. Judge Potter motions them to stop. The clerk walks up to witness and raises the Bible to Savage.*)

Put your right hand on the Bible. Do you swear to tell the truth, the whole truth, and nothing but truth, so help you God?

SAVAGE: (*Places his left, then his right hand on the Bible.*) I do.

(*Now the clerk himself sits to the sides on the back-rest of a chair and mimes typing the proceedings.*)

POTTER: How do you plead, Officer Savage?

SAVAGE: Not guilty.

(*In the visitors gallery, Dexter's family shouts in disbelief.*)

POTTER: You may proceed Mr Giscard.

GISCARD: Thank you Your Honour.

(*Approaches the witness box.*)

(*To Savage.*) Officer Savage, on the date in question, while on duty, the trigger of your gun went off. Is that correct?

SAVAGE: No you've got it all backwards. The trigger hit my finger. My finger did not hit the trigger.

(*Holds his twitching finger in the air.*)

POTTER: (*To the jury.*) Jury, point to be noted.

GISCARD: However the shot was fired.

SAVAGE: Well I didn't know my gun was loaded.

GISCARD: But guns only work when they are loaded.

SAVAGE: But I didn't know the guy would die.

POTTER: (*To the jury.*) Jury, point to be noted.

GISCARD: However bullets do kill, and your bullet killed him.

SAVAGE: But I wanted him to stop.

GISCARD: That's precisely the point. He did stop! After all, you did not shoot him in the back, did you?

SAVAGE: That's just coincidental.

GISCARD: Officer Savage, is it also coincidental that in 1984, you were found responsible for using excessive force while arresting another black man?

POTTER: Out of order. That's past history, not relevant in this trial. The case must be tried as an *isolated incident.*

SAVAGE: *(To the jury.)* Jury, point to be noted.

GISCARD: Did you think the man was armed and dangerous?

SAVAGE: Of course not, that's why I didn't handcuff him.

GISCARD: But you shot him dead.

SAVAGE: *(Jumps up.)* It was an accident! *(Sits down.)*

POTTER: *(To the jury.)* Jury–

JUROR 1: *(Cuts the judge off.)* Yes, we know Judge,

ALL JURORS: Point to be noted.

GISCARD: Officer Savage, how could you possibly call this an accident?

SAVAGE: Well, it was an accident, just like a bus driver running a red light and killing a pedestrian.

POTTER: *(Stroking his beard, in deep thoughts.)* Oh I see. So it was an accident just like a bus driver running a red light and killing a pedestrian.

(Savage nods in agreement.)

Proceed with your final statement, Officer Savage.

SAVAGE: Thank you, Your Honour. Members of the Jury, I've been a loyal public servant for over 10 years on the force. I have testified that the trigger hit my finger and not vice versa. I stopped the black man with shifty eyes da . . . da . . . da . . . black umbrella da . . . da . . . da . . . warned him not to move da . . . da . . . da . . . pure accident. da . . . da . . . da . . . I rest my case Your Honour.

POTTER: I advise the jury that you must convict the accused if you believe beyond a shadow of a doubt that the accused showed criminal intent–that means he wanted to commit a racist murder–and not otherwise.

(Jurors nod their heads in unison and twiddle their fingers.)

Take as long as you need to deliberate. *(Potter continues.)* Well, have you reached the verdict yet?

FOREMAN: Yes your honour, we have.

POTTER: Will the accused please rise.

(Savage rises slowly.)

(To jury.) Do you find the defendant guilty or not guilty?

FOREMAN: Not guilty your honour.

(Savage sighs loudly with relief. Cacophony breaks out in the visitor's gallery as people whisper in confusion. Dexter's mother, Grace, sobs un-

controllably.)
    POTTER: Order order . . . please.
    (*All silent.*)
    I must first congratulate Office Savage for presenting such a con-
cise and logical defense and for making us aware that bullets kill even
though fired accidentally. And secondly a warning to people of this
country to be cautious of black men carrying umbrellas, I mean carrying black umbrellas . . . clerk, strike that from the record. And the
jury deserves full credit for reaffirming the legal tradition of judging
such a case as an isolated incident. Court is . . . one last point. To the
family of the deceased, I extend my sympathy. Court is adjourned.

    (*There is chaos in the visitor's gallery. Judge Potter exits dragging his
feet in a cartoonish manner, stepping over Dexter's corpse without a
notice. The jury exits upstage lights out. A spot appears downstage left
on a TV reporter. He broadcasts his report with Savage, next to him
smoking a cigarette.*)

    REPORTER: In the follow up to the controversial court acquittal of
a police officer charged in the shooting of an unarmed black teenager,
the police enquiry into the incident now finds the officer negligent and
recommends he be dismissed. Racism is ruled out as a factor in the
shooting. The officer now claims . . .
    (*Extends the microphone to Savage.*)
    SAVAGE: . . . I am as much a victim as Dexter Gibson.
    (*Savage flicks his cigarette to the ground and exits with the reporter.
Spot light fades-out on them and fades-in on Dexter's family, downstage
right.*)

    GRACE: (*Stands angrily.*) What is he talking about? Saying he's as
much a victim as Dexter. My son is dead. (*Sits down sobbing.*) Where
is my son?
    JOYCE: Grace, come here, Honey. You just have yourself a good
cry.
    ALFRED: You know, some things just haven't changed all that
much. My Grandpa used to tell me stories about the Klan. And Uncle
Marcus, he bussed down to Washington to march with Martin Luther
King, god rest his soul. Now Dexter's gone, and they are trying to tell
us that the anguish of a white man somehow equals the death of a

black man.

UNCLE: You mean the "accidental" death of a black man.

ALFRED: Ya, "accidental." Can you imagine that the cop still claims his gun went off by itself?

UNCLE: What's worse is that a lot of people believe him.

JOYCE: Well, it doesn't take any court to convince folks I know that when an unarmed kid is shot you call it murder. Enough of this talk. Don't you see how upset Grace is?

GRACE: No, it's alright. (*Regaining her composure.*) I've cried too many tears. No amount of crying is going to bring Dexter back. All I wish is that something good would come out of his death, not only for blacks but for everyone. I want to see justice done, so that everybody, even that officer, realizes that what happened was wrong. We are not going to turn the clocks back to the past. There is too much to be done now. (*To the audience.*) What I'm saying to each and everyone of you tonight is that people are going to remember the day my son was killed. They are going to remember it for a long time to come.

(*Curtain.*)

Biographical Notes

Himani Bannerji was born in 1942 in Bangladesh, which was then part of preindependence India; she was educated and taught in Calcutta. She came to Canada in 1969, and now teaches social science at York University, Toronto. Her poetry, short stories, critical articles, and film and theatre reviews have appeared in the *Toronto South Asian Review*; *Fuse*; *Fireweed: A Feminist Journal*; *Asianadian*; *Parallelogram*; and *Tiger Lily*. Bannerji's scholarly essay "But Who Speaks for Us? Experience and Agency in Conventional Feminist Paradigms" was included in *Unsettling Relations: The University as a Site of Feminist Struggles*. She has two collections of poetry *A Separate Sky* (1982) and *doing time* (1986). The poems in the present volume are from these collections. A broader selection of her poetry appears in *Shakti's Words: An Anthology of South Asian Canadian Women's Poetry* (TSAR, 1990).

Krisantha Sri Bhaggiyadatta is a poet who lives in Toronto. His publications include *Domestic Bliss* (1982) and *The Only Minority is the Bourgeoisie* (1985). His poems have also appeared in the *Toronto South Asian Review*. The poems here are from *The Only Minority is the Bourgeoisie*.

Rienzi Crusz was born in Sri Lanka (Ceylon) and came to Canada in 1965. He was educated at the Universities of Ceylon, London (England), Toronto, and Waterloo, and is now Reference and Collections Librarian at the University of Waterloo. Crusz's poems have appeared in most major Canadian literary magazines and journals. His books include *Flesh and Thorn* (1974), *Elephant and Ice* (1980), *Singing Against the Wind* (1985), *A Time for Loving* (TSAR, 1986), *Still Close to the Raven* (TSAR, 1989), and *The Rain Doesn't Know Me Any More* (TSAR, 1992). The poems here are from *Singing Against the Wind*; *A Time for Loving*; *Still Close to the Raven*; and *The Rain Doesn't Know Me Any More*.

Cyril Dabydeen was born in Guyana and has lived in Canada for more than twenty years. He completed his formal education at Queen's University with postgraduate degrees in English and in Public Administration. He is a race relations practitioner and an educator. For many years he has taught at Algonquin College, and now teaches Creative Writing (fiction) at the University of Ottawa. His work has appeared in periodicals and anthologies in Canada, the UK, Europe, the Caribbean, India, Malaysia, and New Zealand. He has published six collections of poetry, two volumes of short stories, and two novels. He has edited two anthologies, *A Shapely Fire: Changing the Literary Landscape* (1986) and *Another Way to Dance* (1990). Two books are scheduled for publication in 1992, *Jogging in Havana* and *Discussing Columbus*. Dabydeen was the poet laureate of Ottawa from 1984 to 1987. The poems here are from the *Toronto South Asian Review* 5,1 (Summer 1986), *Islands Lovelier Than a Vision* (1986) and *Coastland: New and Selected Poems* (1989).

Ramabai Espinet was born in Trinidad and has lived in Canada for many years. She lives in Toronto and writes poetry, fiction and cultural commentary. Her work has appeared in several anthologies, including *Jahaji Bhai: An Anthology of Indo Caribbean Literature* (TSAR, 1988). She is the editor of *Creation Fire: An Anthology of Caribbean Women's Poetry*, and some of her poems are scheduled to appear in the second edition of *Shakti's Words: An Anthology of South Asian Canadian Women's Poetry*. She is a member of the editorial board of the South Asian cultural quarterly *Rungh*.

Lakshmi Gill was born in 1943. She was educated at Western Washington University, University of British Columbia, and Mount Allison University. Lakshmi Gill and Dorothy Livesay were the first two women to become members of the League of Canadian Poets.

Gill published her first poem when she was fourteen and since then has published several volumes of poetry, including: *During Rain, I Plant Chrysanthemums* (1966), *Mind-Walls* (1970), *First Clearing* (1972), and *Novena to St Jude Thaddeus* (1979). Gill now resides in British Columbia. The poems here are all from *Novena to St Jude Thaddeus*. A different selection of her work appears in *Shakti's Words: An Anthology of South Asian Canadian Women's Poetry* (TSAR, 1990).

Arnold Itwaru was born in Guyana and has lived in Toronto since 1969. He is the author of three books of poetry, *Shattered Songs* (1982), *The Sacred Presence* (1985), and most recently, *Body Rites: Beyond the Darkening* (TSAR, 1991); one novel, *Shanti* (1988); a work of literary criticism, *The Invention of Canada: Literary Text and the Immigrant Imaginary* (TSAR, 1990); and two scholarly books, *Mass Communication and Mass Deception* and *Critiques of Power*. The poems here are from *Body Rites*. The opening chapter from *Shanti* appears in the Fiction section of this anthology.

Surjeet Kalsey was born in India, came to Canada in 1974, and now lives in British Columbia. She received a master's degree in English and Punjabi Literature from Punjab University, Chandigarh and a master's in creative writing from the University of British Columbia. Kalsey edited the Punjabi issue of *Contemporary Literature in Translation* (1977) and has edited and translated an anthology of poetry, *Modern Punjabi Poetry*. As well, she is an associate editor of the *Toronto South Asian Review*. Her poems and short stories have appeared in many literary journals and magazines. She has written and directed three plays on violence against women and currently works as a counsellor for battered women. Kalsey has published one book of poetry in Punjabi, *Paunan Nal Guftagoo* (1979) and two in English, *Speaking to the Winds* (1982) and *Foot Prints of Silence* (1988). A book of short stories and a fourth book of poetry are scheduled for publication. The poems here are all from *Foot Prints of Silence*. *Shakti's Words: An Anthology of South Asian Canadian Women's Poetry* (TSAR, 1990) offers a different selection of her work.

Suniti Namjoshi was born in Bombay and in 1969 immigrated to

Canada in order to study at McGill University in Montreal. In 1972, she joined the Department of English, the University of Toronto, and resigned in 1988. Namjoshi now lives in Devon, England and earns her living as a writer. Her publications include *Feminist Fables* (1981; rpt. 1984), *The Authentic Lie* (1982), *From the Bedside Book of Nightmares* (1984), *The Conversations of Cow* (1985), *Aditi and the One-Eyed Monkey* (1986), *The Blue Donkey Fables* (1988), *Because of India: Selected Poems and Fables* (1989), and *The Mothers of Maya Diip* (1989). As well, Namjoshi and Gillian Hanscombe co-authored *Flesh and Paper* (1986). The poems and fables here are from *Feminist Fables* and *The Blue Donkey Fables*. *Shakti's Words: An Anthology of South Asian Canadian Women's Poetry* (TSAR, 1990) includes a different selection of her work.

Uma Parameswaran was born in Madras, India. As the recipient of a Smith-Mundt Fulbright Fellowship, she came to the United States to study English Literature and in 1966 immigrated to Canada. She teaches at the University of Winnipeg; her special interests are Commonwealth Literature, Indo-English Literature, and Creative Writing. A writer of poetry, short fiction, drama, and literary criticism, she has published several books: *Cyclic Hope Cyclic Pain* (1974), *A Study of Representative Indo-English Novelists* (1976), *The Perforated Sheet: Essays on Salman Rushdie's Art* (1988), *Trishanku* (TSAR, 1988), and *The Door I Shut Behind Me* (1990). Uma Parameswaran has contributed to the community and cultural life of Winnipeg: she has organized instruction in classical Indian dance; founded, produced and hosted a weekly television show PALI (Performing Arts and Literature of India); and written plays for the local stage. Three of the poems here are from *Trishanku*; the other two have not yet been published. *Shakti's Words: An Anthology of South Asian Canadian Women's Poetry* (TSAR, 1990) includes a different selection of her poetry. Her short story "How We Won the Olympic Gold," published in the *Toronto South Asian Review* 8, 1 (Summer 1989), appears in the Fiction section of this anthology.

Ajmer Rode, a poet and playwright, was born in India and immigrated to Canada in 1966. He has lived most of the past twenty years on the West Coast, writing in English and in Punjabi. His books include *Blue*

Meditations (1985); *Surti*; *Komagata Maru*; *Dooja Pasa*; and *Poems at My Doorstep* (1990). His work has appeared in literary magazines in India, Great Britain, and Canada; his poems are included in several Punjabi anthologies. Rode has produced and directed a number of plays in Vancouver and is a founding member of several Indo-Canadian literary and performing arts associations. The poems here are from *Blue Meditations* and from his most recent book *Poems at My Doorstep*.

Suwanda Sugunasiri was born in Sri Lanka. The recipient of a Fulbright Fellowship, he studied in the United States before immigrating to Canada where he completed his graduate studies. He has taught at the University of Sri Lanka, the Ontario Institute for Studies in Education, and the University of Toronto. Sugunasiri is a teacher, a scholar, a critic, a journalist, and a poet. His published works include "Sri Lankan Canadian Poets: the Bourgeoisie that Fled the Revolution," *Canadian Literature* (Spring 1992); *In Search of Meaning: The Literature of Canadians of South Asian Origin* (1989); *A Bibliography of South Asian Canadian Literature in English, Punjabi, and Gujerati* (1987); and *The Faces of Galle Face Green*, a forthcoming collection of his poems.

Asoka Weerasinghe was born in Sri Lanka and lived in England for 12 years before coming to Canada in 1968 and completing his formal education with an M Sc in Palaeontology from Memorial University in Newfoundland. He has published his poems in journals and magazines in England, Wales, Sri Lanka, Canada and the US. His published books include *Lotus and Other Poems* (1968), *Another Good-bye for Alfie* (1969), *Spring Quartet* (1972), *Poems for Jeannie* (1976), *Poems in November* (1978), *Hot Tea and Cinnamon Buns* (1980) and *Home Again Lanka* (1981). Weerasinghe has won several awards for his poetry, among them the Welsh University Eisteddfod Poetry Award and the Government of Newfoundland and Labrador's Arts and Letters Gold Medal for Poetry. He now lives and works in Ottawa. The poems here are from *Spring Quartet*; *Home Again Lanka*; and the *Toronto South Asian Review* (Fall, 1985).

DRAMATISTS

Rana Bose was born in Calcutta and immigrated to North America to study chemical engineering. He works as an engineer and executive for a Canadian aerospace company. Bose has written articles, film and theatre reviews, short stories, and poems, but improvisational-experimental theatre is his passion. He directs and writes plays, designs lighting and sets, acts in and produces plays, and composes music for the stage. He is a founding member of *Montreal Serai*, a crosscultural magazine of literature and music, and of Le Groupe Culturel Montreal Serai, an intercultural theatre troupe. His plays include *Baba Jacques Dass and Turmoil at Cote-des-Neiges Cemetery*; *On the Double*; *Who to Please*; *Nobody Gets Laid*; and *The Death of Abbie Hoffman*.

Rahul Varma and Stephen Orlov:

Rahul Varma is a founding member and the artistic director of Teesri Duniya, a multicultural theatre group based in Montreal. His earliest plays were written in Hindustani and his theatrical style borrows from Nautanki, a theatrical form popular in the villages of North India. His work is political and contemporary. *Equal wages* is a satirical comedy about the inequality of women's wages; *Land Where the Trees Talk* considers the question of native lands rights amidst growing environmental awareness; *Simply a Crime*, his work in progress, combats violence against women. *Isolated Incident*, written with Stephen Orlov, won several awards at the 1988 Quebec Drama Festival.

Stephen Orlov is a playwright and the president of Playwrights' Workshop Montreal, Canada's major centre for the development of new plays. His work includes *Salaam-Shalom*, a serio-comic play which peers over the ghetto walls dividing Jews and Palestinians in Canada and *Isolated Incident*. Orlov is an actor who has played numerous lead roles in Montreal theatre, among them his critically acclaimed performance as Officer Savage in Teesri Duniya's production of *Isolated Incident*.

FICTION WRITERS

Ven Begamudré was born in South India and moved to Canada when he was six. He has also lived on the island of Mauritius and in the United States. He studied public administration in Ottawa and in Paris. His first book, the novella *Sacrifices,* was published by The Porcupine's Quill in 1986. He received the Okanagan Short Story Award for summer 1989 and the 1990 City of Regina Writing Award. *A Planet of Eccentrics* was published in 1990, and was followed in 1991 by *Out of Place* (Coteau), an anthology edited by Begamudré and Judith Krause. His upcoming publications include a novel, *Van de Graaff Days* (Oolichan Books) and an anthology of stories by Regina writers for Fifth House Publishers. "The Evil Eye" is from his collection of short stories, *A Planet of Eccentrics.*

Neil Bissoondath was born in Trinidad in 1955. He came to Toronto in 1973 to attend York University, where he majored in French and began his writing career. After graduation, Bissoondath taught English and French, and continued his work as a writer. Bissoondath has been a full time writer since 1985. *Digging Up the Mountains*, a collection of short stories, was published in 1985, followed by a novel, *A Casual Brutality* (1988) and then a second collection of short stories *On the Eve Of Uncertain Tomorrows* (1990). In 1986 Bissoondath was awarded the McClelland and Stewart fiction award for his story "Dancing," which appears here and is from his first book, *Digging Up the Mountains.*

Ved Devajee was a pseudonym for Réshard Gool, who was born in London in 1931 and came to Canada in the mid-sixties to pursue graduate studies in political science. He taught at the University of the West Indies in Jamaica and at several Canadian universities, including the University of Prince Edward Island. Réshard Gool died in 1989. He was a novelist, poet, critic, scholar, journalist, editor, and film script researcher. During the seventies he founded, owned, and operated Square Deal Press in Charlottetown and in cooperation with his wife, the artist Hilda Woolnough, established, in Charlottetown, a craft cooperative and alternative gallery, "Gallery on Demand." His publications include *In Medusa's Eye* (poetry, 1972),

Price (novel, 1973), which was reissued with the author's changes in 1989 as *Cape Town Coolie* (TSAR), and *The Nemesis Casket* (1979) published under the pseudonym Ved Devajee. The excerpt here is from "Marshall," Part One of the trilogy which forms *The Nemesis Casket.*

Farida Karodia was born and brought up in South Africa. She taught there for four years and then in Zambia for three before emigrating to Canada. After three years in Canada, she left teaching so that she could concentrate on her writing. She wrote several radio dramas for CBC before publishing her first novel, *Daughters of the Twilight* (1986), set in South Africa during the fifties, the time of apartheid's enforcement of "separate development." In 1989 Karodia published a collection of short stories, *Coming Home.*

Rohinton Mistry was born in Bombay in 1953. He immigrated to Canada in 1975, and now lives in Toronto. He started writing short stories in 1983, while attending the University of Toronto. He has won two Hart House literary prizes and, in 1985, he won *Canadian Fiction Magazine*'s annual Contributor's Prize. His first book, a collection of short stories, *Tales from Firozsha Baag* (1987), was published in Canada, the US and the UK and is scheduled to appear in translation in France and Japan. *Tales from Firozsha Baag* was short-listed for the Governor-General's Award in 1988. His second book, *Such a Long Journey* (1991), won the 1991 Governor-General's Award for Fiction, the 1991 Smithbooks/Books in Canada First Novel Award and was nominated for the Booker Prize. The story included here, "The Ghost of Firozsha Baag" from *Tales from Firozsha Baag*, has recently been adapted for radio.

Bharati Mukherjee was born in Calcutta and lived in Toronto and Montreal before moving to Iowa with her husband, writer Clark Blaise. She is the author of three novels, *The Tiger's Daughter* (1972), *Wife* (1975), and *Jasmine* (1989); she has coauthored two books with Clark Blaise *Days and Nights in Calcutta* (1977) and *The Sorrow and the Terror: The Haunting Legacy of the Air India Tragedy* (1987); and two collections of short stories *Darkness* (1985) and *The Middleman and Other Stories* (1988). She has received several major writing awards. "The Management of Grief" is from *The Middleman and Other Stories*.

Nazneen Sadiq was born in Kashmir and immigrated to Canada in 1964. She has published a children's book, *Camels Can Make You Homesick and Other Stories* (1985), and a novel, *Ice Bangles* (1988). She lives in Toronto where she works as a writer and journalist. The selections here are from *Ice Bangles*.

Sam Selvon was born in Trinidad and immigrated to England in 1950 where he lived in London. Selvon has written television scripts and radio plays; he is a poet, a short-story writer, and a novelist. In addition to wining two Guggenheim Fellowships to America, he was awarded the Humming Bird Medal for work in Caribbean Literature. His more than ten books include *The Plains of Caroni* (1970; rpt. 1985), *Those Who Eat the Cascadura* (1972; rpt. TSAR, 1990), and *Moses Ascending* (1973). He lives in Calgary. The selection here named "The Harvester," is from his novel *The Plains of Caroni*.

M G Vassanji was born in Kenya and raised in Tanzania. Before coming to Canada in 1978, he trained as a physicist at MIT in Cambridge, Massachusetts. In 1989 he was international writer-in-residence at the University of Iowa's International Writing Program. Vassanji's first novel, *The Gunny Sack* (1989), was awarded the Commonwealth Literary Prize for a first novel in the African section. His second novel, *No New Land*, was published in1991 and a collection of short stories *Uhuru Street* appeared in 1992. A children's story for radio, *The Ghost of Bagamoyo*, is scheduled for broadcast by the CBC in Fall 1992. His work has appeared in several anthologies, including *Contemporary African Stories* (1992) edited by Achebe and Innes. Vassanji is active in promoting writing and supporting the arts, especially in his capacity as co-founder and editor of *The Toronto South Asian Review*. He now lives and writes in Toronto. The selection here is from his novel *No New Land*.

THE EDITOR

Diane McGifford received her Ph D in literature from the University of Manitoba. She has taught English at the Universities of Manitoba, Saskatchewan and Winnipeg. She was co-editor of *Shakti's Words: An Anthology of South Asian Canadian Women's Poetry* (TSAR, 1990), and has published several scholarly articles, including studies of Suniti Namjoshi and Uma Parameswaran. Currently she is a member of *Contemporary Verse II*'s editorial collective. She lives in Winnipeg and makes her living as a community researcher, writer, and educator.

Sources

I: POETRY

HIMANI BANNERJI.
"A Letter for Home," "Upon Hearing Beverly Glen Copeland": *A Separate Sky* (Toronto: Domestic Bliss,1982); "Paki Go Home," "to Sylvia Plath ": *doing time* (Toronto: Sister Vision,1986).

KRISANTHA SRI BHAGGIYADATTA
"Barbara Frum the sun sets early," "Winter '84," "in the valley of the towers," : *The Only Minority is the Bourgeoisie* (Toronto: Black Moon,1985); rpt. in *The Toronto South Asian Review* 5,3 (Spring 1987).

RIENZI CRUSZ
"Elegy": *Flesh and Thorn* (1976); "Sun-Man in Suburbia," "The Elephant Who Would Be a Poet," "Love Poem" "Dark Antonyms in Paradise": *Singing Against the Wind* (Erin, Ontario: Porcupine's Quill, 1985); "Elegy #2":*A Time for Loving* (Toronto: TSAR, 1986); "Song of the Immigrant": *Still Close to the Raven* (Toronto: TSAR, 1989); "Song for the Indian River Man" "The Geography of Voice," "Bouquet to My Colonial Masters," "The Rain Doesn't Know Me Any More," "Poem," "He Who Talks to the Raven": *The Rain Doesn't Know Me Any More* (Toronto: TSAR,1992).

CYRIL DABYDEEN
"Interludes": *The Toronto South Asian Review* 5,1 (Summer 1986); "Exiles: A Sequence (#101, 102)": *Islands Lovelier Than a Vision* (Leeds, England: Peepal Tree, 1986); "The Forest," "Foreign

Legions," "Elephants Make Good Stepladders": *Coastland: New and Selected Poems* (Toronto: Mosaic, 1989).

RAMABAI ESPINET
"Hosay Night," "In the Jungle," "Instruments of Love and War": *Nuclear Seasons* (Toronto: Sister Vision, 1991).

LAKSHMI GILL
"Letter to a Prospective Immigrant," "Marshland Wind," "Honor Roll," "Night Watch," "Third Street," "Letter to Gemma, Activist," "Out of Canada": *Novena to St Jude Thaddeus* (Fredericton, Nova Scotia: Fiddlehead, 1979).

ARNOLD ITWARU
"visit," "arrival," "matin mornings," "body rites (chant seven)": *Body Rites (beyond the darkening)* (Toronto: TSAR,1991).

SURJEET KALSEY
"I Want My Chaos Back," "A Woman with a Hole in Her Heart," "Voices of the Dead": *Foot Prints of Silence* (London, Ontario: Third Eye,1988).

SUNITI NAMJOSHI
"Further Adventures of the One-Eyed Monkey," "Philomel": *Feminist Fables* (London: Sheba Feminist Publishers, 1981); "On that island . . . ," "It's not that the landscape," "Eurydice," "Transit Gloria": *The Blue Donkey Fables* (London: Women's Press, 1988).

UMA PARAMESWARAN
"Tara's mother-in-law: What kind of place you've brought me to, Son?" "Dilip: Amma, I like school," "Usha: A river meandering motherly through the plain": *Trishanku* (Toronto: TSAR,1988); "Demeter I miss you": unpublished; "A Wedding Song": unpublished.

AJMER RODE
"Try a Red Hot Coal," "Under a Sewer Bridge": *Blue Meditations*

(London, Ontario: Third Eye, 1985); "Mustard Flowers," "Once She Drowned," "Spanish Banks": *Poems at My Doorstep* (Vancouver: Caitlin Press, 1990).

SUWANDA SUGUNASIRI
"Women on Tape": *The Toronto South Asian Review* 4,3 (Spring 1986).

ASOKA WEERASINGHE
"Trilogy," "The Birth of Insurgents," "The Insurgents," "The Plight of Insurgents" : *Spring Quartet* (Hayward's Heath, England: Breakthru Publications, 1972); "Metamorphosis": *Home Again Lanka* (Ottawa: Commoners', 1981); "Four Poems For Anikka Maya": *The Toronto South Asian Review* 4,2 (Fall 1985).

II: FICTION

VEN BEGAMUDRE
"The Evil Eye": *A Planet of Eccentrics* (Lantzville, BC: Oolichan, 1990), pp. 48-57.

NEIL BISSOONDATH
"Dancing": *Digging Up the Mountains* (Toronto: Macmillan, 1985), pp. 187-209.

VED DEVAJEE (Réshard Gool)
The Nemesis Casket (Charlottetown: Square Deal, 1979), pp. 1-7.

ARNOLD ITWARU
Chapter I, *Shanti* (Toronto: Coach House,1990).

FARIDA KARODIA
Chapters 15 and 21, *Daughter of the Twilight* (London: Women's Press,1986).

ROHINTON MISTRY
"The Ghost of Firozsha Baag": *Tales From Firozsha Baag* (Toron-

to: Penguin,1987).

BHARATI MUKHERJEE
"The Management of Grief": *The Middleman and Other Stories* (Toronto: Penguin, 1988), pp. 179-197.

UMA PARAMESWARAN
"How We Won the Olympic Gold" *The Toronto South Asian Review* 8,1 (Summer 1989).

NAZNEEN SADIQ
Selected passages: *Ice Bangles* (Toronto: Lorimer, 1988).

SAM SELVON
"The Harvester" from *The Plains of Caroni* (1970, rpt. Toronto: Williams Wallace, 1985); rpt. *The Toronto South Asian Review* 5,1 (Summer 1986).

M G VASSANJI
Excerpts from *No New Land* (Toronto: McClelland & Stewart, 1991), pp. 82, 126-128,136-146.

III: DRAMA

RANA BOSE
On the Double first staged by Montreal Serai, 1986, unpublished.

RAHUL VARMA and STEPHEN ORLOV
Isolated Incident first staged by Teesri Duniya, Montreal, 1988, unpublished.